Scott Landry rolled to a stop and threw his pickup into park. He leaned across the seat to crank the passenger window down.

The woman shuffling down the dirt road stopped and turned her head. He peered at her. The thing he noticed first was her emerald-colored eyes. Second, he noted her disheveled appearance. Her face was pretty, but dirty, and her long ebony hair was tangled. She wore sweat pants and a fitted tee shirt, ripped along the shoulder. She didn't carry a purse or a backpack. Not even a bottle of water.

"Hello," he called. "Can I help you?"

The woman stared at him with a blank expression. It was apparent she needed assistance. He pushed open the squeaky door and stepped out. As he sauntered around to the front, the woman's eyes grew wide and then she sprinted down the road.

"Wait!" Scott hollered, running after her. He punched down his cowboy hat to keep it from flying off.

She hadn't gone a hundred feet when she collapsed to the ground like a rag doll. Scott rushed to her, knelt, and found her unconscious. His touch was gentle when he patted her cheek.

"Come on, ma'am. Wake up." He laced his fingers around her neck and raised her into his lap. As she lay limp, he saw an angry purple bruise splotching the inside of her arm. When he brushed the waterfall of hair out of her eyes, he spied a lump on her forehead as big as a goose egg.

When she came to, her eyes got enormous. She struggled to break free from his hold.

"Hang on, lady. I'm not gonna hurt you." Scott released her and she attempted to stand. "Take it easy," he drawled. "Let me help. You just fainted. You might pass out again." He offered his hand.

With a wary look in her eye, she placed her hand in his and let him pull her off the ground.

Praise for Stacey Coverstone

"CHASING HER DREAMS is a rousing read that pulled me in like a net drawing in fishes. I was so mesmerized, it was hard to let go...Though some may not believe that true love can happen so fast, sometimes things happen for a reason that involves one's destiny. This story certainly is one that makes the reader believe. I was completely swept away with this romantic tale."

~Linda L., Fallen Angel Reviews

"I wondered what was so special that [Devin] had the strange imaginary pull to the lighthouse. I loved the surprise ending and thoroughly felt entertained throughout the entire story. I would definitely recommend [CHASING HER DREAMS] to other readers."

~Diana Coyle, Night Owl Romance

"Coverstone more than amply gives her readers a happily-ever-after ending and leaves the reader looking forward to the next book by this talented writer."

~Valerie J. Patterson, on LUCKY IN LOVE

High Lonesome

by

Stacey Coverstone

This is a work of fiction. Names, characters, places, and incidents are either the product of the author's imagination or are used fictitiously, and any resemblance to actual persons living or dead, business establishments, events, or locales, is entirely coincidental.

High Lonesome

Contact Information: info@thewildrosepress.com

Cover Art by *Rae Monet*

The Wild Rose Press
PO Box 706
Adams Basin, NY 14410-0706
Visit us at www.thewildrosepress.com

Publishing History
First Yellow Rose Edition, 2008
Print ISBN 1-60154-473-1

Published in the United States of America

Dedication

To my brother, Brian Marvin,
who never read a book in his life, but now reads all of mine and has become a romance convert.

To my proud, supportive parents,
Don and Bev Marvin.

And to my husband, Paul,
for his love and encouragement in all things I do.

Chapter One

Scott Landry rolled to a stop and threw his pickup into park. He switched off the radio, which had been blaring country music, and leaned across the seat to crank the passenger window all the way down.

The woman shuffling down the dirt road stopped and turned her head. He peered at her. The thing he noticed first was her emerald-colored eyes. Second, he noted her disheveled appearance. He was thirty-two; he guessed her to be close to his age. Her face was pretty, but smudged with dirt, and her long ebony hair was tangled and unkempt. She wore sweatpants and a fitted tee shirt, which outlined the curvature of her small breasts, but the shirt was ripped along the shoulder. She didn't carry a purse or a backpack. Not even a bottle of water.

"Hello," he called. "Can I help you? You look lost."

The woman stared at him with a blank expression.

It was apparent she was out of her element and needed assistance. He pushed open the squeaky door and stepped out of the truck. As he sauntered around to the front, the woman's eyes grew wide and then she sprinted down the road.

"Wait!" Scott hollered, running after her. He punched down his cowboy hat to keep it from flying off.

She hadn't gotten a hundred feet when she collapsed to the ground like a rag doll. Scott rushed to her, knelt down, and found her unconscious. His touch was gentle when he lifted her head and patted her cheek.

"Come on, ma'am. Wake up." He laced his fingers around her neck and raised her into his lap. As she lay limp, he saw an angry purple bruise splotching the inside of her arm. When he brushed the waterfall of hair out of her eyes, he spied a lump on her forehead as big as a goose egg.

Scott's gaze raked over the angelic-looking woman. She was built small—no heavier than a feather in his arms—and her skin was flawless. He noted the smattering of freckles across her upturned nose, long eyelashes, and heart-shaped lips. He couldn't begin to imagine how she'd found herself wandering the desert in the shape she was in. He placed his hand on her uninjured arm and jiggled until she stirred.

When she came to, her eyes got enormous. She gasped and struggled to break free from his hold.

"Hang on, lady. I'm not gonna hurt you." Scott released her and she attempted to stand. "Take it easy," he drawled. "Let me help. You just fainted. You might pass out again." He offered his hand.

She searched his face for a moment. With a wary look in her eye, she placed her hand in his and let him pull her off the ground.

"Thank you," she whispered.

"You're welcome. My name's Scott. I think you oughtta go over there and sit in my truck. You need to get out of the hot sun. I've got a bottle of water inside."

The woman gave her head a vigorous shake. Her eyes darted up and down the long, meandering road.

"Don't *even* think about making a run for it again," he warned in a good-natured tone. Though he could see she was as scared and jittery as a caged animal, he wasn't interested in another jog. "I'm not wearing running shoes, as you can see." He pointed to his cowboy boots.

He sidestepped past and opened the passenger door of his truck. After reaching in for the water bottle, which sat on the console, he took one easy step forward and offered it to her. She accepted with a tentative hand.

"You go ahead and have a seat in the truck and I'll stand way over there." Scott nodded toward a clump of sagebrush at the side of the road. "I understand your wanting to be cautious. I won't even go near the driver's side. In fact, you can hold my keys if it makes you feel better." He tossed his truck keys to her.

The woman caught the keys, but didn't make a move toward the truck.

The spurs on Scott's boots jingled as he walked with a leisurely gait and stood next to the sage. He shoved his hands into the back pockets of his Wranglers.

"You don't need to be afraid of me. I was just coming home from picking up grain for my horses." To assure her he was telling the truth, he jerked his head in the direction of the truck bed where bags of grain were stacked. "I have a ranch right down this road. You're lucky I came along when I did. You don't look well. Now, go ahead and drink all that water. I think you're dehydrated."

Still guarded, the woman watched him as she raised the bottle to her lips and gulped the entire contents. Some water dribbled down her chin. She wiped her mouth with the back of her hand and tossed him the empty bottle. She took one step and began to sway. Her eyes rolled back in her head.

"Whoa." Scott rushed forward and grabbed her, just in time to break her fall. She slid into his arms like a stick of melting butter. He swept her into his arms, carried her to the truck and deposited her in the front seat. Again, he patted her cheek in order to wake her.

Her eyes opened. "What happened?" she asked. "I feel lightheaded."

"You fainted. Again."

"Oh." She rested her head on the back of the seat. Sighing, she raised her hand to her forehead—wincing when she felt the bump.

"You have a pretty big knot there," Scott told her.

"How did that happen?"

"I was hoping you might be able to tell me."

She stared at him like she was trying to place him. "Do I know you?"

"Nope. If you don't mind my asking, what are you doing out here in the middle of nowhere? Where's your car?"

The woman rotated her head. Scott wondered what she was thinking as her eyes scanned the miles of desert land, flowering cactus, turquoise skies, and red mountains in the near distance. She wore a confused expression when she turned back to him.

"Where am I?"

"Where are you supposed to be?"

"I asked you first."

A grin tugged at his lips. "Do you want to know which road you're on?"

"No. Yes. Oh…I don't know. What town are we in? What state? None of this looks familiar." She glanced around again.

"You're on the outskirts of Ghost Rock, New Mexico. Did your car break down?"

She ignored the question and cast him a surprised look. "New Mexico? Are you sure?"

"Of course I'm sure. I was born and raised close by. I don't recall seeing you before. I take it you're not from around here."

She thought a minute. "I don't know." As she studied her dirty, torn clothes, the realization of the situation must have sunk in. “What’s going on? Did you do this to me? Did you hurt me?” Shear panic crossed her face.

“No,” Scott replied. He purposefully spoke with a calm demeanor. “I was driving by and saw you stumbling down this road. I’m just a guy trying to help.”

She touched her bruised arm and cringed. “My arm hurts. Who did this to me?”

“Don’t you remember how that happened?”

She shook her head.

Scott crouched, placed his knee on the running board and looked her square in the eye. His tone was compassionate when he asked, “What’s your name?”

Her professionally groomed eyebrows furrowed as she considered the question. A single tear welled in the corner of her eye as she answered. “I have no idea.”

Scott lifted his cowboy hat and raked his fingers through his hair. “You’re not carrying a purse, and those sweats don’t have pockets, so I’m guessing you have no ID on you.”

She shrugged.

“I don’t suppose you recall how you got that knot on your head either?”

“No.” The woman touched the lump again and grimaced. “I have a headache.”

“I bet you do.” He pushed the passenger door closed, walked around to the driver’s side of the truck, hopped in and slammed the door. Their gazes locked. “You’re gonna have to trust me, ma’am. My ranch is just a couple of miles on down this way. If you give me my keys, I’ll drive you there, and I’ll get you something to eat and drink. I have a friend who’s a doctor. I’ll call her and she can take a look at your injuries. What do you say?”

She nodded. “I guess I don’t have much choice.”

“No, I don’t think you do,” Scott said in

agreement.

"I'm sorry to put you out like this," she said softly.

"Don't be sorry. Just promise you're not going to jump out of my truck and run away again." He winked.

She offered him a weak smile. "I promise."

"Okay." He stretched out his palm and she placed the keys in it. "Buckle your seat belt, ma'am. This pile of rust jerks when I start 'er up."

****

They passed under a wooden arch with a sign reading *High Lonesome Guest Ranch*. She stared as they drove by a large barn and corral, where a half dozen people saddled horses tied to posts. Off in the distance, she spotted some rustic cabins nestled at the foot of red sandstone mountains.

Up a short but steep hill, situated on a green lawn, was a two-story pine log dwelling with a metal roof and a covered porch stretching the entire length of the house. On the porch sat eight white wooden rockers, as well as huge terracotta pots bursting with pink and purple petunias. Another sign, posted above the front door, read *Headquarters.*

She glanced at Scott for an explanation. He pulled into a gravel lot next to the house and parked in front of a hitching post.

Shutting off the motor, he told her, "This is a dude ranch. I own seven thousand acres, and guests come here to ride horses, take in the scenery, and enjoy the climate. We call this place the High Lonesome. You probably saw the sign."

"It's very beautiful."

"Thanks. We have miles of trails leading up into the mountains, a lake, and caves which were inhabited by ancient Indians." Scott exited the truck, slammed the door and walked around to open her door. He extended his hand to help her out. Her trembling palm slid into his.

"I feel so weak," she said. "I think I might faint again."

"I'll help you into the house."

She linked her arm through his, and he led her into the log home by way of the back door, which opened to the kitchen. An older Mexican woman stood behind the counter mixing batter in a large stainless steel bowl.

Scott spoke but didn't bother with introductions. "Carmen, could you please get me a glass of ice water and grab a bottle of aspirin and bring them to my bedroom?"

The cook plunked the bowl down on the counter. She ran her curious eyes up and down the woman.

"*Si*," she replied. "I'll be right up." She wiped her hands on her apron then shuffled to the refrigerator to pour cold water from a big glass pitcher.

"Did you say your bedroom?" the woman inquired, fixing an anxious look on Scott.

He kept a firm hand at the small of her back and guided her up the rear stairway. "Yeah, but don't get any funny ideas. I don't even kiss on the first date." His blue eyes sparkled and teased.

The woman lost her balance and slumped against Scott's shoulder. "I don't feel so good."

Once again, he lifted her into his arms, and her head sunk into his chest as he carried her up the stairs. He kicked open the bedroom door with his boot and carted her to the iron bed.

The Mexican woman rushed in behind them and turned back the covers. The woman moaned as Scott eased her onto the mattress. Carmen handed him the glass of water and pill bottle, then stood at the footboard.

Scott perched on the edge of the bed and offered cold water. "Drink this, ma'am. Here are some aspirin for your headache, too." He opened his palm, which held two little white pills.

She scooped them up, popped them into her mouth and sipped from the glass, then let her eyes drift shut.

"Mr. Scott, who is she?" Carmen asked.

"I don't know. I just found her a couple of miles down the road. It looks like she's been in an accident. Could you please call Doctor Coleman's office and see if she has time to run out here and take a look at her? I'm going to get a wet wash cloth for her face."

He disappeared into the master bathroom as Carmen picked up the phone on the bedside table and dialed. As she waited for an answer, Scott returned and wiped dirt and sweat from the woman's face. His touch was gentle and caring.

"*Buenos dias*. This is Carmen Rios calling from the High Lonesome," the cook said into the phone. "We have an injured guest out here, and Mr. Landry would like to know if Doctor Coleman could come out and take a look at her. Uh huh. I'll hold." Carmen placed her hand over the receiver and said, "The receptionist is going to check."

"Thank you." Scott hung the washcloth over the footboard rail, while his gaze remained glued to the woman.

He took a seat in the overstuffed club chair next to the bed that he'd slept in ever since he was a boy and watched her curl herself into a ball.

"The lady's cold, Mr. Scott. Cover her up," Carmen ordered.

He jumped up and tucked the well-worn comforter around her shoulders.

"Look at that," the cook said, amazed. "Asleep already."

"She must be exhausted. I think she's been through quite an ordeal," Scott replied. "I don't think she's from these parts. I've never seen her before."

Carmen had a habit of being blunt. "She looks a mess. What do you think happened to her?"

"Something bad. She has a big knot on her head, as well as bruising on her arm. It looks like she's been attacked, to me. She was surprised to learn she was in New Mexico, and she can't remember her name."

Carmen gasped and made the sign of the cross. "Oh my. She has amnesia?"

"Yeah, from what I can tell."

Removing her hand from the telephone mouthpiece, Carmen said, "*Si*, I'm here. Okay. Thank you very much." As she hung up the phone, she told Scott, "Doctor Coleman will be by in a few minutes. Apparently she's not far from here."

"That's great. Thanks. Is there anything else we can do for her while we wait?"

"I'll fix her some hot tea and reheat the leftover soup from dinner last night. I think she's very weak. She can eat when she wakes up."

"Good idea. God knows how long she's been wandering around out there. It's a wonder she was able to make it down the road."

"She looks at peace right now—like a sweet angel." The older woman's lips curled into a smile.

"That was my exact thought when I first saw her. The poor thing sure was scared. She tried to run away from me, but didn't have the physical strength to get far. Of course, I don't blame her for running. She was disoriented and frightened."

Scott glanced at his watch. He may have found himself involved in a mystery at the moment, but he still had a business to run. "When we drove in I saw Cody and the guests saddling the horses. Is he taking them out for a trail ride?"

"*Si*. I packed them sack lunches. They won't be back until late afternoon."

"Good. You can go back to what you were doing,

Carmen. I'll stay here with her. Just send Joanna up when she arrives. Please," he added.

"Will do. I'll get a tray ready for the lady for when she wakes."

Carmen left the room and Scott sunk back down into the chair next to the bed. He watched the woman's chest rise and fall steadily beneath the cover, and wondered aloud, "Who are you, and where did you come from?"

With sudden, unexpected ferocity, she groaned and kicked the comforter off. Tossing her head back and forth, a blood-curdling scream erupted from her throat.

Scott shot to his feet and shook her arm. When her eyes flew open, he leaned forward and asked, "Did you have a bad dream?"

She nodded. Her forehead glistened with perspiration.

Carmen yelled from the bottom of the stairs. "What happened, Mr. Scott?"

"It was just a bad dream. She's all right," he called back. As an afterthought, he hollered, "You can go ahead and bring up the soup when it's ready."

"Sure thing."

Scott knelt at the edge of the bed. "Are you okay?"

"I think so," the woman whispered.

"My cook is bringing some food up for you, and I've called a doctor. She'll be here real soon to check you out. Do you still not remember how you got hurt or where you're from?"

"No. What's wrong with me? My brain feels fuzzy."

"You sustained a blow to your head. I'm sure that's why you feel strange. Try not to worry. The amnesia is probably temporary."

"Amnesia?" Her deep green eyes grew wide. "You think I have amnesia? That's my problem?

That's why I can't remember anything?"

"Well, yeah. I guess so. It appears that way. We'll see what the doc has to say."

Carmen entered the room carrying a tray with a bowl of soup, some bread, and a cup of tea on it. Scott formally introduced the two women. "This is Carmen Rios. She's the best cook in all of New Mexico."

"Nice to meet you." The woman nodded hello.

"Same here," Carmen said, returning the greeting.

Scott asked, "Do you think you can sit up? I think you'll feel better if you eat something."

She scooted to a sitting position and leaned back against the pillow. "I *am* hungry. My stomach feels empty."

Carmen lowered the bed tray across the woman's lap and asked, "Do you like tortilla soup?"

"I'm not sure I've ever had it before. It smells good."

Placing the spoon in the woman's hands, as if she were a child, Carmen drew it to her mouth. "Eat all of this. I guarantee it will make you feel one hundred percent better."

"Thank you." The woman swallowed, licked her lips, and requested more.

Grinning with pride, the cook said, "When you're finished with the soup, you can drink my special tea with chili pepper. It will invigorate you."

The woman threw Scott a questioning look.

"You'll want to do as she says. I own the ranch, but she's the real boss around here," he joked. "Keep eating that soup. I think the color is already starting to come back into your face."

"Hello? Scott?" a feminine voice called from downstairs.

"That'll be the doctor. I'll be right back." He excused himself and stepped into the hallway.

Peering over the railed balcony to the great room below, he waved and said, "We're up here."

Wearing a white physician's jacket over a navy pencil skirt perfect for showing off her slender physique, Joanna Coleman ascended the main staircase, carrying her black medical bag.

"Thanks for coming over so quickly," Scott told her when she reached the top. "Hope I didn't take you away from anything important."

"No problem. I happened to be in the neighborhood. My receptionist reached me on my cell phone." She flashed him a bright smile under short blonde hair. "She said it was an emergency."

"Yeah, I'd call it that for sure." Scott lowered his voice and explained the situation while they stood in the hall. "I was coming home from town and came across this woman stumbling down the road. It's obvious she's been in an accident. You'll see she has a lump on her head and a nasty bruise on the inside of her arm. I think she has amnesia as well."

Joanna cast him a surprised look. "Why do you think that?"

"She doesn't know where her car is, and she can't remember her name or where she's from. She doesn't know how she got hurt. She has no ID on her, but I'm sure she's not from around here. I've never seen her before, and she said none of the area looked familiar."

"Let me take a look at her." Doctor Coleman strode into the bedroom. "Good morning, Carmen," she said, acknowledging Scott's longtime cook.

"Morning, Miss Joanna."

Joanna stood at the side of Scott's bed and introduced herself to the woman. She glanced at the tray on her lap. "Hello. I'm Doctor Coleman. I see Ms. Rios has been treating you with her fabulous cooking."

"Yes. It was delicious. Made me feel better.

Thank you again," she said, handing the empty soup bowl to the cook.

"You're welcome. I'm happy to see rosy pink cheeks on you. I told you it would help," Carmen boasted.

"Carmen's food can cure more ailments than modern medicine," Scott added, sounding more like a proud son than her employer.

Joanna pulled on plastic gloves and leaned over the patient. "Do you mind if I take a look at that bump on your head before I check your vitals?"

The woman shook her head. "I don't mind."

"Let me move this out of the way," Carmen said, taking away the tray.

Joanna examined the knot, and then took the woman's blood pressure and temperature. "Mr. Landry tells me you can't remember your name." She placed a stethoscope against the brunette's chest and listened.

Responding to the doctor with a bob of her head, the patient replied, "That's right. I don't seem to remember much of anything right now. I've been racking my brains, but it feels like I'm in a fog."

"You've got quite a hematoma on your forehead, but your vitals are good. Is your arm sore?" Joanna turned it over and examined the bruising.

The woman flinched and nodded.

"I apologize. Does anything else hurt? Your legs or your back?"

"I feel sore all over—like I've been run over or beaten with a club or something."

Scott and Carmen exchanged subtle glances. Carmen made the sign of the cross again.

Joanna straightened and studied the woman. "With your consent, I think it'd be prudent to do a rape kit." Her manner was all businesslike.

The woman glanced at Scott then bowed her head, flush with embarrassment. When he met

Joanna's gaze, Scott's cheeks were burning as well. Carmen looked down at her shoes.

"Mr. Landry, perhaps you and Carmen could wait downstairs," Joanna said, steering them out of the bedroom. "I'll let you know when I'm done here."

"Sure." Scott stuck his hands in his pockets and nodded for Carmen to follow him out of the room, which she did with no hesitation.

An hour later, Joanna found Scott and Carmen in the kitchen sitting at the island having coffee.

"There's no signs of rape," she reported, "but I'll take the evidence I collected back to the lab to be one hundred percent sure."

Carmen sighed and stood, then stepped over to the sink.

"That's a relief," Scott replied. "Can I go back up now?"

"Yes. I'll go with you."

The two of them took the back stairs up to the bedroom. The doctor reached into her bag and pulled out a small pad. "I'll prescribe something for your pain," Joanna told the woman once they'd returned to her side. "I'd also like to schedule you for an EEG and a CT scan, in order to assess your head injury. It's obvious you've suffered some kind of blunt trauma, but it's impossible to know whether you hit your head on something hard or were struck with an object."

The woman cringed. "Are you suggesting someone intentionally hurt me?"

"I'm sorry," Joanna said. "The idea of that must be difficult to fathom. I apologize for blurting it out that way. It's a definite possibility, but let's not jump to any conclusions. Either way, the injury has caused you to suffer a neurological deficit. In layman's terms, you're suffering from amnesia, which Mr. Landry already suspected. We need to be sure there's no skull fracture. How soon could you arrange to go to the clinic and have those tests run?"

Scott spoke up. "I can take her whenever you can get her in. You name the time and we'll be there."

"All right." Joanna pulled her day planner out of the black bag and consulted it. "How about later this afternoon? I have an acquaintance at the clinic who owes me a favor. I'll arrange for an appointment around three o'clock, if that suits you."

Scott nodded once, firmly. "The sooner the better. For her sake."

"Okay, then. See you both later today."

"Thank you, doctor." The woman extended her hand to shake.

Scott noticed she was still trembling.

Joanna took her hand and pumped it. "You're welcome. Try and get some rest, drink lots of liquids, and," her voice took on a lighter note, "I'd suggest enjoying more of Ms. Rios's cooking." She picked up her medical bag and said goodbye.

"I'll be right back," Scott told the woman as he trailed Joanna out the door. She walked down the stairs ahead of him and bypassed the hall that led to the kitchen, heading to the front door instead. Her heels clicked on the hardwood floors.

She and Scott didn't speak until they were in the foyer, out of his guest's hearing range.

He flung open the door and they stepped onto the front porch. "I appreciate you interrupting your schedule and running out here. Who would have thought when I woke up this morning that something like this was gonna happen?" The question was rhetorical, but the wheels in Scott's brain were spinning like whirlwinds. "One of the first things I need to do is try to find out where she came from and if she has any family."

"They must be frantic, worrying about what's happened to her," Joanna concurred.

"I'll call Buddy. The sheriff's department is the natural place to start."

"Of course you should call him, but the one missing person case he worked was the time Connor Russell's sister thought he'd been kidnapped by some drug dealers. If you'll recall, Buddy found Con under the high school bleachers all liquored up, and the only thing missing was his pants. Here in podunk Ghost Rock, hunting out of season is about the biggest crime Buddy ever has to deal with. He won't know where to begin with a real case like this." Joanna rolled her eyes.

"You shouldn't talk about your ex-husband that way," Scott teased. "He's good at his job. He wouldn't have been elected sheriff two years ago at the age of thirty if he wasn't. You never want to give him any credit."

She sighed. "You're always defending that goofball."

"No I'm not. Anyway, he doesn't need defending. He's a damn good sheriff." Scott leaned against the side of the house with his boot hiked up.

Joanna patted his shoulder. "You have to say that. He's your best friend. You're very loyal, Scott, but sometimes you let your friendship with Buddy stand in the way of *our* relationship."

"I don't think I do," he retorted. "He's been my best friend since we were kids. You knew when we started dating that I'd never give that friendship up. Buddy and I talked about it—about you and me going out—and he told me he was okay with it, but I still question whether he's being honest with himself. I wouldn't be okay if the situation was reversed. It's still uncomfortable for me, at times."

"How did we get on this subject?" Joanna pulled a stick of gum from the pocket of her jacket and offered him one. "Buddy and I are history," she reminded him. "Our relationship ended years ago.

It's about time you stop worrying what he thinks. He doesn't care that we're together."

"I'm not so sure about that." Scott stuck the gum in his mouth, wadded up the paper and tucked it into his shirt pocket.

"Scott, you and I have been going out for almost a year now. Buddy cares about both of us and wants us to be happy. He and I were not meant for each other. We both realized that and ended our marriage before either of us got hurt. He accepts that you and I are together now."

Scott's grin was half-hearted. "I'm not convinced you know your ex as well as you think you do."

"I know him better than anyone—even you." She stabbed her finger into his chest. "And I know he and I were too young and impetuous when we married. It was a big mistake. That's the one thing we ever agreed on. Neither of us knew what true love really was."

"And you do now?"

"Yes. I know the *exact* kind of man I want and need now." She leaned in close and nuzzled Scott's neck. "Speaking of wants and needs...As I recall, we have a date planned for tonight. Will you be getting that woman a room at the motel?"

He backed up and threw her a stunned look. "No. She's going to stay here. Since I'm the one who found her, it's up to me to keep her safe. Someone most likely did this to her on purpose—you said so yourself. He or she might still be after her."

Joanna grabbed his hand. "Yes, I said that, but it doesn't make you responsible, honey. She's very lucky you came along when you did, but you did what any good citizen would. You've opened your home to her. You're bringing her in for tests. She can't expect more than that. Hand her off to Buddy this afternoon and let him do his job. Let him take care of her."

"Hand her off?" Scott shook his head. "She's not a pair of used shoes. I'm sure she doesn't expect anything, but the poor girl doesn't even know her own name. She's scared to death. I'm not about to leave her alone in some crummy motel room. Carmen and I will look after her until Buddy locates her family, or someone who can identify her."

Joanna stuck out her lower lip and feigned a pout. "You called her a girl. She's not a girl, Scott. She's a full-grown woman. I don't think I like the idea of her sleeping in your bed, either."

Joanna had a way of getting his ire up, but he didn't want to argue. He snaked an arm around her waist and kissed the tip of her nose. "I've never seen you jealous before. You're always so confident and sure of yourself. What's all this about?"

"I don't know. I suppose it's because she's so beautiful, and she's going to think of you as her knight in shining armor. Since you rescued her, she'll feel indebted to you. I'm not comfortable with that."

Scott squeezed her waist and chuckled. "I'm no knight. I just happened to be in the right place at the right time."

"A lot of men are attracted to helpless women." Joanna eyed him.

"I'm not. You're far from helpless. Besides, this lady is not that way by choice."

"You feel sorry for her, don't you?"

"Of course I do. Someone beat her up, dumped her and left her for dead. Don't you?"

She didn't answer—just moved her fingers through his shaggy hair.

Joanna sure knew how to push his buttons. "She *is* lucky I found her," Scott said stiffly, "because I'm not the kind of man to look the other way when someone's in trouble. We've known each other all our lives, Jo. You know that about me."

She shrugged out of Scott's embrace. "Of course I know. You've taken care of other people your entire life."

He leveled a solemn gaze at her. "I've had to."

"I realize that," she responded at once, "but you finally have your own life to live, Scott. And in case you've forgotten, I'm a part of it, limited as it may be."

He frowned. "I don't understand where this attitude is coming from, Jo. You're a doctor. Of all people, you should be understanding and sympathetic. Instead, you're coming off like a jealous teenage girl, and I have to say, it's not very becoming."

Her eyes flashed and she opened her mouth to retaliate, but the look on his face must have given her pause. The blaze in his temper dared her to go on. He was generally mild mannered and easy going, but he could get fired up when pushed. She clamped her mouth shut.

Instead, she snuggled closer and purred, "I'm sorry...I'm just tired…and a little jealous. I do admit it. Walking in and seeing a woman in your bed threw me for a loop. It's been so long since *I've* shared your bed. I've been missing you. Will you forgive me?" She set her lips on his cheek and let them linger—for a couple of seconds. Backing away, she scrunched her nose and complained, "You need a shave, darlin'."

Scott put his hand at the small of her back and guided her out to the driveway where she had parked her car, a red Audi Roadster.

"Do us both a favor and admit it," she hounded. "You think she's beautiful, too."

"Oh, Joanna. Please. I hadn't even noticed." He opened the car door and thanked her again for rushing out. "I'll see you this afternoon at three. Okay?"

"Okay." She climbed in, not bothering to pull

down her skirt when it shimmied up her thigh, and slammed the door.

He leaned in and they shared a brief kiss, then Scott watched her put the convertible in gear and speed down the drive, kicking up rocks in her wake. “Slow down!” he hollered through the dust.

Joanna stuck her arm out the window and gave him a backhanded wave.

He entered the house and tromped back up the stairs, feeling guilty about lying to Joanna just then. The truth was he *was* attracted to the woman ensconced in his bed. But more than that—strange as it seemed—he'd felt not just a physical connection, but also a strong emotional bond to her the moment he'd laid eyes on her. It unnerved him. How could a perfect stranger cause his heart to race the way it was right now? And why was he imagining what it'd be like to kiss her?

Even though the bedroom door was open, and it was *his* room, Scott knocked on the door just the same, out of courtesy. He peeked in and discovered the old iron bed was empty.

Just then, Carmen stepped out of the master bathroom like she owned the place and said, “Hi, Mr. Scott. I hope you don't mind, but the lady asked if she could take a bath. She said she felt grimy, and she wanted to wash her hair. I ran a bath and got her some clean towels.”

“I should have thought of it myself,” Scott admitted.

“Men don't think like women,” Carmen replied as she passed by. “Come on out of here. Go unload your grain sacks. Let her have some privacy.”

“Okay, okay. You're getting bossier every day. Doesn't she need some clean clothes to change into when she's done?”

“*Si,* Mr. Scott. She needs clothes. I'm going to throw away those rags she came in here with.”

"Don't do that," he said. "The sheriff might want to test them. Maybe he can take DNA from them. That could identify her."

"You're right. I wasn't thinking this time," Carmen confessed. "As for the clean clothes, I know where there is a closet full of things she could borrow."

A dull ache pulsed through Scott's veins.

Carmen must have noted the shadow that passed across his face—the face she'd seen change from lanky young boy to the man he was now. She lowered her voice and said, "If you approve, I'll pick out a few basics for the nice lady. She's about the same size as Maggie, don't you think?"

"Yes," he answered in a soft voice. "Go ahead and get what she needs. I'll buy her some new clothes later when we go to town."

"She will appreciate that, Mr. Scott. She seems like a real sweet person." Carmen gave him a tender hug before leaving the bedroom.

He waited there a moment. As he paused in the doorframe, he heard a soft sound coming from behind the bathroom door. Listening, he heard the drip...drip...drip of the hot water faucet he hadn't yet gotten around to fixing.

He thought about the woman and tried to imagine how she was feeling and what she was thinking, all alone in an unfamiliar place, not knowing what was going to happen to her. Dependant on total strangers to protect her and take care of her.

He took a step and stopped. She was humming. It was barely audible, but as he listened, he could make out a familiar tune. The lyrical sound lilted under the bathroom door. He closed his eyes and allowed the music to transport him back to a time when his heart was full and the future was bright. It had been so long since he'd heard such a sweet sound.

Frozen, he stood listening and remembering. Maggie always hummed when she mucked the stalls or cleaned the house. She hummed her favorite country songs. Later, those country tunes were replaced by lullabies.

Scott let the peaceful feeling wash over him.

When the humming abruptly stopped, he opened his eyes, spun on his heel and took the stairs down two at a time, hoping she hadn't sensed him eavesdropping. Cruising into his office, he flipped open his cell phone and punched in Buddy's number.

Chapter Two

She ran the warm, soapy washcloth across her aching body. Squeezing the rag over each shoulder, she watched the lather slither down her arms. She stared at the discolored bruise glaring at her from the inside of her arm and recoiled after touching it. When she laid her head on the back of the tub, she allowed the questions to swim around in her mind.

What happened to me? Why can't I remember who I am, or where I'm from? How did I get hurt? Was it an accident, or did someone do this to me on purpose? Why wasn't I carrying any ID? Is anyone looking for me?

Her body relaxed after a while, and the image of the rancher's face floated in front of her. He was a good, kind man. Amnesia couldn't erase the intuition she sensed about him. He was special. Eyes and hands were the first two things she had always noticed on a man, because the eyes were the mirrors to a person's soul, and the hands were tools for causing a body either pleasure or pain. She had a strange feeling she'd experienced both.

Even though she'd been dazed and in a weakened state, she had noticed Mr. Landry's sparkling blue eyes and strong, powerful hands.

There was a lot for her to be worried about, but she didn't *feel* worried. It seemed odd to her, since she'd just met the man, but she knew she'd be safe in his home under his care and protection. She knew nothing about Scott Landry, but she had a strong feeling he was a man of integrity and trustworthiness. After all, he'd exhibited those qualities within the first ten minutes of their meeting.

The water sloshed as she leaned back and dunked her head into it. It felt wonderful to lather her long hair with the fruit-scented shampoo. She scrubbed her scalp until it tingled, rinsed her hair, then pulled the plug and watched the water swirl down the drain as she stepped out onto the bath rug.

The aspirin had taken effect and her head had stopped throbbing. She reached for the fluffy white towels the Mexican lady had hung on the rack. After wrapping her head in one towel and drying off with the other, she was starting to feel human again.

There was a rap on the door and Carmen's pleasant voice called out to her. "Ma'am, I've brought some fresh clothes for you. I'll leave them on the bed."

"Thank you." The woman peeked out from behind the bathroom door.

"Do you feel better?" Carmen asked, as she spread an outfit out on the bed.

"Yes. Like a brand new person."

The two women looked at each other and then broke out laughing.

"I see you didn't lose your sense of humor along with your memory," the cook chuckled. She shuffled to the door with one hand on her hip. "I hope those things fit. Take your time dressing. We do everything slow around here. Come downstairs when you feel up to it."

"You've been so kind, missus..."

"I'm not a missus. I was once, but it didn't work out. Just call me Carmen."

The woman smiled. "Okay. Carmen, it is. Thank you for the loan of the clothes. I'll be down soon."

She held the pair of jeans and top against her body. They looked about the right size. When she slipped them on, she was delighted at the perfect fit. She buckled the leather belt and slipped on the socks and canvas tennis shoes, then dried her hair. Finding no rubber bands in the bathroom, or anything similar to use for pulling her hair into a ponytail, she stepped back into the bedroom and ran a gaze over the furniture.

A gold frame sitting in the back corner of the tall oak dresser drew her gaze. It was a family photo of the cowboy, his pretty wife, and their baby, swaddled in pink, held in her mother's arms.

What a beautiful family. They look very happy.

She let her finger drift along the edge of the frame. She picked it up with both hands and studied the photo with an inquisitive eye. Something about the baby stirred a sense of familiarity in her. A snippet of a memory assaulted her.

An image flooded her mind of a woman running with a child in her arms, and a man chasing them—reaching out for them.

She laid the picture frame down with a jolt. The image lasted a mere second or two, but it was enough to unhinge her. She'd never experienced anything like it before. She stumbled into the bathroom, hung her head over the sink, and splashed cold water into her face. Raising her eyes to the mirror, she stared at her reflection.

What just happened? Was that a flashback of a real memory?

She wondered what had brought it on. Had something in the rancher's family photo triggered a memory from her own life?

After a few moments, she took a deep breath and left the bedroom, deciding some fresh air was what she needed. She descended the stairs, holding onto the wooden handrail, just in case she got dizzy again.

She heard country music blaring and pots and

pans banging in the kitchen. On quiet feet, she followed the noises down the hallway. Halfway down, a door flung open next to her and out popped her host, talking on a cell phone. He wore the same well-worn cowboy hat over Keith Urban-style shaggy blond hair that touched the collar of his work shirt. A five o'clock shadow dusted his chin and cheeks, and his eyes were as blue as sapphire. His voice was low and his southwestern drawl sexy. He finished up his conversation.

"Thanks, Buddy. I'll bring her by this afternoon. I appreciate it." He snapped the phone shut and said, "Hello."

"Hello."

"How are you feeling? You look...refreshed." His gaze took her all in, top to bottom, from her wet hair to the old-school tennis shoes.

"I am. My headache is gone, and getting something in my stomach helped bring me back to life. Thank you for letting me use the tub in your bathroom. The bath worked wonders on my sore muscles."

"I'm glad to hear that."

The woman couldn't help but notice he was staring at the clothes she wore. Perhaps the cook had loaned the clothing without her boss's permission. She stammered, "Carmen brought me these things to wear. I don't know where they came from, but I promise I'll return them as soon as I can buy some more."

She thought she saw pain behind his eyes. But maybe she had just imagined it. His lips curved into a crooked grin.

"Don't worry about it," Scott responded. "I'll take you shopping when we're in town later today. It'll be my treat."

"Oh, no. I can't allow you to do that. I've already imposed on you as it is. You don't know me, or anything about me. You don't have to buy me anything."

Scott insisted. "You need a little help right now and I have the means to give it to you. I'm more than happy to buy you some clothes."

"Is there a shelter in town? A mission, perhaps?" she asked.

"Yeah, but why do you want to know?"

"I could room there while I figure out what I'm going to do about my situation. I really feel bad putting you out."

"You'll do no such thing," he said. "You're going to stay here at the ranch and we're going to help you find your family." He cocked his head. "Let me ask you a question. Have you ever read the Good Book?"

"The Good Book? Are you referring to the Bible?" she asked, curious. "Yes. I've read it."

"Then you know I'm just doing what it says. I'm being a Good Samaritan. If you don't allow me to do what the Good Book says, then you'll be making it harder for me to get to Heaven. Do you understand?"

He flashed that lopsided grin again, and she realized he was pulling her leg.

"Besides," he continued more seriously, "you're not imposing. We have people coming and going around here all the time. That's how it is in the guest ranch business. There are six guests staying here this week, so one more person is no big deal."

She smiled. "Well, okay. Since you put it that way."

Scott held up his cell phone. "I was just speaking to the county sheriff. I explained your situation. He wants us to stop by before I take you to the clinic for the CT scan. He'd like to interview you and take your photo. He's going to put out a multi-state APB. By the time I got off the phone with him, he was already planning a media blitz."

"That's fast work," she said, pleased.

"To be honest with you, it's reasonable to expect you'll become somewhat of a local celebrity in Ghost Rock. Not much happens around here. It's a pretty small community, so a pretty young lady with amnesia is gonna set tongues to wagging."

She chuckled, picturing the little old blue-haired gossips whispering on the street corner.

"Are you still hungry?" Scott asked. "I want to make sure you get your strength back. We don't know how long you were out in the desert. Carmen can fix you a sandwich."

"No, I'm fine," she assured him. "The soup and bread was perfect, but I'd love something cold to drink. I'm still parched."

"Come with me." They stepped into the kitchen and Scott's nose tilted upward. He sniffed the air as Carmen popped a cake into the oven.

The cook grinned. "Hello, miss. You look so clean."

"I think she means that as a compliment," Scott said, chuckling.

Carmen frowned. "Of course I do. Cleanliness is next to godliness."

The woman smiled. "Well, thank you. I couldn't agree with you more."

"Smells like spice cake in here," Scott guessed, pouring a glass of tea for her and one for himself.

Carmen removed quilted oven mitts from her hands and began gathering ingredients from the refrigerator. "It's your favorite, Mr. Scott. It has lots of pecans and thick cream cheese icing."

"Mmmm. Can't wait." He looked at his watch then glanced at the woman. "I've got to unload the grain in the back of my pickup. We have a little time before we need to head in to town. Would you like to come outside with me? If you feel up to it, I'll give you a tour of the place when I'm done unloading."

"I'd love to see the ranch."

"Great. Bring your tea with you."

"Have fun," Carmen called as they exited the kitchen. "Glad to see you're feeling better!"

Like a gentleman, Scott held the door open for her.

"Your cook is very sweet," she said as they strolled down the sidewalk to the pickup.

Scott lifted his hat, ran a hand through his hair, then punched the hat back down on his head. "Carmen's more than our cook. She's a part of the family. She's been with us since I was a boy."

She urged him to elaborate.

"She's been cooking at High Lonesome for close to thirty years. My father hired her after my mother passed away, and she's been here ever since."

"Oh. I'm sorry about the loss of your mother."

"I was just a little kid when she died. She had cancer."

"That must have been very hard on you. A boy needs his mother. What about your father? Is he still alive?"

Scott sidestepped a reply while opening the passenger door for her. "Jump in. We're going down to the barn." He slammed the door shut then climbed in on his side and started up the engine as he revisited her question. "My dad passed away two years ago. He died right here on the ranch because he refused to go to the hospital. Stubborn as a mule, that one. We ran this place together up until the time he got sick. He was my rock. I miss him."

Scott put the truck in gear and started down the gravel drive.

"Do you run the business by yourself now?" she asked.

"Oh, no, I have a lot of help."

She bounced up and down on the springy seat. Her voice jiggled while trying to hold a conversation. "Seven thousand acres and a guest ranch must be very demanding on your time and energy."

"It is, but we never have more than ten guests at a time, and I've got a good crew backing me up. Besides Carmen, I have a girl named Amber. She's our housekeeper. She's only nineteen but does a bang-up job. Has a good work ethic. It took a lot of trial and error before I found her. I also have two young wranglers who handle most of the guest activities. Taking them on trail rides or on local excursions around the county. Cody was the cowboy we saw earlier when we drove in. You weren't feeling too well, so I don't know if you noticed him."

"I did see a young man helping people saddle their horses."

"Yep. That was Cody. I don't know where Rowdy is right now." Scott stopped the pickup at the barn then stuck his head out the window and peered around. "He's supposed to be repairing some broken bridles."

"Is Rowdy his real name?"

"No. The boy's given name is George, but he didn't think George sounded like a cowboy, so he came up with Rowdy. I don't know how. I think he got it from one of the old western re-runs they show on TV. He's an Apache. He lives on the reservation with his uncle."

"Is that so? How far is the reservation from here?"

"About a thirty-minute drive. Not that far by general standards, but it may as well be a continent away to a young person with a busy social calendar. Rowdy tends to stay up late and sleep in. I helped him secure a loan for a little Toyota truck so he can get to work on time. Before he got the truck, it was typical for him to arrive late, or not show up at all."

"What a generous thing for you to do. Helping him buy a truck."

"It's used, but it serves the purpose."

"Still, you didn't have to do it."

Scott jerked the keys out of the ignition and tossed them on the seat. He pushed the door open and went around her side to open the passenger door. "I like the kid," he continued, "but I confess I had an ulterior motive. With a business like this, I need dependable people. They have to be here when they're supposed to be. Besides, he's a pretty good worker and I believe in giving everyone a chance."

"Rowdy is lucky to know you...and so am I." She smiled and followed him to the back of the truck. He unlatched the rear gate. "What kinds of opportunities are there for young people on the reservation?" she asked.

"Not many. Most of the kids leave and go to the big city. They want adventures and fun. There aren't many jobs to be had on the rez anyway. Even if there were, a good many of the young folks seem to be allergic to hard work. It's not like when I was growing up. My dad had me baling hay and shoeing horses with him when I was seven or eight years old. I didn't have a choice. It was expected when you grew up on a working ranch."

Scott began to lift and haul fifty-pound bags of grain one at a time from the back of the truck. She leaned against the pickup and watched with interest as he went back and forth. His legs looked as sturdy as tree trunks, and his arm muscles bulged with each exertion.

"What about you? You never decided to strike out from this ranch?" she asked on one of his return trips. "You never wanted to go to the big city and seek out adventures?"

He shook his head. "The High Lonesome is my home. The horses are my life. I love it here. Besides, I don't know how to do anything else but cowboy."

"There's nothing wrong with being a cowboy," she replied. "And from the looks of this ranch, I'd venture to guess you're a savvy businessman."

"I do all right," he admitted. "I've been blessed, in many ways."

She stared out across the pasture, her mind drifting. She said, "I envy you, Mr. Landry. You love your home and your life. I'm not so sure I do."

"Pardon me?" He yanked a bandana from his back pocket and wiped his brow, then strode over and stood in front of her. "Why did you say that?"

Snapped from her reverie, she gazed at him. Her face felt blank from the inside. "I haven't the foggiest."

"That was an unusual thing to say," Scott noted.

"It *was*, wasn't it? I don't know where that thought came from. I don't believe my brain's functioning the way it should."

"Maybe it was a memory," Scott offered. He reached into the truck bed and pulled out another bag. Heaving it over his shoulder, he strode a few steps into the barn and dropped the bag into a wooden bin on top of the others. "Have you remembered anything about your life yet?" he asked, walking back.

She hesitated before she answered. "Yes, I think so."

He stopped and said, "Tell me."

"Right after I got out of the bath, I experienced what I think was a flashback. It all happened so fast, it almost didn't seem real."

"What was it like?"

"I don't know if you could call it a memory. It was like a scene from a movie. I couldn't make out any details. The people in it were fuzzy, just like my brain."

"The people? Who was in this movie of yours?" Scott shifted from one foot to another.

"A man and a woman, and a child. The woman was running. She was carrying the child in her arms. I think the man was chasing them. It wasn't a good feeling."

"Did you recognize them? Was the woman in this flashback you?"

She frowned. "I don't know. It lasted a moment then faded away. It was a blur. It's strange to see something in your mind that way and not know if it's real or imagined."

Scott wagged his head as though he didn't understand either. He grunted as he lifted the final sack of grain out of the truck bed and carried it into the barn. He deposited it into the bin. When he returned to her side, he said, "We need to tell Buddy—I mean Sheriff Griggs—when we see him today. Any little detail could be important."

"All right."

Scott bent over and plucked a rusty nail from off the ground. She couldn't help but admire his firm backside.

His wife sure is a lucky woman.

As fast as a shooting star, a man's face entered her mind. His mouth was twisted into a scream and his eyes were red and wild. Her fist flew to her mouth and she braced herself against the side of the truck.

"What is it?" Scott asked, taking long strides toward her. "Is it another flashback?"

"Yes." She took a deep breath and assured him, "It's over now, but it was frightening. It came so quick, with no warning."

"What did you see this time?" His brow creased with sincere concern.

"A horrible man with crazed eyes." She closed her own eyes and shuddered, trying to shake away the vision.

"Do you have any idea what triggered this image? What were you thinking about just before it came on?"

Her gaze flew to the ground. She nibbled her lower lip. "I was thinking your wife is a lucky woman," she admitted. Her mouth twitched in a nervous grin, but when she looked up, she saw his face had grown pale.

"I'm sorry," she stammered. "I should have censored myself before I said that. I'm pretty sure complete honesty is not the best policy when you just meet someone." She rolled her eyes and sighed in embarrassment.

Scott cleared his throat and said, "No. Honesty is a good trait." His mouth drew into a line, and he kicked at some rocks with the toe of his boot then met her gaze.

They stood for a moment, their eyes fastened on one another.

"I can tell I've upset you," she apologized. "I'm not even sure why I said that. I don't think it's the real me to be so forward. I think I'll blame it on the head trauma." The tease came out half-hearted.

"It's okay. I'm not upset." Scott jerked off his hat and slid his fingers through his long hair. When he plopped the hat back on, he changed the subject by asking, "Would you like to see the horses?"

She replied she would, but it bothered her to know she'd caused him any kind of distress. They'd just met, and it was the second time she'd seen a cloud pass in front of his beautiful blue eyes. It was her good fortune, however, that whatever had rattled him was short lived. He grinned, as if nothing had happened, and they walked to the other side of the barn.

"There are a few horses in here. The rest are out on the trails with Cody and the guests this morning."

She sauntered up to the first stall and stroked the velvety nose of a chestnut. He had a wide white blaze down his nose and two white socks. "He's beautiful. They all are," she remarked as she strolled down the aisle, awestruck.

"You can give them each a treat if you'd like." Scott opened a plastic container and handed her some peppermints.

"I didn't know horses like candy." She moved down the row, holding her palm out to each animal. They slurped up the mints, leaving her palm wet, and made loud crunching noises as they chomped.

"Horses want good breath, too," he joked. "You look natural around the animals. I wonder if you've ever ridden. Can you remember ever being on a horse?"

"No," she replied. "I'd sure love to try though. They seem to trust me, don't they? I feel a kinship to them."

"Come with me. I want to show you something else."

She followed him to a large corner stall where a tall painted horse with a flowing white mane and tail stood. The animal exuded pride and confidence. When the horse spied Scott, she whinnied. He reached into his shirt pocket and held a piece of carrot under her flapping lips. "She gets a special treat." The mare yanked the carrot out of his hand and bit down. "Her name is Pepper. This girl is mine."

"Oh, she's wonderful," she cried, as she patted the paint's neck and threaded her fingers through the horse's silky mane. "How old is she?"

"She's just a baby. Just turned three years old. She was born right here in this stall and I broke her. She's the best trail horse I've ever had." He rubbed the paint's ears then said, "Let's hop back in the truck and I'll drive you down to see the guest cabins now."

They climbed back into the pickup and rambled down a gravel road to the base of the red rock mountains. Nestled among juniper trees and wildflowers were five rustic cottages, spread out over a couple of acres. They all had wooden decks with rocking chairs out front. Scott turned off the truck engine and the two of them got out and moseyed over to one of the cabins.

"This one's empty this week so I'll show you the inside of it."

Hanging on the front door was a bleached cattle skull with a lasso and pair of spurs decorating the space between the double windows. Under the windows sat a barrel full of flowers. A table with a wagon wheel and glass top sat next to a weather-beaten rocker.

Scott pulled a ring full of jangling keys from his shirt pocket. He stuck one key in the door and turned the knob. When the door creaked opened, they heard a gasp come from inside.

A young couple was lying on the loveseat, fully clothed, but locked in a passionate embrace. They were kissing. Caught, they jerked apart and sat up. The young girl's cheeks flamed and her dark gaze flew to the ground. The young man slicked back his black hair and acted as if nothing was out of the ordinary. He glanced at the girl then said, "Hey, Scott. What are you doing here?"

"I was about to ask you the same question, Rowdy," the ranch owner replied in an even tone.

Rowdy stood and strutted to the door, leaving the girl behind. "Guess I should be getting back to the barn. Got some work to do." He plucked a wide-brimmed hat off a wall hook and slammed it on his head, shading his chocolate brown eyes.

"Not so fast, pardner," Scott said, gripping the lean wrangler's shoulder with a firm hand.

The girl remained on the loveseat with her head bent. She began to whimper. "Please don't fire me, Scott. I'm so sorry. I told Rowdy we shouldn't come in here. Especially not during work hours." She cast an angry look at her boyfriend.

Scott wanted his employees to understand he wasn't going to tolerate any monkey business while on his time clock, but there wasn't any reason to lose his cool or humiliate them in front of his guest. That wasn't his style. He and his companion exchanged a knowing glance.

Rowdy's eyes blinked like he had a nervous tick. When he met Scott's cool stare, the young wrangler's bravado shrunk. He shoved his hands into his pockets. "Amber's right," he apologized. "It's all my fault, Scott. If you're going to fire anyone, it should be me. I told her we could hide out here for a little while, but I should have known better."

Scott glanced back and forth between the couple. Amber's lower lip quivered. He could see she was embarrassed to death. And for all his cocksure attitude, Rowdy knew when he'd done something wrong.

"Oh, hush, both of you. Nobody's getting fired." Scott released his hold on Rowdy and pointed a finger at Amber. "You, come here, Miss Amber. And wipe your tears."

The girl rubbed the back of her hand across her cheek, stood, and shuffled over to her employer.

Her legs were shaking.

Scott stared at the couple for one of the longest minutes ever recorded. Kind but firm, he came right to the point, his words measured.

"This is a place of business. The two of you are my employees. I don't care what you do on your own time, but when you're on my clock, I expect you to be doing what I pay you to do, which is wrangling and housekeeping. Understood?"

"Yes, Scott," they replied in tandem.

"All right, then. Get back to work. Break is over."

"Yes, sir," Rowdy said, saluting his boss. Amber rose up on her tiptoes and gave Scott a quick peck on the cheek. Relief flooded her face.

The couple grasped hands and ran out the door and up the hill toward the barn.

"No more make-out sessions in the cabins!" Scott hollered after them.

He and the woman looked at each other and started laughing.

"You're a real toughie," she teased.

"Ah, they're just two kids in love. They don't mean any harm. Don't you remember what it feels like to be young and in love?" As soon as the words left his mouth, he regretted them. "I'm sorry," he said. "That was an insensitive thing for me to say, considering your amnesia and all."

"Don't be sorry. I *do* remember what it's like to be in love. I just don't know whether I'm in love right now."

"It must be strange not to have any idea about the elemental things in life, like your own name, or whether you're single or married." He wondered about her marital status himself.

"This morning in the bath, I was thinking about that. If there *is* someone in my life, I hope he's looking for me."

"If I were him, I'd be pounding the sidewalks until I found you." Scott pierced her with his eyes and an unexpected tremor coursed through his body when their gazed fastened.

She blushed, and did not respond.

He cleared his throat. "I guess you can see that I say what's on my mind, too." Changing the subject again, he rubbed his hands together and said, "Well, now you've seen what the cabins look like."

"Thanks for giving me the grand tour."

"You're welcome, but that's not the grand tour. There's a whole lot more to this ranch. I'll show you the rest of it later, when we have time and you're up to it." He looked at his watch. "We should probably get started in to town. We'll stop by the sheriff's department before we head over to the clinic."

"I'm ready if you are."

The two of them hopped back into Scott's truck and he swung by the house to tell Carmen they were leaving.

As they motored to town, she remarked about how unique and pretty the area was.

"None of this looks even vaguely familiar to you?" Scott asked.

"No. I wish something...anything would come to me. I'm just blank."

Scott drove in the manner of a man with nowhere to be at no particular time. His arm dangled out the window and he slumped in his seat. She appraised his profile. He had a strong jaw and there was a slight bend in his nose. She wondered if a horse had kicked him, or if he'd broken it playing some high school sport. His lashes were long and thick, for a man. His skin was tan, no doubt from long hours working in the sun, and his long sandy blond hair looked soft and well conditioned.

She gathered up her courage and decided to broach the subject of his family. She was curious as to the whereabouts of his wife and child. She'd been in his home for several hours and there'd been no mention or sign of them. "Mr. Landry—"

"Call me Scott," he said, interrupting her.

"Okay. Scott. I'm not a nosey person, I don't think, but when I was in your bedroom, I noticed the photo of your family on your dresser. You have a lovely wife and precious little baby. Will I get to meet them later?"

He took his eyes off the road just for a moment. He met her stare, and his answer was straightforward. "My wife, Maggie, passed away four years ago."

She sighed. *I've done it again.* "Oh, I'm so sorry. No wonder you reacted the way you did a while ago when I brought her up."

"You had no way of knowing. It would have come up sooner or later."

"Are these your wife's clothes I'm wearing?" She fingered the shirt.

"Yes. It was Carmen's idea for you to borrow them. But I didn't mind," he added quickly. "I hope you don't feel weird about wearing them."

"It's fine with me, as long as you're okay with it. Her things must be precious to you."

He kept his eye on the road. "I haven't looked at any of her things for a long time. *She* was precious, but clothes are just clothes. It was a shock to see you wearing them, that's all. I'm over it now."

Since they were being candid, she went ahead and asked, "If you don't mind talking about it, what happened to your wife?"

"She suffered a brain aneurism. One minute she was laughing and playing with our daughter, and the next minute she was gone. There was nothing anyone could have done. It was just one of those bad things that happen to good people."

"That's tragic. She must have been quite young."

"Twenty-six. We were high school sweethearts, but she was two years behind me. We had a good life together, while it lasted. I thought we'd grow old together, but the universe had other plans."

She waited, not speaking, sensing he had more to say.

He continued. "Maggie played a major role in making the ranch as successful as it is today. And she gave me my little daughter." Scott smiled then, a smile so radiant it could have lit up a moonless sky. "Willow is seven, and she's a real pistol. She's ornery and precocious as all get out. You'll get to meet her tomorrow. Tonight she's spending the night with a horse riding friend."

"Willow. That's a darling name."

Scott chuckled. "Maggie chose it. She was involved with a local environmental group for a while when she was pregnant. They wanted to save the trees. If we'd had a son, Maggie planned on naming him Oak. Oak Landry." He laughed out loud at the remembrance. "Maggie was as curious as a cat. That girl liked to read the encyclopedia for fun. Can you believe that?" He shook his head. "Willow means the world to me. I don't know what I would have done if I hadn't had her when Maggie died. I suppose I would have gone crazy."

Their frank conversation about something so personal seemed natural. His ability to open up to her, a stranger, about his loss said so much about the man. It said a lot about the way they connected. "You're a lucky man," she told him. "You'll always have a part of your wife with you, through your daughter."

He nodded. "Yeah, but there are so many regrets."

"What kind of regrets?"

"The biggest is that Willow doesn't remember much about her mommy. She was so young. To her, Mommy is just a photograph. She'll never know what a special lady her mother was."

"She'll know if you tell her. It's important for you to share your memories and stories with her. As I'm sure you do," she added. "That coming from a person who can't even remember her own name." She rolled her eyes playfully.

Scott smiled. "You seem to know what children need. Do you think you might have a child?"

"I don't know," she replied. "That's the kind of gut feeling I'd think even amnesia couldn't erase."

They both reflected on that.

All of a sudden, Scott said, "Willow needs a mother. As she grows and gets older, she's going to have lots of questions about things I don't understand or know anything about. What will I do then? I won't be able to give her the kind of advice a mother can. She's already such a tomboy. I'm worried about what will happen when it comes time for her to date and go to dances...I don't know how to raise a girl."

The woman flashed him a sincere smile. "I'm sure you're doing just fine. All any child needs is a loving parent. Willow is lucky to have you as her father. You're a good man. I can sense that. Anyway, there's nothing wrong with tomboys," she added. "I have a sneaking suspicion I may have been one when I was a girl."

Scott whipped into a parking space at the sheriff's department and cut the motor off. He was still in a philosophical mood. "Most people think it's too painful for me, so they never talk about Maggie. They act as if she never existed. I suppose they think it's better for me, but it's not. Maggie was my wife, and the mother of my child, and I loved her. Sometimes it's therapeutic to talk about her. I think you understand."

The woman nodded. "Of course I do. It's perfectly natural to want to keep memories alive. Maggie was your love. You expected to spend your life with her. She was taken from you too soon."

He bowed his head, then looked up and peered into her eyes. "Thank you for asking about my family. That was real kind of you." Scott rubbed his chin.

"I'm glad you felt comfortable enough to tell me about your wife."

"That's unusual for me. It usually takes a while for me to warm up to people, but you're very easy to talk to."

When they got out of the truck, he shook his head and said, “Here you are, not able to remember whether you have a family or not, and you’re listening to me jabber on about mine. I’m sorry about that. It was insensitive of me. Again.”

“Don’t be silly,” she replied. “You can return the favor when I need to talk.”

“That’s a deal.” He stuck out his hand to shake. When they touched, a spark ignited between them. He wondered if she’d felt it.

They entered the brick building and Scott greeted the secretary with a high five. “Linda and I were classmates,” he told the woman, as she and the secretary nodded greetings. “The sheriff told us to drop by, Lin. Is he here?”

“Yep. You can go on in.”

Scott peeked into the office. Buddy was sitting ramrod straight in a swivel chair staring at the computer screen. The door was open, but Scott still rapped on it before entering.

“Come in.” Buddy stood and pumped his friend’s hand. “How you doing, Scotty?”

“I’m good. Buddy, this is the lady I called you about.”

“Ma’am.” The sheriff shook her hand. “I’m Sheriff Griggs. Pleased to meet you.”

“Same here.”

Scott watched her scan the man, and looked at his friend as a stranger might see him. Buddy was big and stocky but had a round, boyish, clean-shaven face, dimples, and a warm smile. His hair was a nest of thick, dark curls. Far from intimidating—more reassuring. The woman visibly relaxed.

“Both of you go ahead and have a seat. I’ve been doing a check to see if any other county or state offices have issued a missing person’s announcement.”

“And?” Scott asked.

"So far there's been nothing fitting your description, ma'am, so we're going to get the ball rolling on our end." He slid a notepad out of his desk drawer. "Let me take down all the pertinent information we can come up with so we have an accurate description for our bulletin. I'm going to have Linda snap your photo and we'll print up some color flyers. We'll plaster them all over the county and send them out on the wire across New Mexico, as well as Colorado, Arizona and Utah. I'll also get you up on the internet."

The smile on the woman's face echoed Scott's as she looked at him.

"Thanks for getting right on this," Scott told Buddy, pleased.

"Hey, when my best friend says jump, I ask how high."

"Buddy and I have been friends since we were in elementary school," Scott said.

"I lived down the road from the High Lonesome, and Scotty and I used to play all over those mountains. Didn't we?"

"Yep. We sure did."

The sheriff laughed, and leaned back in his chair. "We'd ride our horses from sunrise to sundown, and go swimming in the lake. I bet we explored every hideout on the ranch when we were boys. Did Scotty tell you about all the caves up in the hills yet?"

She nodded. "He mentioned something about them. Sounds like you two have a lot of shared history."

"Yeah, and it doesn't stop there," Buddy remarked. "Now he's dating my ex-wife. Get a load of that!"

She threw Scott a curious glance.

He said nothing, but narrowed his eyes at his pal.

Buddy's laugh was robust. "I see our mutual friend is going to remain mum on that topic."

Scott leaned over and plucked a donut out of the box sitting on the corner of Buddy's desk. "I have an idea. Why don't we get back to figuring out how we can help this lady? I'll go ask Linda to bring her camera in." He sank his teeth into the donut and complained, "Stale" as he sauntered out of the room.

"My ex-wife is a touchy subject," Buddy explained, grinning. "Not for me, but for him."

Linda stepped in and took several photos as the sheriff typed up a physical description of the woman.

"I'll get those flyers printed up and your picture on the internet as soon as possible," he told her. "I'll let you know as soon as I get any leads or phone calls."

"Thank you so much," she replied, shaking his hand again.

"You're welcome, ma'am. I'll do my best to help you find your way back home—wherever that may be. In the meantime, enjoy your stay at the High Lonesome. Scotty knows how to show his guests a good time." The sheriff touched the brim of his hat with his finger then clamped a hand on his friend's shoulder. "*Adios*, pardner. Talk to you later."

Scott nodded. "Appreciate it, Bud."

****

They sat in the clinic waiting room. Scott held a clipboard with blanks yet unfilled on the informational form. He took it up to the front desk. The young receptionist stared at the empty spaces on the paper.

"I'm going to pay for this appointment," he whispered. "Doctor Coleman referred us and she knows all about this situation. It's kind of unique. The problem is the lady doesn't know what to put in these blanks."

"Huh?" The girl cracked the gum in her mouth

and loudly said, "You still have to put a name and address on here, even if you're not using insurance. How are we supposed to make a file folder if we don't have a name?"

"Could you please lower your voice?" Scott raised a finger to his lips and made a shushing sound.

"Don't shush me, sir," the girl said, firing him a rude look.

"I'm sorry. Can't you just put Jane Doe on the file folder? The patient"—he nodded toward the woman—"doesn't know her real name." He sighed. "As I mentioned before, Dr. Joanna Coleman is aware of all this." He glanced back and saw all the people in the waiting room staring at the pretty brunette, and her looking as if she wanted to crawl under the chair.

Just then, Joanna burst through the door. She made a beeline straight to Scott. "Hello, Mr. Landry." Taking long strides to the front counter, she spoke to the receptionist in her usual assertive manner. "I called in and arranged for a three o'clock CT scan with Doug. Can you check to see if he's ready for us?"

"Yes, doctor." The receptionist flipped through the notes on her calendar and then made a quick call. "You all can go on back." Her tone changed from surly to polite under Joanna's bold gaze.

"Thank you. Follow me," Joanna ordered both Scott and the woman. They all walked through a set of double doors and treaded down the sterile hallway toward the x-ray department. "Hello again," Joanna said, turning to acknowledge her temporary patient.

"Hello, Doctor Coleman."

"You're looking much better than you did earlier today," Joanna noted.

"It's remarkable what a hot bath and some fresh air will do for a body."

"Better than modern medicine in some cases,"

Scott added.

Joanna arched an eyebrow at the pair. "Here we are. Hello Doug," she said, greeting the x-ray technician with a handshake. "This is Scott Landry. He's the owner of the High Lonesome Ranch, and this is Mr. Landry's guest. She has a hematoma on her forehead and is experiencing some memory loss."

"I have your orders right here, Doctor Coleman." The technician tapped a file. "You can come with me," Doug told the woman. "Doctor, you and Mr. Landry can wait in my office if you'd like. I'll let you know when we're done."

"Thank you. I appreciate your squeezing us in like this."

"Glad to help."

Joanna tugged at Scott's arm as the technician led the woman down another hall. She directed him into a small office and they plopped into leather chairs.

"I couldn't wait to see you." Joanna leaned over and surprised Scott with a juicy kiss on the lips. "What have you and the little princess been up to the last couple of hours?"

Scott frowned. "Don't call her names. Why would you refer to her that way?"

"Oh, I'm just teasing. Don't be so sensitive."

"I'm not. I don't think possible assault and amnesia is anything to joke about, that's all."

"Come on, Scott. How often do we see a case of amnesia around this little podunk town? Never. It's kind of exciting."

"I doubt she would consider getting cracked in the head and dumped in the desert exciting," he answered.

"And what would *she* call it?" Joanna glared at him.

"Disconcerting. Frightening. Confusing. Those are a few adjectives which come to mind."

"Uh-huh. It's possible she could be faking the whole thing. Has that occurred to you?"

He cast her a look of bewilderment. "Don't be ridiculous. Why would someone like her fake amnesia?"

"Someone like her? What's that supposed to mean?"

"Nothing. I used the wrong phrasing. It's just that I spent some time talking to her today and she doesn't seem like the kind of person who would go to the trouble of faking amnesia. What would be the purpose? Anyway, she didn't give herself that lump on the head, and she didn't twist her own arm. Someone violently attacked her, and we both know it."

"I've seen stranger things before, honey." Joanna crossed her legs. "You'd be surprised at the crazy things people will do for attention. Especially women."

"Well I don't buy it," Scott replied. "I don't understand why you're being critical. You're a physician. You took an oath to show compassion and care for those in need. This lady fits the bill."

"I'm an M.D., not a mental health counselor," Joanna answered with a smug expression.

"She's not mentally ill." Scott jumped up then shoved his hands in his pockets and walked around in circles.

Joanna uncrossed her legs, rose and sidled up close to him. "Why are you acting so nervous? Stop pacing," she demanded. Stroking his thigh with her nails, she asked, "Are you coming over tonight?"

"I don't think so."

She backed up and snapped, "But Willow's gone. You told me you'd be free to spend the night."

"That was before all this happened. I should stay home and help this lady settle in. She's having terrifying flashbacks. That's normal with amnesia, right?"

Joanna flopped into the chair again and answered with a big sigh. "Yes, it's normal. I'm having flashbacks, too—in case you care to know. I'm flashing back to when Buddy preferred spending his time hunting, fishing or riding the range, rather than be with me."

"What's Buddy got to do with this?" Scott asked.

"You seem to be falling into the same pattern."

"That's not fair, Jo. Don't lump this unique situation in with whatever irrational thoughts you're having about you and me."

She shot him a look that could kill.

Wishing to keep the peace, he sat and patted her knee. "Come on now. Let's not fuss. Buddy's already sending out bulletins all over the state and beyond. I'm sure we're going to hear from someone in no time. Someone who can identify her. Then you and I can take a weekend and go somewhere together."

Jo brightened a little. "Really?"

"Sure."

"Okay. That makes me happier." Reverting to doctor mode, she inquired, "What has she remembered today? You said she's having flashbacks."

"Yeah. She saw a vision of a child and a man."

"Maybe they're memories of her family. But, I didn't notice a wedding band on her hand."

"Me either, but maybe it slipped off if she had to fight off her attacker."

"That's assuming she's married. Are you figuring she is, just because she's so attractive?" Joanna asked through clenched teeth.

Scott rolled his eyes and rested his chin in his hand. "Don't start again," he begged. "I don't want to argue with you."

"Okay. Sorry. Forget I said anything."

They sat not speaking for a while. Finally,

Joanna said, “Scott, I do understand why you’re helping her. Part of the reason I love you is because you’re such a decent man. But the main reason I love you is because you’re so damn sexy.” She squeezed his thigh, causing him to jump. “I’m just disappointed because I was planning a very romantic evening with you tonight. It’s been a while since you’ve been over.”

He covered her hand with his. “I know. It’s been so hectic around the ranch, and now this. I promise—we’ll go off together soon.” He tried to sound excited, but his mind was elsewhere.

The door opened and the technician stepped in. “All done. She’s out in the waiting room. Doctor Coleman, I’ll put a rush on this and call your office personally with the results.”

She and Scott stood and each shook his hand, then she replied, “Thank you, Doug. Mr. Landry and I appreciate your help and cooperation.”

The two of them strolled out to the waiting room and found the woman sitting alone, looking forlorn.

“Hey, how did it go?” Scott asked, touching her shoulder.

“Fine, I guess. Thank you, Doctor Coleman, for arranging this.”

“It’s my pleasure.” Joanna fired a glance at Scott’s hand.

“If we’re done, then I guess we’re ready to go,” he said.

Joanna spoke to the receptionist for a moment, and then the trio stepped outside and walked to Scott’s pickup. Joanna spoke in a professional tone when she said, “Mr. Landry, I’ll call as soon as I get the results. I’ve got to head back to the office now. See you both later. Be sure and call if you have any concerns.” She waited until the woman turned her back then winked at Scott before jumping into her Audi and peeling away.

He climbed into the old truck. The woman had already gotten in and laid her head back against the seat.

"I was planning on taking you shopping," he reminded her, "but maybe I should get you back to the ranch instead. It's been a long day and you look exhausted."

"I am. Do you mind very much if I wear Maggie's clothes for another day?"

"Of course not. You're welcome to anything in my home that you need, for as long as you're there. I'll call Amber on my cell right now and ask her to get the downstairs guest room ready for you. It has its own bathroom. I think you'll find it very comfortable."

She nodded her approval and closed her eyes. Sheriff Griggs' words rolled over and over like a tumbleweed in her mind. *He's dating my ex-wife.* How were Scott and the sheriff able to maintain their friendship with a woman between them? What kind of woman was he attracted to? He and Sheriff Griggs were, physically, very different types of men, yet they'd both become involved with the same girl.

It was a disappointing bit of news—to learn Scott had a girlfriend. She felt a definite attraction to him. What was she thinking, anyway? *Why on earth am I disappointed? Why am I thinking about him that way? For all I know, I might have a boyfriend, or a husband.* She stared at her left hand. No ring. *Maybe I'm not spoken for. I wonder how long it will be before I learn the truth.*

She opened her eyes and let them linger on the cowboy. He was focused on the winding road ahead.

I need to do the same thing. Focus. Prepare for the twists and turns that are sure to come.

Chapter Three

The next morning, she woke in a cold sweat. She sprang up in bed and gazed around. *Where am I? It doesn't look like my...Oh, yeah...this is his house. I'm sleeping in Scott's guest room.*

She rubbed her eyes with the back of her hand. He'd been in the erotic dream she'd just had. Heat coursed through her veins as it replayed in her head.

Why am I dreaming about the man? Didn't I just learn he has a girlfriend? I might have a man of my own, she reminded herself. *Stop thinking about him!* She stretched her arms above her head, ran a toe down her clean-shaven leg and smiled. *Oh well. There's nothing to get all worked up about. It was just a little dream, after all.*

Delicious smells wafted down the hallway and under the door of the bedroom. Her appetite had returned with a full vengeance, and she couldn't wait to dig into some more of Carmen's food. She jumped in the shower then dressed quickly—humming to drown out the growls her stomach was making.

When she was dressed, she walked down the hall, passing the rancher's office door, which was closed, and prayed she wouldn't run into him first thing. The dream was fresh, and she knew she'd not be able to look him in the eye without turning pink as a salmon. Fortunately, he was not in the kitchen either when she entered.

"*Buenos dias*!" Carmen greeted her with a huge smile as she stabbed slabs of bacon with a fork.

Pancakes and eggs were bubbling on a griddle and bread was toasting. Coffee was brewing, a pitcher of orange juice sat on the counter next to a bowl of bananas, and potatoes were sizzling in a cast iron pan. The cook resembled an octopus with her hands reaching out in several directions.

A small person sitting on a stool at the island peered up from a magazine and grinned. She was missing a front tooth.

"Howdy. You're the lady who don't remember nothin', ain't ya?"

Carmen reprimanded the girl in a low growl reminiscent of a mother bear. "Willow, that's a rude thing to say to someone you just met. And don't say ain't."

"Sorry, Carmen."

"And one more thing. Quit speaking improper English. Your daddy sends you to school for a reason."

"Sorry *again*, Carmen." The girl rolled her eyes, but didn't bother to hide her mischievous grin.

Seeing the little blonde triggered a strange sensation in the woman. She clutched the edge of the island as the vision of another small child formed in her mind. She was a young child with dark hair who was laughing and yelling the words, *Higher! Higher!*

The flash was over in a second, but the image shook her to the core, because along with it came a strong sense of familiarity.

"You *are* the lady, right?" The girl tapped the countertop with her finger to get the woman's attention.

Realizing she'd blanked out for a moment, she regained her composure and climbed onto a bar stool to study the young girl. Her hair was the color of a stalk of wheat, and she wore a pink cowgirl hat with rhinestones dotting the band.

She smiled. "Yes. I'm the lady. You must be

Willow. Your dad told me about you."

"Carmen told me about *you.*" Willow glanced at the cook with her eyebrow arched.

"Sorry, ma'am," Carmen apologized. "But I thought I should give Willow a heads up about you and the..."

"That's okay, Carmen."

"Is it true you don't know your own name?" Willow asked.

"I'm afraid so."

"Can I see the bump on your head?" Willow tucked her feet under her bottom and leaned forward, propping herself on her elbows.

"Okay. But are you sure it won't make you queasy? It's starting to turn a weird shade of green."

"Oh, no. I'm tough as nails. I saw a baby colt born before. There was a lot of blood and guts all over. A little knot on your head ain't gonna bother me none."

"Willow!" Carmen slammed a spatula down on the counter. "The way you talk, child. I warned you. Speak correctly, *por favor.*"

"Sorry, Carmen." Willow emphasized the *sorry* and winked at her table companion.

The woman lifted her bangs as the girl pulled a small magnifying glass out of her back jeans pocket and proceeded to inspect the bump as if she were a detective.

Laughing, she asked the girl, "Where did you get a magnifying glass?"

"Out of a spy catalog," Willow replied. "Mmmm. That's a right nasty looking bump, all right. May I see your arm, *por favor*? You'll notice I speak Spanish, too."

Carmen chuckled with her expansive bosom vibrating. She was unable to hide her amusement.

The woman stretched out her arm to show the girl the large purple and blue bruise.

"Did somebody try to twist it off?" Willow asked.

"I'm not sure. I don't remember anything about my accident."

There was a bag labeled *Beth's Banana Bread* sitting in front of the girl. She pulled out a thick slice and took a bite. "That's a shame for you, but lucky for me. I've never met anybody who had amnesia before."

The woman and Carmen exchanged glances.

"She's seven going on seventeen," the cook replied, shaking her head.

Willow offered her new friend a slice of bread. "Would you like some? Carmen orders it special because it's my favorite. It has loads of pecans in it. It's delish!"

"Thanks. To tell you the truth, I'm so hungry I could eat an elephant."

"Me, too. Have you ever eaten an elephant before, lady?"

She giggled. "No. Can't say that I have. I don't believe anyone in the world eats elephant. At least I hope not. I think it's just a funny expression."

"Maybe the people in India do."

"If I'm remembering my world history, Indian people revere elephants. I don't think they want to have them for dinner."

"What does revere mean?"

"It means to honor."

"I see." Willow took another big bite of bread. "I revere my horse."

"Excuse me." Carmen interrupted the conversation and asked, "Ma'am, would you like to have your breakfast here in the kitchen this morning, or in the dining room with the other guests?"

"Oh, this is fine. If I'm not in your way," she added. "I'm not sure I'm up to explaining my situation to strangers over casual chit-chat."

"I understand." Carmen retrieved a butter dish and two jars of jam from the fridge. "I'll get you a plate."

"Take your time. I can wait until the other guests are served."

"I've been contemplating something," Willow said in complete seriousness.

"Is that so?" The woman folded her hands in front of her.

"Yep."

Grinning, she said, "Contemplating is a very big word for a seven year old."

"I'm good at vocabulary and I'm a voracious reader."

"Voracious? That's another word I didn't expect out of the mouth of a babe. I'm very impressed."

"Thank you," Willow replied. "My mama was very smart. Daddy says I get it from her."

"I'm sure your mama is very proud of you."

"She's in heaven. She can't be proud of me." Willow's statement was matter-of-fact.

"Well, sure she can. Even if she's not right here with you, she's always in your heart and she's still watching over you."

"My daddy tells me the same thing."

"Your daddy's very smart, too. Now, go ahead and tell me what it is you've been contemplating."

Willow peeled a banana and stuffed a bite of it in her mouth. When she finished chewing she said, "If you're going to be staying with us, I think it's important you have a name. We can't call you lady all the time. And Carmen would get after my butt if I yelled *hey* at you. Do you have any ideas?"

Carmen wagged a piece of bacon at the girl. "Willow, don't talk about butts at the table."

"To be honest," the woman told Willow, "I hadn't thought about what my name could be. I have a sneaking suspicion you have though. What's your suggestion?"

"I want to call you Beth."

The woman stared at the banana bread bag, dumbfounded. "You want to name me after your favorite quick bread?"

"Yep. I think it's a real pretty name. I wish that was *my* name. What do you think about it?

The woman considered it. "I think it's very pretty, too."

"Do you think Beth could be your actual real name?" Willow asked with excitement. "Wouldn't that be something if it was?"

"I hate to burst your bubble, Willow, but it doesn't ring a bell."

"Oh." The child frowned, and then the frown turned upside down again. "Well, what would you think about being called Beth anyway? It would be just until you find out what your real name is."

Carmen placed a big round plate in front of the guest. "Willow, maybe the nice lady doesn't want to be named after a hunk of dough."

"Would you mind being named after my favorite bread?" Willow asked with glitter in her eyes. "It's the best bread in the world." She rubbed her tummy and licked her lips.

"You're very thoughtful," the woman answered with a chuckle. "It's pretty and it's simple. I should be able to remember it," she joked. "You may call me that if you'd like."

"Yippee!" Willow shouted. She clapped her hands and jumped off the bar stool and did a happy dance around the island.

"Beth" grinned when she noticed the girl was wearing pink boots to match her hat. She also had on a rhinestone belt, looking quite the little cowgirl.

"Is there a party going on in here?" Scott asked as he sauntered through the back door. He jerked off his cowboy hat and hung it on a hook just inside the door. He ran his hands through his blond hair and grinned.

Beth's heart gripped at the sight of him—and at the remembrance of the sexy dream. He looked the essence of western masculinity in his tight Wranglers, dusty boots, and blue denim shirt. He also wore a silk scarf tied around his neck.

He said, "It smells delicious in here. I'm as hungry as a bear."

"Daddy!" Willow skipped over and threw herself into his arms. He heaved her over his shoulder, they hugged, and she planted a big kiss on his stubbly cheek.

"Did you just get home, baby?"

"A little while ago. Wait till you see what Midnight can do."

"I'm looking forward to it. Let me say hi to our guest." Scott plopped Willow on the island counter and his gaze raked over Beth. He thought she looked pretty as a picture. Her green eyes twinkled and her dark hair looked so shiny lying soft as flower petals across her shoulders. "Good mornin'."

"Good morning." Her eyelashes fluttered.

"Did you sleep well?"

"Like a log, as they say."

"Daddy, guess what?" Willow interrupted, bouncing up and down.

"What?"

"The lady has a name."

Scott threw them a shocked look. "You remember your name?" he asked.

"No, Daddy," Willow giggled. "I thought up a new name for her. She's going to be Beth from now on."

"Beth, huh? How did you come up with that?"

Willow pointed to the label on the bread bag and Scott laughed. "It works as well as anything, I guess. Beth. I like it. It's pretty. It fits her. Good job, honey." His eyes lingered on the newly christened Beth.

"Do you want to eat now, Mr. Scott?" Carmen asked, reaching for another breakfast plate.

He washed his hands in the kitchen sink and dried them on a dishtowel. "Yeah. I'll join these two lovely ladies, if they don't mind," he answered, straddling an island stool.

"When do your guests eat?" Beth asked.

Scott answered. "They'll be coming in any minute. They all eat together in the dining room. I normally take breakfast with them, but I asked the wranglers to act as hosts this morning."

As they chatted, the cook hurried back and forth from the kitchen. She delivered bowl after bowl of food to the long wooden table in the dining room, in preparation for the arrival of the guests.

Beth jumped up. "Let me help you with those."

Carmen shooed her away. "No thank you. Eat before it gets cold. This is my job." Right on cue, she set the last bowl down as the guests came through the front door and took their places at the dining room table.

Beth heard them chattering like jays. She didn't have to be told twice. She delved into her plate of eggs and watched Scott douse his potatoes with ketchup.

"Willow, tell the lady what you were doing at your friend's house yesterday." Scott poured a cup of coffee then swiped some bacon off the heating plate on the counter behind him.

"She's not the lady, Daddy. She's *Beth.*"

"I'm sorry. I forgot already. Go ahead and tell Beth."

"I was practicing for the Little Wranglers Rodeo."

"You're going to be in a rodeo?"

"Yep. I've been in plenty of rodeos already. I

compete in pole bending on my horse, Midnight."

"What's pole bending?" Beth asked.

Willow looked to her father to explain. He finished swallowing a link of sausage before he spoke.

"The object of pole bending is to ride through a pattern of upright poles in the shortest time without toppling any of them. There are six plastic poles set in rubber bases. The first one is about twenty-one feet from the start/finish line, with the others placed progressively farther from the line at twenty-one foot intervals. Willow gallops at full speed down one side. Then, at the end, she turns one hundred eighty degrees and weaves through the serpentine path. When she reaches the last pole, she turns and goes back through the pattern again until she reaches the far end. When the pattern is completed, she dashes to the finish line."

Beth blinked. "My gosh. You do all that on a horse? Without falling off?"

"Yep. Would you like to see Midnight? Come on, I'll show you." Willow reached for her hand and tugged.

When their hands touched, Beth felt a spark, and the image of the dark-haired child flashed in front of her again. This time, the vision was of the little girl lying in a canopy bed listening to a bedtime story.

I feel a connection to that little girl. But, who is she? What does she mean to me?

"Later," Scott told Willow. His forehead wrinkled. "Beth, what is it? Are you getting a headache?" He gave her a knowing look, and she nodded confirmation, realizing he understood what was happening to her.

"It was just a sharp pain, but it's gone now. I'm okay." The image disappeared as quickly as it had come on. She took a drink of juice. She couldn't help but wonder if the flashbacks were random pictures, or pieces of a puzzle associated with her life. Whatever they meant, they were disconcerting. She snapped back to reality, realizing Willow was staring. "I'd love to meet Midnight when we're done here."

"Goodie!" The child clapped her hands.

"I'll go out to the barn with you," Scott said. He devoured the eggs, pancakes and potatoes, but Beth noticed his gaze remained on her as she patiently listen to Willow, who chattered on like a monkey about her horse and pole bending.

After breakfast, the three of them washed then went to the barn where Willow introduced Beth to her black quarter horse. Scott excused himself and said he had to scoop poop. Beth fed the bay treats as the little girl brushed his mane and combed his tail, and talked non-stop.

"You're bending more than poles today, Willow," Scott joked as he pushed a third wheelbarrow of horse poop past them. "You're talking the poor lady's ear off. You can give her a demonstration on your horse another time. As soon as I dump this load, she and I are going in to town." He unloaded the manure, whipped a kerchief out of his pocket and wiped it across his glistening forehead.

"We are?" Beth's eyebrow rose.

"Yesterday I promised you a shopping trip. Remember?"

"Oh. So you did."

"I'm glad to see your short-term memory is intact."

"Can I go?" Willow begged.

"Not this time, cowgirl. Maybe next time."

Willow didn't argue. She put away the brush and comb and kissed her horse on the nose.

"Go on now. Scoot," Scott told his daughter as he patted her bottom. They stepped into the sunshine.

"Tell Carmen I've taken Beth to town. And behave yourself. We'll be back later."

"Okay, Daddy." Willow gave him a kiss and started running up the hill toward the house. "Bye, Beth!" she called.

Beth waved and hollered back. "She sure is a doll," she told Scott as they climbed into the pickup.

"She's quite a character," he replied, grinning.

As they bumped along the dirt road toward Ghost Rock, Beth said, "I still can't get over the fact that your daughter races that big horse around poles—and doesn't fall off! What an incredible feat for a girl her age. I'm going to have to watch her sometime."

Scott's ocean blue eyes slid toward her and lingered for a moment before returning to the road. Again, she'd caught him looking. She was flattered. He must like what he sees, she thought. *I like what I see, too.* Her heart flip-flopped.

"So, were you comfortable in the guest room last night?" he inquired for the second time.

She knew he was fishing for small talk. It was sweet. He acted like a teenager with a crush.

"No bad dreams?" he asked.

"No bad dreams. As a matter of fact, I had a rather pleasant one this morning."

She felt a compulsion to tell him about the erotic dream in which he played the starring role. She squeezed her eyes shut and shook her head as if she was trying to shake the cobwebs out. *What's wrong with me? I'm thinking like a reckless fool. You don't just tell a perfect stranger about a sexy dream you had. Even if he's ruggedly handsome and you feel a connection to the man. Get a grip, Beth! Or whatever your name is.*

"So did I," she heard him answer. Their eyes locked, but Scott didn't elaborate. He only smiled that crooked smile that caused her insides to melt like ice cream in summer.

She felt two suns warm her cheeks. *Can the man read my mind?* Half afraid to look at him again, Beth stared out the passenger window and watched the cactus fly by.

When they reached town, he drove down Main Street and parked in front of a women's clothing store.

"This is a quaint little town," she remarked, as she exited the truck and looked up and down the street. Buildings painted vibrant shades of purple, red, orange and yellow lined both sides of the avenue, some with murals on the walls and some with detailed tile work around the doors and windows. At the end of the street, a Mexican-style fountain occupied the space in front of a building with a big clock on top. The water cascaded over the rim and splashed into a circular pool. People on the sidewalks came and went from shops like bees buzzing to and from the hive.

"After you," Scott said, holding the store door open. "I don't know anything about this place except they sell ladies clothing, so I'll follow you."

Racks of clothes filled the cavernous space. Beth glanced around. "It's a lot bigger than it looks from outside. I don't know where to begin. I guess I need another pair of jeans, and a couple of shirts, and some underthings."

Scott lifted his eyes to the ceiling at her mention of undergarments. "You're going to need a pair of boots, too," he said quickly.

Her curiosity was aroused. "Cowgirl boots?"

"You bet. I'd like to take you riding up in the mountains—if you're up to it. Tennis shoes won't do. We can get you a nice pair of boots at Shady's Boot Emporium when we're done here. They have a great selection."

She graced him with a warm smile. "I'd love to

go into the mountains, even though I don't know a thing about horseback riding. Can you give me the Reader's Digest version of a lesson before we go?"

"Sure. I have no doubt you're a fast learner." He took a seat on a padded bench in the center of the store. "I'll sit right here. Go on now. Pick out whatever you want."

She walked up and down the aisles, choosing a few items here and there. When she had an armful, she asked the sales clerk if she could try them on. "I won't be long," she assured the cowboy, who had removed his hat and balanced it on his knee.

"Take your time. I'm in no hurry."

Beth stepped into the dressing room. As she tried on the clothes, it was difficult to keep her mind on anything except the good-looking rancher.

He wants to take me riding. She reprimanded herself again. *Don't read anything into it. He's just being nice. He's a Good Samaritan. He told me that himself. There's nothing more to it. He's simply a good man being kind to a lost soul.*

Sheriff Griggs' words ran though her mind again. Scott was dating his ex-wife. *So, if he has a girlfriend, why have I caught him looking at me the way he does? I know the look of interest when I see it. Should a man with a girlfriend be buying another woman clothes and offering to take her riding in the mountains?*

After trying everything on, Beth changed back into Maggie Landry's clothes and stepped out of the dressing room with the selected items draped over her arm. She *had* to shake Scott from her thoughts. She would exorcise out the daydreams—and, by all means, the night dreams. After all, he was taken—and she probably was, too.

She inched toward him with a determination to keep emotionally distanced from the man from that moment on. As she neared, she saw him talking to a woman with fire engine red lips, high hair, and a low-cut blouse, which exposed ample cleavage.

Beth slowed her approach. She was aware that she was about to intrude on his life again. A knot suddenly formed in the pit of her stomach. *Could this woman be his girlfriend? Sheriff Griggs' ex-wife?* She and Scott appeared very chummy with one another. Beth didn't expect to come face to face with her so soon. Particularly when she was just having daydreams about him.

Scott turned his head and saw her. He stood and stuck his hands in his pockets. "Did you have any luck?"

"Yes. I found some things that will work just fine."

"Great. Beth, I'd like to introduce you to Sherry Martin. Sherry, this is Beth. She's a guest at the High Lonesome."

Sherry gave her the once over, taking her in from head to toe. A thinly tweezed eyebrow arched. "Since when do you take your guests on personal shopping expeditions, Scott?"

Beth's heart dropped. This *is* his girlfriend, she thought.

He ignored the question and told Beth, "Sherry and I went to high school together. Back then, she was a cheerleader, honor student, and the class president. Now she's the number one realtor in the county."

Sherry playfully slapped him on the arm and cried, "Oh, don't embarrass me, sugar. Pleased to meet you, Beth." She thrust out her hand to shake.

"Same here. So, you both went to school with Sheriff Griggs?" Thinking this was Buddy's ex-wife and the cowboy's current love interest, Beth was intent on gauging the woman's reaction at the mention of the sheriff.

"Yep. We ran in different crowds back then, but

everyone knew everyone else. It's a small town, you know."

There was no rolling of the eyes. No odd expression at the mention of the sheriff's name. Nothing.

"So, you're a guest at the ranch," Sherry said, reversing the topic back. "Where you from?"

"Uh…"

Scott broke in and said, "This is her first time in New Mexico."

Sherry gave him a sideways glance. "I'm sure your guest can speak for herself, Scott. For heaven's sakes." She rolled her eyes and returned her gaze to Beth. "Well, I hope you enjoy our beautiful Land of Enchantment. Scott owns seven thousand acres of the most pristine land you'll ever lay eyes on. I could retire on my commission alone if he'd ever let me sell his place. But I suppose hell will freeze over before that ever happens. Isn't that right, hon?" She elbowed him in the ribs.

"I'm afraid so, Sherr. You'll have to make your fortune another way."

"How long are you planning on staying at the ranch?" Sherry drawled, her attention drawn back to Beth.

"I haven't decided yet. I'm playing it by ear." She glanced back and forth between the couple. It was difficult to imagine the rancher with the heavily made-up woman. She wore too much pancake makeup and was squeezed into her skirt like a sausage in a casing. She just didn't seem his type.

"Scott, it's been *ages* since I've seen Joanna," the realtor exclaimed. "What have you two been up to lately? You must be hiding away in a little love nest on the ranch."

Beth's ears pricked. Joanna? Wasn't that Doctor Coleman's first name? Her chest seized as she searched Scott's face and waited for him to respond to Sherry.

He cleared his throat and his cheeks pinked. "Jo's been very busy with her patients, and I'm up to my ears with guests out at the ranch. You know how it is when two people lead very different lives."

He took hold of Beth's elbow and steered her toward the checkout counter as if they were rushing away from a fire. "It was real nice seeing you, Sherry."

Beth's mind flew into a tailspin. *Is Doctor Coleman Sheriff Griggs' ex-wife, and Scott's girlfriend?* She never would have guessed the cool and aloof M.D. to be Scott's type either, but she'd only known the man for a day. What did she know about his type? Still, the news surprised her.

She allowed him to nudge her toward the counter. She got the distinct impression he was trying to make a fast getaway from his former classmate, but the realtor wasn't going to let him off so easy.

Sherry's high heels clicked on the floor as she trailed behind them. When she caught up to them, she grabbed hold of his shoulder, spun him around and asked, "When are you two going to do it?"

"Beg your pardon?" Scott's mouth gaped.

"You know what I'm referring to, Scott Landry."

He shifted from one foot to another.

Sherry was like a bulldog. She'd sunk her teeth in and was going to hound Scott until he gave her a straight answer. "It's been, what? Almost a year now you've been going together? When are you going to make an honest woman out of Joanna?"

His face heated to a lovely crimson color. He cleared his throat again and replied, "We're nowhere near discussing marriage, if that's what you're talking about."

"Of *course* that's what I'm talking about, dummy."

"Joanna's very focused on her career," he answered—clearly uncomfortable as his eyes darted between Sherry and Beth. "She's not interested in that kind of commitment right now."

"Oh, fiddlesticks!" Sherry retorted. "Jo would marry you in a heartbeat. All you have to do is ask, you silly man! What are you waiting for?" She laughed and punched his arm. To Beth, she chortled, "Men! I swear. Sometimes we have to hit them over the head with a brick."

Beth forced a polite smile and shrugged.

"Well, I can see I'm getting nowhere, so I'll run, kids. Time is money in my business, and I don't have enough of either. Nice to meet you honey," she said to Beth. "Scott, you better think about what I just told you. Joanna might not wait forever on you—and we both know what a catch she is." The realtor exited the shop, her broad hips swaying like a boat rocking on the sea.

Beth laid her bundle down on the counter, and Scott took out his credit card and paid for the items—neither one speaking during the transaction.

When they stepped out onto the sidewalk, she said, "So...you're dating the doctor. No wonder she rushed over so fast yesterday. I thought she was just being a *Good Samaritan.*"

Although he thought she was teasing, the words stung. He opened the truck door for her then hopped into his side, pursing his lips. He slipped the key into the ignition and explained. "I've known Joanna all my life. We dated briefly in high school, before Maggie and I got together. After graduation, she left town for college and medical school. When she came home years later, she and Buddy got married, and then they got divorced. One day she invited me to some shindig at the hospital..."

"And the rest, as they say, is history." Beth finished the well-known line for him.

"I guess so." He revved the engine, put the truck in reverse, and then drove in the direction of Shady's Boot Emporium, feeling like he'd betrayed her by hiding the truth about his relationship with Joanna.

Why do I feel I owe her an explanation? I barely know the woman. Why didn't I want her to know I'm seeing Jo?

"Look!" he said, pointing, as they headed down Main Street. Several teenagers were slapping a photo of Beth's face up in shop windows and on telephone poles.

"The sheriff sure got those flyers out fast," she replied, craning her neck as they passed by the teens.

"Let's hope someone will recognize you and come forward," he said.

She nodded and gazed out the passenger window.

Scott wondered what she was thinking. She didn't seem too excited about seeing the posters. Of course, a lot was being thrown at her all at once. She was bound to be overwhelmed. That big-mouth Sherry Martin didn't help any either. He wished she hadn't spilled the beans about him and Joanna. Beth had caught him staring at her more than once. He could just imagine what she'd think of him now. A real cad—or some kind of cowboy Casanova. Flirting with her while he had a girlfriend! Damn. He didn't expect to be feeling what he was feeling. He stared at the back of her head, wanting to say something, but not sure what to say.

All Beth could think about was Scott and Doctor Coleman together as life mates. She just couldn't picture it. The doctor was so put-together. Perfectly coiffed. Confident in an arrogant way. And a little uptight, if she was being honest about first impressions. Scott, on the other hand, was laid back, funny, drove this old pickup truck, and lived the real life of a Marlboro man. He was comfortable in his cowboy skin and didn't need to prove anything to anyone.

They seemed polar opposites from one another. But then, who was she to judge? She knew nothing about either of them. What she did know, however, was that neither of them gave off the vibes of being madly in love. She may not remember her own name, but she certainly knew how people reacted and behaved when they were in love.

Once again, she recalled the sexy dream. *He and I have more chemistry together.*

The strong bond she felt for Scott defied explanation, but she was sure it was not one-sided. Amnesia or not, she knew when a man was interested.

Beth twisted around and set her gaze on his profile. She was curious as to why he hadn't popped the question to the doctor. He'd been a widower for four years and hadn't he told her Willow needed a mother? As for his own needs—well, he was a young, vital man who, by his own admission, had once shared a satisfying emotional and, no doubt, physical life with his wife.

She'd heard the statistics before. Men who lost a spouse after being in a good marriage were more likely to seek out marriage a second time. So why was Scott waiting when he had a woman ready to take the plunge, according to his friend Sherry? Joanna Coleman *was* a good catch from all accounts. She was beautiful, sophisticated and a doctor.

Beth felt like kicking herself. *Why am I even speculating about the man and his love life? It's none of my business. Rescuing me and offering me a place to stay doesn't give me the right to question his motives or intentions with another woman.*

She vowed right then to push all romantic and irrational thoughts of the rancher out of her mind.

Since Sheriff Griggs had set the wheels in motion, she had high hopes that it might not take long for someone to come forward and claim her. Then she'd never see Scott again anyway. Besides, maybe—just maybe—she was happily married, or engaged, herself. She held mixed emotions about that possibility while, deep inside, a brooding suspicion nagged at her.

Chapter Four

Scott and Beth grabbed some lunch at a small diner after shopping at Shady's. The restaurant patrons all gawked at her, proof that Buddy Griggs' media blitz was already working. It bugged Scott that she was being scrutinized like a sideshow act, but she didn't seem to mind or take offense.

Beth admired aloud her new cowgirl purchases all the way home. "I never knew a girl could fall in love so fast," she sighed.

When Scott shot her a surprised look, she chuckled and pointed to the Ariat leather boots on her feet.

"This is the first cowboy hat I've ever owned, too," she said. "I think I'd remember if I had one."

The cocoa brown felt hat complimented her dark cascade of hair. She tipped the brim back with her finger, the way cowboys did in the movies.

"I feel like I belong on the ranch now."

It was an innocent statement, but one which caused Scott to imagine a myriad of possibilities. He glanced at her. She couldn't realize what effect that simple comment had on him.

When they returned to the ranch that afternoon, he carried her shopping bags into the house and headed straight to the guest bedroom while she showed off her new duds to Carmen. He laid the bags on the bed and stood at the footboard. Her scent lingered in the air, and he noticed a slight indentation in the pillow where her head had lain. The thought of her in that bed caused his chest to grow tight. Sweat popped up on his forehead and goosebumps pricked his arms. Feeling the fabric of his denim jeans grow tight with a hard-on, he rushed out of the room and about collided with Amber in the hall.

"Hey, Scott. Going to a fire?" Amber greeted him with a tease. She tried to act nonchalant, but the twitch at the corner of her mouth and the blush in her cheeks were sure signs that she was still embarrassed about being caught in the cabin with Rowdy. She clutched a bucket of cleaning supplies in one hand and pushed away some flyaway hair with the other.

"Sorry, Amber. Beth and I just got back from town. I was putting her new stuff in here for her."

"That was real nice of you to buy her some things, Scott."

He rubbed his chin the way he tended to do when he was reflecting. "How's your day going?" he asked to change the subject. There was still a little tension between them, but he was not a man to beat a dead horse. He'd stated his peace earlier and hoped both she and Rowdy had learned a lesson.

"Fine. I'm getting ready to wash the cabin towels. How's that lady doing anyway? Has she remembered anything about her life yet?"

"No. Not really. Buddy's putting an APB out on the wire. There has to be someone somewhere who knows her. Have you seen Willow lately?"

"I think she's in her room taking a nap. I heard her tell Carmen she stayed up too late last night at her friend's house."

"Thanks. I'll go check on her." He turned to leave, and then stopped. "Are Rowdy and Cody out with the guests right now?" he asked over his shoulder. He wanted to make sure Rowdy was doing his share and not leaving the other wrangler with all the work.

"Yep. They were both taking them down on the lower trails today."

"Okay. See ya later."

Scott peeked into Willow's room and found her snoring away. He tiptoed over to her bed and placed a light kiss on her forehead; he didn't want to wake her. He grinned when he saw she was still wearing her pink boots. Closing the door softly behind him, he strolled down the hall to the kitchen, where he found Beth and Carmen sharing tea and conversation around the island.

"Willow's asleep," he announced.

"She's tired," Carmen said. "The girl's just a baby. Too young for sleepovers." She gave Scott the eye. She was quick to reprimand the man who was more of a son than a boss, but just as eager to serve him. "Do you want a cup of coffee? I can fix you a snack if you want one." She stood and started for the fridge.

"No, I'm good. We had lunch in town. Sit back down and take it easy. There's nothing for you to do right now. The guests are out with the boys. Relax for a change."

"Okay." Carmen resumed her seat without further argument.

"I see Beth has shown you a couple of her new purchases," Scott said.

Kicking her leg out, Beth grinned and reiterated, "I just love these boots. And the hat, too. I feel so empowered in these things. Weird, huh?"

"They say clothes make the woman," Carmen said. "Take me for example." She balled her apron up into her fist and laughed.

"You're going to love those boots even more once they're broken in and all scuffed up," Scott said. "If you're not tired and ready to give it a try, I thought we could go riding."

"Right now?"

"Yeah."

Beth's face lit up. "I'm not tired. Let's go."

"Finish your tea first. There's no rush."

"I'll watch Willow," Carmen offered. "She can help me make biscuits when she wakes up. You two have fun. It's a perfect day for a horseback ride." She gave Scott a subtle wink as he passed by to grab two water bottles from the fridge.

****

Down at the barn, Scott chose an older chestnut quarter horse by the name of Sundance for her. "Since we have no idea whether you've ridden before, I don't want to take any chances. We call Sundance old reliable around here. He likes to take it slow down the trail." Scott tied both the quarter horse and his mare to an iron rail outside the tack room. "Time for your first lesson."

Beth accepted a curry brush and he showed her how to groom the horse. "Brushing's not just for looks. It's also to guarantee a good fit and safe ride. We make sure there are no burrs or clumps of mud under their bellies or on their backs so the saddle and cinch don't rub."

Both horses had good manners. Sundance stood still as she brushed him, aside from swishing his tail at flies now and then. Next, Scott demonstrated how to detangle the horse's hair by rubbing oil from a bottle called *Cowboy Magic* into the mane. Then he showed her how to adjust the pad on the horse's withers before slinging the saddle on.

She watched, mesmerized, as he made quick time of yanking the girth in place, hooking it, pulling the leather tight, and checking the stirrups.

"This is the bridle, and this is the bit," he instructed, holding up the leather and metal contraption. "We don't allow the guests to put the bits in the horses' mouths. Only the wranglers and I do that. Horses are like people in a lot of ways. They don't want a bunch of different hands fishing around in their mouths."

"I don't blame them," she said, chuckling. She watched, impressed, as he whispered in Sundance's ear and eased the bit into his mouth. "Ah. You're a horse whisperer. What did you say to him?"

"I told him he'd better give you a nice ride or else he'll get sent to the dog food factory."

"You didn't!" Beth cried.

He smiled. "No. I didn't. He's a good boy. I like teasing you." He scratched the horse's nose and fed him a peppermint.

"I can see that." She took her turn speaking into the horse's ear. "Your owner likes to joke around, doesn't he? But we're going to get along just fine, aren't we?"

She watched Scott saddle Pepper in the same manner he'd saddled Sundance, only faster. "I can't believe what all is involved in getting a horse ready for a ride. Do we do it all in reverse when we get back?"

"Yep. It takes a lot of patience to work with horses."

"Something I see you're an expert at," she replied, meaning it.

"Horses are second nature to me. You're a natural, too. I can tell that already. You're calm around them and you have a gentle touch. I think you're going to do just fine."

"Thanks. I hope you're right. They're such big, strong animals."

She had enjoyed watching Scott's hands move swiftly over the horseflesh. Again, her mind drifted back to the dream she'd had that morning. In it, his hands had moved over *her* flesh in much the same way, only a lot slower and with the ultimate goal of pleasing her. She grew warm all over, just recalling the sensations she'd felt.

His sense of humor and confident attitude was very attractive—not to mention how easy he was on the eyes. Her heart fluttered, watching him bend and move in his tight jeans. Sighing, she rebuked herself for not sticking to her recent promise.

"Okay, if you're ready, let's go. Let me give you a boost up." He cupped his hand and Beth stepped into it. "Heave ho!" he said. He lifted and she swung her right leg over the saddle with no effort at all.

"Wow, it's pretty high up here." She took up the reins and patted Sundance on the neck.

Scott stuck his foot into the stirrup and hauled himself up—the leather creaking as he settled into his saddle. Clucking his tongue and lowering the reins, he nodded at her to follow his lead. "You look like you were born to ride. You look great in your hat and boots. You're a real cowgirl now."

"Just like Willow," Beth replied, tugging at the brim of her hat.

****

They had ridden deep into the mountains on unmarked trails and were now walking the horses through a narrow canyon filled with fragrant wildflowers of all hues. They talked some, but mostly just enjoyed each other's company and the company of their animals. Beth found it difficult to speak. Peace and tranquility washed over her, and moved her as she experienced nature in its most primitive state.

Scott reined Pepper to the left, onto a path less traveled. "This was an Indian thoroughfare a thousand years ago. We've discovered shards of pottery along these trails."

Off in the distance, the chattering of Piñon Jays brought a smile to her face.

"I can almost feel the ancient spirits riding alongside us," she said in reverence.

"I often sense a power bordering on the

paranormal when I'm up here." He leaned back and rode with his right hand resting on Pepper's rump. Both mounts walked with the confidence of animals who'd been on the trails hundreds of times. They grabbed at leaves from low-hanging branches every once in awhile. The sounds of their munching and the thumps of their hooves, along with the chirps of insects and the scurrying feet of small animals, all combined to form a beautiful musical symphony.

"Do you bring Willow out on the trails?" she asked.

"Sometimes, but she doesn't appreciate the quiet like grownups do. She wants to go fast all the time."

Beth chuckled and shook her head. "I still can't get over that little girl racing a horse around poles. I'm sure I wasn't that gutsy when I was her age."

"You seem very brave to me. What you're going through—being hurt and stranded in the desert, losing your memory, and now trusting me to take care of you—that takes courage."

"You're easy to trust," she replied. When she locked onto his brilliant blue eyes, she thought she might swoon and fall out of the saddle. She faced forward and began asking him safe questions. "When did you begin teaching Willow about horses?"

"My child was literally born to ride. She was on a horse before she was even out of her mother's womb. Maggie was helping a neighbor track a lost calf two weeks before she delivered."

"That's amazing. Maggie must have been quite a lady."

"She was. Most of us around here grew up with the notion that we could do anything we set our minds to. That's the way New Mexicans are. My friends all lived on ranches and we were raised with animals. We were all in 4-H and competed in local rodeos. We all rode horses before we could walk."

"What about Doctor Coleman?" Beth was

tentative, but curious. “Does she ride with you?”

Scott didn’t seem to mind the question. “No. Jo was a townie. She never liked to get her hands dirty, and she still doesn’t. I guess that’s why she became an M.D. and not a surgeon. She’s kind of prissy.” He flashed a lopsided grin. “That’s the way I’ve always seen her anyway. Strong and secure, but real prissy.”

“How do you see *me*?” Beth blurted.

Scott commanded his horse to whoa, and when Pepper stopped on a dime, Sundance followed suit. The reins slipped out of Beth’s hand as the animal lowered his head and began yanking weeds from the ground. Scott twisted in his saddle and rested his hand over the horn. He stared at Beth with such intensity she felt her face flame.

He took his time before answering, as if he were considering his words very carefully. When he answered, he looked straight into her eyes. “I see you as the kind of woman a man would ride to the ends of the earth for.”

His gaze settled on her like a soft, downy blanket.

Her heart thumped—she could not find her voice. Hot tears stung her eyes. It had been an emotional couple of days, and the sweetness and absolute purity of his heartfelt words sent her senses reeling. “That is the nicest thing anyone’s ever said to me,” she finally managed to say.

He ran a hand across his five o’clock shadow. “Begging your pardon ma’am, but how would you know that’s the nicest thing that’s ever been said to you?”

When she realized he was teasing again—this time about the amnesia, she broke into a wide grin and began to laugh. “You got me there, Scott. You know, I appreciate the way you keep things light-hearted. Your sense of humor sets me at ease. You keep me from worrying too much about what's going to happen to me."

"Life is too short to be too serious," he replied. "With that said, however, I want you to know that I don't *always* joke around. For instance, when you just asked me how I see you—that was an honest reaction. I meant what I said."

Their gazes fastened again, and thoughts of Joanna nagged at Beth.

Pepper's ears flopped back just as a tremendous clap of thunder rumbled through the mountains. It sounded like a locomotive steaming down the track at full speed. Sundance tossed his head and began to prance. Scott urged Pepper forward so he could pick up the reins that had slipped from Beth's hands. Grasping the saddle horn with his left hand, he leaned and reached down to get them, then placed the reins in her fist and instructed her to pull back gently if the horse became unruly.

Although a novice, Beth took control of the gelding. The horse's antsy behavior didn't appear to frighten her. "Storm is comin'," Scott announced, peering up at the darkening sky. "Rain storms are fast and furious when they strike up here in the mountains. We're gonna get soaked if we don't get to shelter in a hurry. We're not far from a cave. Do you feel comfortable trotting?"

She nodded.

"Kick him hard in the sides with your boot heels and keep your balance. You'll be fine."

They urged their horses into a jolting trot down the narrow trail, maneuvering their way through sticky brush and downed tree limbs. Another boom of thunder followed a crack of lightning, and then an angry storm cloud opened, spilling out a light mist. "Here it comes!" Scott called. "We've just got a little farther to go."

Beth grasped the reins in a loose hold, allowing

Sundance to do his job. She knew he'd been over the same trails hundreds of times, so she put her trust in the gelding to get her to their destination safely. Drops of water rolled off the brim of her hat onto her pant legs. Sundance huffed and snorted, and his muscles bulged as his pancake-sized hooves pounded the hard ground. He was doing a fine job of keeping up with Pepper, who was sailing down the trail as if she had wings.

"There's the cave," Scott hollered, pointing ahead. A hundred feet up, Pepper slid to a stop and Scott leaped off her back. Beth rode up behind them and hollered, "Whoa."

They hadn't expected a storm when they set off, but it had come up in a hurry. The wind howled through the forest of juniper and piñon trees like a pack of coyotes. Scott hastily tied Pepper to a wooden hitching post under the cave's natural rock overhang.

"Will the horses be all right here?" Beth yelled above the wind. As she attempted to dismount, Sundance proved uncooperative—dancing in a circle and tossing his head. His nostrils flared and his ears were pinned back. Beth flung her leg back over and held tight to the saddle horn.

"They'll be safe," Scott hollered back. "Your horse does not like storms though!" He grabbed hold of Sundance's halter.

Just then, the clouds that darkened the sky unleashed a barrel of rain.

As Scott tried to settle Sundance, Beth's natural instincts took over. She tugged the lead rope out from under the saddle horn and lifted her right foot out of the stirrup. Swinging out of the saddle in one fluid motion, she bounced on her boot tips as she hit the ground. She tossed Scott her reins, and he knotted the lead rope around the hitching post then reached for her hand. They ran into the mouth of the cave, hand in hand. Drenched, she began to shiver.

"Sit here," Scott said, leading her to a rock formation jutting out from the wall of the cave. It resembled a big easy chair. "I'll start a fire and we'll be dried out and warm in no time."

"Hhhhow are you gggoing to start a fire?" she stuttered. She wrapped her arms around herself, but her whole body convulsed with shivers.

He marched to the back of the dark cave and returned holding a bundle containing sticks, some matches, and a striped wool Indian blanket. "I keep a cache of supplies here for times like this." He wrapped the blanket snug around her shoulders then dropped to his knees in front of a blackened fire pit dug into the ground.

She watched as he built a teepee out of sticks, struck a match on the bottom of his boot, and tossed it onto the sticks. A tiny spark ignited and he bent down, cupped his hand around it, and blew short puffs of air onto the flame to coax it out. When the fire lit, he fanned it with his hands. It wasn't but a moment before a small fire was crackling.

"I was kind of expecting you to rub two sticks together," she teased, her voice still quivering.

"Ah shucks, ma'am." He attempted to do a John Wayne impression. "Sticks only work in the movies. Round here we like to use that newfangled technology called the match."

She chuckled and patted the spot next to her. "You're soaked, too. Sit beside me and get warm. I'll be glad to share the blanket."

When he obliged, she opened the Indian blanket and draped it across his back and over one shoulder. The moment their wet shoulders and legs touched, a jolt of electricity jumped off him and sent a zing straight to her heart. They looked at each other, but neither commented. She wondered if he'd felt the electricity.

They watched the orange flames flicker, leap and dance. Despite the chill, Beth could feel heat radiating from Scott's body. They pressed together like a sandwich, neither of them moving even an inch.

"Do your wranglers bring the guests up here?" she asked, breaking the silence between them. The fire was beginning to dry out her bones and her teeth were no longer clicking together.

"Yep. There are several caves on the property. We've built hitching posts at all of them, and they all have some kind of protective covering so the horses can stay out of the weather on days like this. I like to be up here when it rains."

"I like it, too. There's something about being here in this storm—just us and nature at its wildest. It's exciting. It must not be much different now than when the Native Americans roamed the area and made caves like this one their home."

Scott tossed a couple more sticks on the fire. "You're right. Not much has changed up here in a thousand years. Cody and Rowdy know the entire history of the ranch and Cody, in particular, has become very interested in how the Indians lived. I guess it's old hat to Rowdy since he's grown up on the reservation, but he seems to enjoy playing it all up for the guests. The boys like to dig around and find bits and pieces of pottery to give to our guests as souvenirs. They also like to throw in a ghost story or two for fun."

"I can see why. This is the perfect setting for ghosts."

The wind continued to blow and the rain fell like daggers outside the opening of the cave, but inside they were as cozy as bedbugs.

"Are you starting to warm up?" he asked.

"Yes. Thank you for starting the fire. I can see you're a good guy to have around in times like this."

She gazed into the incandescent blaze.

On the outside, Scott appeared calm and in control, but inside, his heart pounded like an Apache drum. *What is it about this woman? I met her two days ago, but I feel like I've known her all my life.*

He'd never thought love at first sight was possible until he set eyes on her. At that moment, he knew she was special, and as each day passed, she proved to be more and more so. No matter how he tried, he couldn't stop thinking about her. He was falling for the mysterious woman—and he was falling hard.

He peeked at her out of the corner of his eye. The desire was so strong—almost uncontrollable—to take her in his arms and kiss her. He wanted to hold her and tell her everything was going to be all right—that she had nothing to worry about—that he'd take care of her. Now and always. Scott Landry, Mr. Dependable, had never felt so reckless before.

His chest tightened like a vice. *What if she's married*? That thought was never far from his mind. But imagining her with another man just about drove him crazy. He must be falling in love, he thought. He didn't want her gazing into another man's eyes. He didn't want someone else to touch her. He glanced down at her hands folded in her lap. There was no wedding band on her finger, but he knew the absence of a ring didn't mean anything. She could have lost it, or it could have been stolen or removed on purpose. He'd already considered all the possible scenarios.

What's wrong with me? I'm imagining a future with this perfect stranger, when I should be thinking about the woman who's already in my life.

Joanna. The two of them had known each other their entire lives. She was strong, outspoken, and independent, and she made it plain as rain that she wanted him.

What is it that keeps me from committing to her? Why can't I even tell her I love her? He knew Jo longed to hear the words, but a lead weight dropped to the bottom of his belly anytime he thought of appeasing her by saying those three little words. For him, the L word was too powerful and precious to toss out in a casual way. The last woman he had completely given his heart to was Maggie, and he'd lost her. It was a frightening prospect to open up to those kind of feelings again. At least where Joanna was concerned.

After almost a year, it was still hard to think about giving himself to Joanna, but Beth…it just felt right somehow. He was thinking about her in ways he'd never thought about Joanna.

Why was she brought into my life? It could have easily been someone else driving down the road the other morning. Any number of ranchers in the area could have found her. Why me? Why now?

He was falling in love with her, but he couldn't bear to lose another woman he cared for—and he was bound to lose this one. She had amnesia now, but she would eventually regain her memory and go back to wherever she came from. No doubt she'd return to another man—perhaps a husband and children who loved her and wanted her home.

Then again, maybe...Don't even go there. He turned his face back to the fire and set his chin in his hand.

The rain continued to pour. The two of them sat, knee touching knee, with the popping and crackling of the fire between them. Their horses' tails swished and the wind howled. And it seemed they were the only two people on earth.

"Have you noticed how neither of us feels the need to fill the air with senseless talk?" Scott asked.

That was important. A couple needed to be able to share silence as well as words.

Beth smiled. "It's nice, isn't it?" She fingered the frayed edge of the Indian blanket. "I've been sitting here thinking."

"About what?"

"What if I never get my memory back? Or, worse, what if I start remembering things I wanted to forget? I believe something real bad happened to me. Maybe I'm keeping it all locked up in my mind on purpose—to protect myself from the truth."

"I can only imagine how confused you are," he said.

"What if someone comes for me," she continued, "but I don't have any recollection of them? What will I do then?"

"I don't know," he answered. "You won't know either, until that moment arrives."

She twisted a knot of fringe around her finger. "I'm so afraid of having to leave the ranch and go off with a stranger. Will I have to?" She looked to him and wanted to be reassured.

Scott shrugged. "I don't know, Beth. Let's cross that bridge when we come to it." He placed his hand over hers. "You're so much stronger than you realize. I've already seen what you're made of. When you're faced with the knowledge of what happened to you, and you'll be forced to do something about it, I have no doubt you'll cowgirl up."

She chuckled. "Cowgirl up? What's that mean?"

"It means to pull yourself up by the boot straps and handle whatever's thrown your way, no matter how difficult or challenging."

She contemplated that, and then sighed in relief. "I like that. And I appreciate your confidence." She paused, stared into his blue eyes, and then changed the subject abruptly as her heart started to race. "Your friend Buddy got right to work sending out bulletins and getting those posters up. I like him, and I trust he knows what he's doing."

"Yeah. Joanna thinks he's incompetent, but she holds a grudge. He's a good man and a capable sheriff. He'll do all he can to help you."

At the mention of Joanna's name, Beth turned away and stared into the flames again.

Scott dug at the dirt with the toe of his boot.

"Are you going to marry Joanna?" Beth blurted.

He looked up, his face so open the question must have caught him off guard. "I don't know. Why do you ask?"

"I was just wondering. Just thinking about what your friend Sherry said."

Before he could respond, lightning struck near the mouth of the cave, followed by a boom of thunder. Flames engulfed the tree.

They both jumped up and ran to the front. The blanket still enveloped her shoulders. The horses whinnied and stomped their hooves.

Another crack reverberated through the mountains and a frightening vision formed in Beth's mind. She heard a man's angry voice shouting, and saw an arm raised above her head. She slumped against the cave wall and moaned softly.

"What is it?" Scott asked, placing his hands on her shoulders. He turned her toward him. "Are you experiencing a flashback?"

She nodded and blinked. "I was, but it's over now. The visions come and go so fast, but they seem so real."

Scott looked deep into her eyes. "Do you want to tell me about it?"

She told him what she saw. "I wonder if I'm remembering what happened to me. I hope not. But why else would I keep seeing these visions?"

"I wish there was something I could do to help," he replied.

Their gazes fastened.

She felt the pressure of his warm hands as they

squeezed her arms. Her eyes raked over his tan face as he leaned in. Their mouths were mere inches apart. As his lips parted, a hot flame crept through her veins.

It would be so easy to let him kiss me. Her heart thumped and her senses reeled.

Then, just like the flashbacks, the face of the other woman appeared in her mind. Beth turned her head sharply and eased out of his hold.

"Look! The rain has stopped." She looked around him and pointed, then strode to the horses and gave each a neck scratch. Every nerve in her body was jumping. She hoped he couldn't see her trembling. She'd almost let him kiss her. Even though she wanted to feel his mouth on hers, more than ever, she knew it wasn't right. Thank goodness for the diversion. If she'd let him kiss her, there'd be no turning back.

Pointing to the sky she exclaimed, "There's a rainbow! It must be a sign."

Without a word, Scott walked up behind her and slid the blanket off her shoulders, sauntered back into the cave and doused the fire by kicking dirt on it.

He disappeared into the dark recesses of the cave and replaced the blanket and matches to their hidden spot. When he returned, Beth was sitting tall in the saddle on Sundance.

"Look at you," Scott said, surprised. "You mounted him by yourself. I guess that means you don't need a knight in shining armor anymore." Taking up his own reins, he placed his foot into the stirrup and climbed onto his mare. The leather of the saddle creaked as he threw his weight into it.

Beth punched down her cowboy hat and pulled the stampede string tight under her chin. "That's right. I've decided I've no use for a white knight anymore, Scott. But an honest, good-hearted cowboy…that could be a whole different story."

"What kind of story?" he asked, arching an eyebrow.

"The kind that ends up happily ever after." She winked, despite herself, then prodded Sundance's sides with her boot heels and shouted, "Let's ride!"

She loped off down the hill, leaving Scott with a dropped jaw.

Chapter Five

Buddy Griggs called Scott around six o'clock that evening. "I've received dozens of phone calls about your mystery lady. Linda and I spent all day checking out every lead."

"And?" Scott was in his office with the door closed.

"Nothing solid. So far, no one has been able to provide me with any concrete proof that they know this woman. Let me tell you, there are some real loonies in this world. One guy told me he's from another planet and she's their queen. Some nut job thinks your friend is her reincarnated cat. And someone else said they knew her back when she was a man."

"Oh, Lord." Scott sighed.

"Something like this brings the crazies out of the woodwork."

"Tell me you're not going to subject her to any of these nuts."

"Of course not. Why do you think Linda and I are screening everyone? Until someone proves this woman's identity beyond a shadow of a doubt, I'm not going to upset her by giving her false hope."

"I appreciate your hard work, Buddy. By the way, her name is Beth."

"Beth? She remembered?" he exclaimed. "Why didn't you tell me at the beginning of our conversation?"

"No. She hasn't remembered anything. Willow didn't think we should keep calling her *the lady* so she gave her the temporary name."

"Mmmm. Sorta like picking out shoes. If this one doesn't fit her, you can always try another one on for size."

"That's an ignorant thing to say, Buddy. This is a situation most people don't find themselves in. We're trying to make it as easy on her as possible."

"Whatever floats y'all's boat," Buddy replied. "Has she had any more nightmares?"

"Yeah. As a matter of fact, she had one just this afternoon. We were up at the cave and she remembered something about a man. She said he was about to hit her. It lasted a second or two then disappeared."

"Sounds like she's recalling domestic abuse. Could she give you a description of him?"

"No. I didn't ask. She's said the man in the flashbacks is in shadows, and she doesn't recall details because they come and go so quick. I bet he's the one who hurt her though. Son of a bitch."

"You seem to be taking this personally," the sheriff noted. "What were you doing at the cave?"

"We rode the horses into the mountains. I thought it would do her good to get out and get some fresh air. It was amazing the way she rode Sundance. She wasn't afraid at all. Makes me believe she's been around horses before. Or else she's just a quick learner."

"Were you up there when the storm hit?"

"Yep. The sky cracked open like an egg just before we reached the cave. We were soaked, but I built a little fire and we warmed up fast."

"Uh, huh. Sounds like you had a nice time together. Do you think that's smart?"

"Do I think *what's* smart?"

"To get close to her. I've got eyes, friend. The girl's a real looker. You're only human. I understand that, but Joanna is not going to like it if she finds out you two were out riding and spent some time alone. In a storm, in a cave, *alone*," Buddy emphasized. "She's the jealous type, in case you haven't noticed."

"I've got nothing to hide," Scott said defensively. "I didn't take Beth up there to be alone. I just thought she needed to have a little fun—something to take her mind off her troubles. She's under a lot of stress. It's called being thoughtful."

"Yeah, well, call it whatever you want. I don't begrudge you trying."

Scott's voice took on an edge. "I wasn't *trying* anything."

"You better watch your P's and Q's, that's all I'm saying. Besides the wrath of Jo, you should also keep in mind that your pretty little houseguest might be married, or engaged, or have a boyfriend. A beautiful lady like her has got to have one or the other. It's dangerous to play with fire. Scotty."

Scott kicked the leg of his desk with the toe of his boot, wishing it were Buddy's shin. He wasn't sure why he was so ticked since Buddy was just calling it like he saw it. "I'm not playing with fire," he grumbled. "She doesn't wear a wedding ring."

Buddy's deep voice rose an octave. "Oh, I see you've noticed."

"Joanna noticed."

The sheriff wheezed out a laugh. "Don't get yourself all riled up, Scotty. You're my best friend. I'm not gonna tell Jo about your secret rendezvous. She doesn't believe a word out of my big mouth anyway."

"There's nothing to tell," Scott repeated. "I'm not keeping a secret. And there was no rendezvous." His patience had run thin. "Thanks for calling. I'll talk to you later." With that, he banged the receiver down.

He took a couple of deep breaths before stepping out of the office. Hearing voices in the great room, he wandered in and found Beth and Willow sitting on the floor in front of the coffee table with a puzzle spread out on top. Joanna, dressed in a blouse and slacks, was perched in the leather chair next to the sofa with her long legs crossed.

He scratched his head. *What a coincidence this is. Did she tell me she was coming over tonight? Have I forgotten about another date?*

"Daddy!" Willow popped up like a piece of bread in a toaster and ran to jump into his arms.

"Hi, sweetie. Hello Joanna. Beth."

"Hello, Mr. Landry," Jo answered formally, still pretending their relationship was purely professional. She stood and smoothed down her slacks with her hands.

"Looks like you and Beth are working on a big puzzle," Scott noticed as he ruffled Willow's hair.

"Yeah, we are. She's so much fun, Daddy. We were playing Old Maid before we got the puzzle out."

"That's nice of her to play with you while I was doing some work in the office." He glanced at Beth and gave her a warm smile. She returned one just as genuine. He swung Willow around in a circle then plunked her down in front of the coffee table, where she scurried back to Beth's side. She sat cross-legged and stuck her nose back into the puzzle.

Scott sauntered over to Joanna. "What brings you over tonight, doc?" When she gave him an icy stare, he whispered, "Do we have a date tonight that I've forgotten?"

"No. We do not." The answer bit. She glanced back and forth between him and Beth, who averted her eyes the moment Joanna met her gaze.

In a snap, Joanna's voice dripped with honey. "I came over to give your guest the results of her CT scan, but she wanted to wait for you, so you could hear the news together."

"Oh." He apologized. "I'm sorry to have kept you

both waiting. You should have sent Carmen in to get me."

"It's okay," Joanna answered. "Beth and I have been chatting. I understand you're calling her that now."

"I made up her name, Joanna!" Willow shouted with enthusiasm.

"It's very nice, dear, but it's not her real name, you know."

Willow frowned. "I know. We're just pretending."

Scott motioned for Joanna to have a seat. "Tell us about the CT scan. We're both anxious to hear the results."

Beth moved up from the floor to the sofa and gave her full attention to the doctor.

"The scan was normal, but I have to warn you, not everything that occurs in a head injury shows up on a scan. It's possible to have a normal scan and still have a brain injury."

"What does that mean with regard to the amnesia?" Scott asked.

Jo addressed Beth. "You have what's called traumatic amnesia. It's the loss of memory due to a head injury in which there was external force upon the brain. As I mentioned before, you could have fallen and hit your head, or you could have come in contact with a blunt instrument. This type of amnesia is often transient, but it could also be permanent."

Scott glanced over and saw Beth's face turn sallow.

"It's impossible to know whether the loss of memory will be temporary or long lasting," Joanna continued. "It's going to be a waiting game, I'm afraid. Actual memories could be triggered by external events, or you might experience dreams that have nothing to do with your life at all. It may be difficult to differentiate between what's real and what are dreams. I know that's of little consolation, but medical science is not so advanced yet that we understand everything there is to know about the complex brain. I can tell you that it's possible you could regain all your memories at once, or some could return little by little. There's honestly no way of knowing."

"Your information doesn't sound very hopeful," Scott said, frowning.

"Well, the good news is her scan shows no brain damage, per se."

"That's a relief," Beth acknowledged.

"I'm sorry I can't tell you more. Is that knot still tender?"

"Yes, but it looks worse than it feels now." Beth raised her bangs to show them both the unsightly discolored lump.

"And the arm?"

"The bruise is fading. It's not hurting anymore."

"Do you have any questions?" Joanna asked.

"I guess not."

"Well, if you need anything more from me, don't hesitate to call. Good luck." Joanna stood and shook Beth's hand.

"Thank you, Doctor Coleman."

Willow, who had been listening to the conversation as she worked on the puzzle, jumped up, skipped over to Joanna and tugged on her sleeve. Her blue eyes twinkled as she asked, "Will you read me a bedtime story?"

Joanna reacted with a startled expression.

Scott was also flabbergasted, since Willow rarely seemed interested in talking to Jo when she came around. He narrowed his eyes at his daughter.

Willow pulled on the doctor's hand. "Come read me a story. Please," she whined.

Joanna slipped out of the child's grasp. "Oh, Willow. I've had a very long day. Could I do it another time, honey?"

"No," the girl said. "I'm tired and I want to hear the troll story right now. It's my favorite." She took a defiant stance and stuck out her bottom lip.

"Willow, you're being rude," Scott said.

"Honey, I came over to visit with your father for a little while. You go on to bed and he'll come tuck you in later." Joanna patted the child on the bottom and gave her a tiny shove. "Night, night, now."

Willow crinkled her nose and stood in the middle of the room with her arms folded across her chest.

Joanna didn't budge either. The two stubborn females glared at one another.

Beth stood and took Willow's hand. "Sweetie, if you put this puzzle and the cards away, I'll read the troll story to you. Deal?"

Willow's eyes brightened at Beth's offer. "Deal!" She scooped the puzzle pieces into their cardboard box and returned it and the Old Maid cards to the game cabinet. "They're put away now. I'm ready to go read the troll book. You're the best, Beth. Good night, Daddy." Willow hugged him.

He gave her a kiss on the cheek and whispered in her ear, "I'll be there soon to tuck you in, baby."

"Take your time, Daddy. Beth is going to read to me! She's the nicest lady on Earth."

Scott's brows knitted in a warning. "All right. Tell Doctor Coleman good night."

She obeyed. "Good night, Doctor Coleman."

"Good night, Willow."

As Beth took her hand and they walked by Scott, he mouthed, "Thank you."

After they'd left the room, Joanna cleared her throat and asked Scott, "What was that all about?"

"Pardon me?"

"Was that woman trying to show me up?"

"Show you up? What are you talking about? She

offered to read my daughter a story after you refused to."

"It's obvious she's infiltrated herself into your daughter's life. I warned you something like this might happen."

Scott shook his head. "Infiltrate is not the term I'd use. She likes Willow. She enjoys spending time with her."

"I like Willow," Joanna said without passion. "I just don't know much about children."

"It doesn't take a brain surgeon to figure out how to please a kid. No pun intended."

"So now you're taking *her* side?"

Scott rolled his eyes. "Not again. Can we please move on to something else?"

Joanna pouted for a minute. "Sure. Now that they're gone, come on over here and give me a little sugar." She glided onto the buttery leather sofa and reached for his hand. He hesitantly sat next to her.

"Kiss me," Joanna purred, puckering up. She planted a hard kiss on his lips, but when he was less than enthusiastic at returning it, she frowned and complained, "I touched warmer cadavers in medical school."

"Sorry, Jo. I'm just thinking about Beth's prognosis."

She crossed her arms. "I don't believe this, Scott. I wish you'd spend less time thinking about *her* and more time thinking about us."

"I'm sorry." He smiled. "I'm glad you came by."

"You are? Really?" She brightened.

"Sure. I'd just been thinking about you." The statement wasn't altogether a lie.

"Good. I've started to wonder since she arrived. What's going to happen to her now?"

"What do you mean?"

"Well, there's nothing obvious on the CT scan. Like I told her, she's just going to have to wait it out and see if her memory returns."

"I guess that's what she'll do then. Buddy called earlier and he's gotten a ton of leads from people claiming to know her, but none are panning out so far."

"Is she going to keep staying here?" Joanna rubbed her hand up and down his thigh.

"Yeah, but for your information, she's staying in the guest room."

"Good. You know, I was thinking you could set her up in one of the cabins. That way she could have more privacy."

Scott saw through her true intentions, but he didn't feel like arguing. "All the cabins are booked starting next week."

"Oh." Joanna didn't bother to hide her disappointment. She removed her hand from his leg. Unable to bite her tongue as usual, she said, "Do you mind if I ask how long you're planning on letting her sponge off you? I know you bought her clothes. I saw Sherry Martin."

Scott wriggled off the sofa and shoved his hands in his pockets. "Joanna," he began, "I'm growing tired of this game you're playing. It's none of your business how I spend my money, and it's certainly none of Sherry Martin's damn business. This discussion is over." He sauntered to the ceiling-to-floor rock fireplace and kicked his boot up against it. He hadn't intended on speaking harshly to her, but the same old conversation was beginning to wear on him.

Jo didn't speak for a moment. She puckered her lips and he could tell she was considering her next move. When she strolled over and tucked her arms around his waist, Scott refused to budge.

"Let's not fight, darlin'," she purred. She scratched the inside of his thigh with her fingernails then reached around to squeeze his butt. "I'm sorry.

I won't bring it up again. Cross my heart. Can we please kiss and make up?" When she started to suck his earlobe, Scott eased away and gave her a quick peck on the cheek. He wasn't interested in making up, or making out.

Jo backed up. "Well! That's not exactly what I call making up."

"Beth could come back into the room anytime," he offered as an excuse.

"Fine!" She rolled her eyes and stalked across the room. "I had another reason for coming over anyway. I wanted to remind you about the ribbon cutting ceremony tomorrow night at the hospital. Is your dark suit clean?"

He leaned his head back against the mantle and closed his eyes. "With everything going on, I completely forgot about the dedication," he groaned.

"Well, you're still coming, aren't you?" Joanna's eyes grew wide. "You know how much this means to me. I'm on the board. What will it look like if my boyfriend doesn't show up?" Her voice rose to a shrewish shriek.

"Calm down," Scott said, taking a step toward her. "Of course I'll be there. I promised you I'd go, and I'm not a man to break promises when I make them. You know that."

"Thank you," she said, calm again. "Meet me in the lobby of the new wing at seven o'clock. Okay?"

"I'll be there." He sighed.

She strode back to him, put her hands on both sides of his face and kissed him again. "And, *please*, get a haircut and shave before tomorrow night. You look like Grizzly Adams." She reached for his hand and dragged him to the front door. "I guess I'll go, but I don't want to. I wish I could stay." Her lower lip plumped.

Scott looked away. "Joanna..."

"I know. I know. I lose out again. At least I'll

have you all to myself tomorrow night."

He felt like a royal jerk as he told her goodbye and watched the taillights of her car dim in the distance. After locking the front door, he tiptoed to Willow's room and stood at the doorframe. His heart constricted at the sight before him.

Beth was stretched out on Willow's bed with her head resting against the headboard. Willow was snuggled in the crook of her arm, and both of them were sound asleep. The troll book was lying open in Beth's lap. Scott stood there for a while, imagining what it would be like to see the two of them that way every night.

He also allowed himself to think about how it would be to have Beth lying in his arms. Kissing her good night. Making love…And waking up next to her warm body each morning.

It's no use hoping for something that's not gonna happen. When someone comes for her, she'll leave and I'll never see her again.

He turned and tramped up the stairs to his bedroom. He knew Beth would stir before long and find her way back to the guest room. There was a night light in the hallway to guide her way. The big question was how was he supposed to sleep when he couldn't get her beautiful, unforgettable face out of his mind?

Chapter Six

Willow crossed the finish line with her little legs pumping and hair flying out from under the pink hat. Midnight's black mane flapped with the wind. He snorted with glee as if he recognized he had just run a good race.

"What's my time, Daddy?" she yelled the moment the bay skidded to a stop. Scott pressed his finger down on the stopwatch.

"Twenty-three point three three six!"

"Yee haw! I'm getting better." The seven-year old waved her hat in the air and bent to nuzzle the gelding's neck.

"Is that good?" Beth asked. "She looks ecstatic, so it must be good."

"It's good," Scott replied, beaming with pride. "It's pretty darn close to being a winning time for pole bending in the Little Wranglers competition."

Willow walked Midnight over to the gate and gave Scott a high five. He and Beth were standing side by side. "What do you think, Beth? Do you think my horse and I can win at the rodeo?"

"I sure do. I've never seen any rider fly as fast as you."

Willow giggled. "I bet you never even seen a rodeo before!"

"Okay. I'm busted. But I still think you're the best."

"I love you," Willow told Beth. "I wish you were my mommy."

Scott's gut gripped. He knew Willow was getting

close to Beth, but his daughter's heartfelt honesty startled him. He had no idea she felt that way. It just went to show, he wasn't as in tune with her feelings as he should be.

Willow needed a woman in her life—someone who would love her and care for her as a mother. The blue eyes that mirrored his gazed longingly up at Beth. He looked to Beth as well. He was too tongue-tied to speak.

Covering the child's hand, Beth smiled and replied, "That's such a sweet thing for you to say. You're very special to me, too, Willow."

Scott could see Beth didn't know what else to say. It was an awkward moment. She'd been put on the spot, but had handled the situation with class and compassion.

He patted Willow on the knee. "That's enough practice for one morning, honey," he said, offering the horse a treat. "Midnight needs his rest. Go put him in his stall. We'll walk up and meet you at the barn."

"Okay, Daddy." Willow nudged her horse forward using her spurs. They started off toward the barn. She got about fifty feet and stopped. Turning the horse in a circle, she shouted, "Daddy, are you going to kiss Beth now?" Then she threw her head back and laughed like a hyena.

"Go on, you squirt!" he hollered.

She spun her horse and kept laughing as she trotted down the path that led to the barn.

The rancher fastened his gaze on Beth and graced her with a crooked grin. He shrugged. "That kid is a real corker. I'm sorry about that. I don't know where she comes up with the things she does."

Beth awarded him with a shy smile and said, "Don't worry about it. She's a sweetheart. Children say what they feel. Wouldn't it be great if adults were half as honest as kids?" When she glanced at him, Scott shoved his hands in his pockets and stared at the ground. The two began strolling down the gravel lane.

"What she said just now..." he began.

"I know what you're thinking," she interjected, "and I won't let her get hurt. She's an amazing little girl. I care for her very much."

"I guess it's natural for her to wish you were her mother. The two of you have grown close in a short time. You act like a mother with her. Playing games, reading to her, watching her ride her horse..."

"I'll talk to her, but I'll be very gentle," Beth assured him. "You know, you're doing a wonderful job raising her. Don't ever doubt that for one minute. She's crazy about you."

Scott thought about that for a moment. What Beth said was true. He was a good father, but he also knew little girls needed a female role model.

"I've had so much help," he said. "My dad was a great grandpa when he was alive, and Carmen, of course, is like a granny or a crotchety old auntie. Willow's been surrounded by a lot of love."

"It shows. That's all a child wants and needs." Beth stopped in the middle of the lane and faced him. "Scott, I'm starting to remember bits and pieces about my life. It's just as Doctor Coleman said. I haven't mentioned it before, but now I realize the flashbacks are more than dreams."

"Tell me." The sun was beating down on them, but neither noticed, nor cared. He wanted to hear what she had to say, even though he feared the words might turn his world upside down.

"I keep having visions of a little girl. She's got dark hair, just like mine, and she's very happy. She giggles and smiles." Beth paused. "I see myself pushing her on a swing. In one image, she was skipping around picking flowers from a garden. I was reading to her in another."

Scott's brow knitted together. "You're sure it's you pushing her in the swing? Maybe she's a neighbor's child, or a niece."

"No. I feel a strong connection to her."

His heart started to beat fast. "Are you able to see her face in these visions?"

Beth took a deep breath before answering. "Yes. The last time, I saw her as clear as if I were standing right in front of her. Her hair is cut into a pixie style, and she has big brown eyes. There's a dimple in each cheek and her eyelashes are long, curled up like a little doll's. I think she's my child."

Scott rubbed his chin and stared into her eyes.

"There's something else," Beth said. "I keep seeing the man, too. He scares me. I think he's dangerous."

"What kind of flashbacks are you having about him?" Scott asked.

"He's yelling. He's very angry. I think he's hurt me before."

Scott scowled. "What do you mean? How has he hurt you? Do you feel he's the one who twisted your arm and whacked you in the head?"

"I don't know about that," she answered. "But I have some memories of being pushed by someone. That could be how I got the knot."

Scott kicked the dirt with the toe of his boot. "That son of a..."

Beth laid her hand on his arm. "What do you think this means? Doctor Coleman said I might not be able to differentiate between what's real and what could just be random thoughts or mixed up dreams. I'm so confused. I hope I'm not having flashbacks of a husband who hits me. I'd be so ashamed to find out I've been living with an abusive man."

Scott lowered his head and started walking again. She fell back in step with him. "Can you see this guy's face?" he asked.

She shook her head. "His face is always blurry. Maybe I just don't want to see it. I know he's tall and he's muscular. And strong. When I have a vision, I can almost feel his powerful grip on my arms. His eyes are wild—they look out of control. That's the best description I have."

"Let's not jump to conclusions about any of it. Let's think this through," Scott suggested. She was living the terror of the flashbacks. Strong emotions could lead to irrational thoughts. He had to be the voice of reason in order to help her.

They were walking without speaking, each lost in their own thoughts, when a piercing scream punctured the air. It came from the far arena.

Scott said, "Come on," and took off running, with her following close on his heels.

At the arena, she saw five of the six guests gathered in a circle.

"What's going on?" Scott broke through the group, his voice concerned, but calm and steady. Cody knelt in the dirt, examining the bloody knee of one of the female guests. The knee of her jeans was ripped and tears streamed down her dust-soaked face. Beth's pulse pounded through her temples.

The young wrangler told Scott, "Diablo kicked her, boss. It's a pretty nasty gash. Rowdy went to get the four-wheeler so we can transport her to headquarters."

"Good job, Cody." Scott clapped him on the back then spoke to his guest. "Marilynne, we're going to take you to town to see a doctor. How are you feeling? You look a little peaked."

"I think I might faint," she replied in a weak voice.

"I'll get her some water," Beth offered. She jogged into the barn and fetched a bottle of water from the cooler in the corner. She'd remembered seeing the cooler the day Scott gave her the tour. After twisting off the cap, she ran back and handed it to a man who had his palm on the injured woman's back.

He thanked her, then tipped the bottle into Marilynne's mouth and said, "Hang in there, honey. Help's on the way."

Rowdy squealed up on the four-wheeler. "Hey, boss. I just called Doc Coleman's office. They said to bring her on in."

"Thanks." Scott and Cody helped Marilynne to her feet and bent so she could sling her arms around their necks. They placed their hands under her legs and lifted her into the four-wheeler. Her husband jumped in the back. The other guests waved and called out good wishes as Rowdy drove up the hill.

Beth stepped inside the barn, hoping no one was paying attention to her. Her head had begun to throb when she saw Marilynne on the ground, hurt. She tried to push away the pictures forming in her mind, but it was no use, so she sat on a wooden stool and closed her eyes.

Another flashback. The same ominous man twisting her arm. As the picture played out, Beth saw her mouth open and heard herself scream. His eyes bulged and he shoved her and then she fell. Just like the end of a movie, the image went black.

"Noooo." The moan slipped from her mouth as if coming from a wounded animal. The group turned to stare.

"Cody, go on and finish what you were doing with these folks," Scott said. "We'll let everyone know how Marilynne is later today." As the group dispersed, he hurried over to her. "What is it?" he asked, placing a hand on her shoulder.

She wagged her head. "I'm sorry, Scott. I didn't mean to call out that way. Your guests must think I'm a nut."

"Don't worry about it. Tell me. Was it another flashback?"

She nodded. "They're coming more often now. This one was more detailed. I remember being attacked."

"You recall the assault? Do you remember how you ended up in the desert?"

"Yes. Well, I'm not sure about that, but seeing your guest injured must have triggered the memory. I'm so afraid I'm getting closer to the truth." Her voice trembled.

"Could you see the man's face this time?"

"No. Why can't I see *him*, when I can see the little girl so clearly?" Tears sprang to her eyes.

"You're probably blocking him out because the whole thing is so frightening. I wonder if it would help for you to see a counselor, or a psychologist or hypnotist. Someone who can bring the visions out into the open so we can determine what's really going on."

She turned from him. When her gaze met his again, her eyes were stinging with tears. "Do you think I'm crazy?"

"No! Of course not. I'm worried about you. I just want to help. I don't know what to do. I feel powerless. It's just like when Maggie died in my arms."

They looked at each other for a long moment, and then she wiped her damp eyes with her shirtsleeve.

"I'm sorry, Scott. I'm being so selfish. I apologize for bringing up painful memories."

"There's no need to apologize. I'm concerned about you. Are you all right now?"

"Yes. Is your guest going to be okay?"

"Yeah. Rowdy's taking her to town. Joanna will stitch her up and she'll be back on the trail within the hour. They always are."

"In other words, she'll cowgirl up."

He smiled. "That's right."

"I should follow her example." Beth got to her feet and took a deep breath. "We better go get Willow. She's going to wonder what happened to us."

"If you're sure you're okay," Scott said.

She nodded. "I'm fine."

On their way to the other side of the barn, Scott placed his hand on the back of her neck. "Everything's going to be all right," he told her.

The lightness of his fingertips grazing her neck sent a shiver racing down her spine, but the sensation of his touch was bittersweet. She desired more than the simple touch of his hand—far from it—but she knew it was never to be. Scott was spoken for by another woman. And she belonged to another man. After this last flashback, there seemed to be no doubt about that.

During lunch, Willow kept them all laughing with a series of knock-knock jokes. It wasn't so much that they were laugh out loud funny, it was her delivery. She made such goofy faces and hee-hawed at her own jokes. Once the giggles started in Beth, she couldn't stop, and the trickle effect took place. Scott and Carmen began laughing so hard, tears streamed down their cheeks.

Now, with the flashbacks coming with more frequency and clarity, Beth needed a distraction more than ever.

"I have an announcement to make," Scott said, pushing his plate back.

"Oh, goodie. What is it, Daddy?"

"Willow, how would you and Beth like to go to a fancy party with me tonight?"

Beth tossed him a surprised look.

"Yes!" Willow screamed, clapping her hands. She jumped off her stool and started to dance around the kitchen, clogging in her pink cowgirl boots. "Where are we going, Daddy?"

"There's a ribbon cutting ceremony being held at the hospital to celebrate the dedication of the new wing."

The girl stopped dancing and sighed. "That sounds boring. I thought you said it was a party."

"Well, they're going to be serving hors d'oeuvres."

"What are those?"

"Tiny sandwiches you eat with your pinkie finger sticking up."

Willow giggled and stuck her pinkie in the air. "What else will they have?"

"Oh, things like miniature cakes and baby pickles and weird cheesy things wrapped in bacon."

"I love bacon." Willow mulled over the possibilities. "Will there be dancing and singing? Will the Four Fiddlers be playing?"

Carmen chuckled. Beth raised her eyebrow, and Scott explained. "They're a local bluegrass band. For some odd reason, Willow loves them. They play at all the rodeos. I don't think the fiddlers will be at this event, honey," he informed his daughter.

"Rats!"

"The best part is," Scott continued, "you can dress up real pretty and be a little lady for once. Wouldn't you like that?"

She pondered the idea. "I guess. Beth, are you going? If you go, I'll go."

Beth's answer was honest. "I don't have anything to wear to a fancy shindig, but I know you'll have fun with your daddy."

Carmen began to clear the dishes. "There are several party dresses upstairs in the closet," she said. "I'm sure you'll find at least one to suit you." She looked to Scott for confirmation.

He nodded. "You're welcome to any of them, Beth, but I think you deserve a new party dress.

What do you think, Willow?"

"Yes! Let's go shopping!"

"No," Beth declared with a firm shake of her head. "You're not going to buy me anything else. You've already done enough for me. But thanks for the offer," she added, with appreciation.

She had her doubts as to whether Scott approved of her continuing to wear Maggie's clothes, particularly a party dress. She could see how a pretty dress his wife wore might conjure up memories that brought sadness or pain. She was determined, however, not to be more indebted to him than she already was. "I've been feeling a little tired today," she offered as an excuse. "It sounds fun, but I think I'll bow out. You can make it a father-daughter date."

Both father and daughter's faces faded.

"You *have* to go," Willow groaned.

Beth and Scott's gazes locked on each other.

"Beth," he said in his soft, sexy drawl, "you are more than welcome to wear any of Maggie's dresses, or I'll buy you something brand new, if you'd feel more comfortable. You choose. I'll do whatever you want. You can wear a feed sack for all I care. I just want you to go tonight. It would do us all good to dress up and get out."

Willow rolled her eyes and laughed. "A feed sack? Dad. That would look stupid."

Beth grinned.

Scott did, too. "I agree, but I think I made my point. Right?" He looked to Beth.

"Right. You made your point," she acknowledged. "Thank you for the invitation. I'd love to go."

His mouth split into a broad grin and Willow hopped up and down like a jackrabbit.

"Beth, can you help me pick out an outfit and fix my hair?" she begged. The little girl's blue eyes twinkled with anticipation.

Beth took hold of her small hands. "I'd be glad to, honey."

The little girl flung herself into Beth's arms and squeezed. When Beth looked into Scott's rugged face, the look of a contented man greeted her.

"Can we pick out my outfit now?" Willow asked with excitement.

"You have plenty of time, sweetheart. The party's not for hours," Scott said.

"Oh. Okay. I'm going out to brush Midnight then." She skipped out of the kitchen, humming.

"Carmen will holler when it's time to come in and wash up," he called out the door as she ran down the sidewalk. Turning to Beth, he said, "I appreciate you agreeing to help her get ready. I think you can see how much it means to her."

"I'm happy to."

He slid a hand through his dishwater blonde locks. "Before the day gets away, I need to go to town and get a haircut. Doctor's orders. I've been told it's too long and shaggy for a fancy shindig."

"Really? I like your hair the way it is," Beth said. He's already about as handsome as they come, she thought, as a tingle shimmied through her body.

"You do?" His eyebrow arched. "Thanks. So do I. It's the no-fuss cowboy style."

"I guess a little trim wouldn't hurt," she added. "I'd be glad to do that for you. It would save you a trip to town."

"That would be great." Scott jumped on the idea. "Do you have time right now?" He didn't want her to change her mind or get busy later. He was already anticipating the touch of her hands on his scalp and skin.

"Sure. I have nothing pressing on my social calendar at the moment," she teased.

Carmen shooed them out of the kitchen with a

broom. "You two go out onto the porch and do that. I already swept up in here. He needs a shave, too."

"He does?" Beth made her eyes wide and pressed a hand to her chest. "I thought the five o'clock shadow was his style, but I can certainly oblige, if a shave is what he wants."

Scott rubbed a hand across his stubbly cheeks and chin, smiling at her jest.

"I'll gather up the barbering equipment and bring them out," Carmen told them.

"You have barbering equipment?" Beth asked.

"What Carmen means is she'll give you a comb and scissors."

Scott escorted her to the front of the house and swung the screen door open, holding it for Beth. He suggested they each take a seat in a wooden rocker where they could enjoy the view while waiting for Carmen. The sun was shining high in the azure sky like a gleaming ball of gold.

"This is such a beautiful ranch," Beth sighed. "The view from here reminds me of a picture postcard. The red sandstone mountains are as pretty as any anything I've ever seen."

Scott's chair squeaked as he rocked back and forth. "Growing up here, I've sometimes taken the beauty for granted. But since you've been with us, I've been seeing New Mexico through your eyes. This *is* a beautiful place, and I'm very proud to be the owner of such a fine ranch."

"Here you go." Carmen pushed the screen door open with her hip and unloaded the barbering tools onto a side table. "Make him look real handsome," she told Beth, before disappearing back into the house.

Scott retrieved a straight-backed chair from the foyer, carried it out to the porch and sat with his legs spread wide. Beth stood at his broad shoulders and removed his hat.

He sucked in a deep breath and tried to still his thudding heart as her fingers began to dance across his scalp.

"Your hair is thick," she noted while fluffing it.

He answered with a low "Uh huh."

She folded a towel around his neck and tucked it into his shirt collar.

The touch of her fingertips brushing against his neck sent a lightning shot straight through him. Beth slid her fingers through his silky hair, massaging his scalp, and then ran the comb over the crown of his head. His Adam's apple pulsed and every cell in his body caught fire.

She took the scissors into her hand and lifted a section of hair, pulled it out, and clipped. Snip, snip, snip went the scissors as she shortened his hair, one piece at a time.

Tingles raced up and down his arms as her nails scraped his neck. She shifted over to the other side, and he had to swallow the lump in his throat when her breasts brushed against his back. His chest rose and fell in rhythm as he tried to control his racing heart.

He suspected she didn't even realize she was humming as she worked. Snip…snip…snip. The warm feeling engulfed him again, just like the first day when he'd heard her humming from inside the bathroom.

The woman did something to him. Something that made him want to act crazy and completely out of character, like, jump up and down on a sofa expressing his feelings.

Scott felt himself grow hard. He laid his hands in his lap in order to cover his awakened, throbbing erection. He closed his eyes and thoughts of them making love filled his mind. He didn't know if he could stand having her so close without pulling her onto his lap and smothering her with kisses.

When Beth finished the trim, she handed him a small mirror. He opened his eyes and pretended to check out the cut from different angles. The truth was he was unable to concentrate on anything except how good she smelled, how soft her hands were, and how rock hard he was. He croaked, “Looks good,” when she asked him what he thought.

“I didn’t take much off. Just shaped it up some. I think longer hair suits you.”

She had no idea the way she affected him. If she did, she was a damn good actress.

He struggled to find his voice. “It’s just the way I like it.” He rubbed a hand over the bristles on his cheeks and attempted to converse without sounding like an idiot. “What about this beard?”

“Personally, I like the five o’clock shadow look, but it seems the orders are to shave you. Don’t move. I’ll be right back.”

In the several minutes she was gone, Scott let his eyes drift shut again and he replayed in his mind the feel of her touch on his neck and scalp. He’d been craving it, dreaming of it for days. When he imagined her hands exploring his naked body, he came to attention again. His eyes flew open when the screen door banged shut.

Beth returned to the porch holding a pair of ice tongs and a fresh white, hot, steaming towel in a bowl. She asked him to scoot the chair up against the side of the house then she stood in front of him and told him to lay his head back. She placed the moist towel over his face.

Scott settled back and said, “Mmmm. That feels real good.”

“I’ll mix up the shaving cream while the steam does it thing.” Beth patted the hot towel down with her hands, gently molding it to his skin. A quick *clack-clack-clack* told him she whipped the shaving cream up in a mug. When she unwound the towel from Scott's face, vapors rolled off his cheeks and chin. "Ready?" she asked.

"Yes, ma'am."

She brushed the thick cream all over his cheeks, chin, and down his neck. It smelled like mint. She seemed in no hurry, as if they had all the time in the world. She dabbed the cream onto his cheeks with the bristle brush. Slow and deliberate were the strokes.

Scott held her gaze. When she took the razor into her hand, she raised it into the air, and the sunlight caught its silvery glint. The melding of metal and sun created a rainbow, which bounced off the glass window next to them.

Beth's voice was so low it was almost inaudible when she asked him, "Do you trust me, cowboy?"

He gazed deep into her emerald pools. "With my life."

Her mouth drifted over his like a spring cloud, and he could feel her warm breath mingle with the mint-scented heat rising from his face.

She sunk the razor into the foam, and the sharp edge rested against his cheek. He held his breath. When she made the first stroke, a shiver spiraled down his spine. Beth slid the razor over his skin, one deliberate stroke at a time. After each, she wiped the excess cream off with a fresh towel. To Scott, it felt like it was all happening in slow motion. He closed his eyes.

Beth continued this routine until his face was bare of foam, and then she ran the razor across his chin and down his neck.

When the shave was complete, she caressed Scott's cheeks and neck with a warm, damp towel one last time in order to remove any residual cream. He opened his eyes again, and she shook some after-shave lotion into both palms and patted it onto the sides of his face.

A hot flame crept up his neck to pulse in his cheeks. Impulsively he reached for her hands. It didn't matter whether he made a fool of himself. He had to tell her how he felt. And he had to tell her now.

"Beth. Things can happen between a man and woman, before they're ever physical. Deep things that can fix a person in somebody's heart for good. Do you understand what I'm saying?"

An easy smile formed on her lips. A smile that was like a slice of sun breaking through on a cloudy day. "I think so."

He fanned her hands open and kissed the inside of her palms, one and then the other. Then he circled her waist with his hands and rocked her toward him. She leaned in, lowered her face to his and shut her eyes. She rested her hands on his knees.

The breath caught in his throat and blood surged through his veins. For the past couple of days he'd imagined their first kiss. It seemed like such a long time coming—because he felt he'd known her all his life. The moment had finally arrived. The time was now. Every nerve in his body quaked with anticipation. He tipped her chin up and their mouths drew near.

Before their lips touched, a horn blared and a car materialized in the drive. Beth leapt away as if she'd been burned. Scott felt the air deflate from his lungs. His heart was about to explode.

The Audi Roadster squealed to a stop in front of the house just as Beth pushed off of Scott's knees. She looked into his face, her cheeks beet red. She reached for a towel and wiped her hands. Momentarily paralyzed, Scott remained sitting in the chair, dizzy with ripe passion and unfulfilled longing.

Joanna bounded out of the car with a garment bag draped over her arm. When she spied the two of them on the porch together, she marched up the stairs with glaring eyes. As she approached, Scott stammered his hello and Beth turned and began gathering up the barbering things.

Joanna eyed the scissors, towels, shaving cream, and other grooming tools lying on the table. She snipped, "Well, well, well. What have we here?"

"Hello, Jo." Scott stood now, stretched his arms above his head, and carried the hard chair back into the house. He slid a subtle glance toward Beth as he walked by. When she turned back to Joanna, the doctor stared at her. Her mouth was pursed tight and her eyes narrowed in suspicion.

When Scott stepped back onto the porch, he ran a hand through his hair and said, "What do ya think, Jo? You told me I needed a haircut, so Beth offered to do the honors. She saved me a trip to the barbershop and a hefty tip." He struggled to keep his voice natural, but he had a feeling Joanna could see through his façade.

She moved around him like a lion stalking its prey. Scrutinizing the trim, her tone was cool when she replied, "I said you needed a hair *cut*, Scott. Your hair is still way too long. This isn't the '60's and you're not a hippie."

"I like my hair." He wasn't smiling. "What brings you out here?" he asked, not wasting any more time with small talk.

She shifted her eyes toward Beth again. "Would you excuse us, please? I need to discuss something with my *boyfriend*."

Narrowing his eyes, Scott opened his mouth to retort, but decided against it when Beth made for the door. As he rushed to open it for her, his eyes searched hers, but she refused to acknowledge him. The door banged shut as she disappeared into the deep shadows of the house.

Scott spoke to Joanna in a controlled, but peeved

tone. "How dare you speak to her that way. What was the point in saying I'm your boyfriend?"

"You *are* my boyfriend! Or have you forgotten? You have the nerve to ask me what *I'm* doing?" Joanna shot back. "I come out here and find you...cavorting with that woman!"

"Lower your voice," he warned. "I wasn't cavorting. She cut my hair and gave me a shave. Like *you* wanted."

"Uh, huh." Joanna slammed her hands upon her hips. "I wasn't born yesterday, Scott. I saw the way she was hovering over you. She was practically sitting in your lap!"

He shook his head. "Joanna, you're getting yourself all riled up over nothing. It was all perfectly innocent. For God's sake, we've been out here on the porch in plain sight."

"You *are* my boyfriend. Why don't you want her to know?"

"I'm not hiding our relationship. She already knows we're dating. I just think it's insensitive of you to throw it in her face, considering her situation."

"Her situation...her situation. I'm sick of hearing you talk about her situation. She's nothing to you and me. She's a stranger, but you're treating her like she's one of the family. What I want to know is when are we going to talk about us and our relationship?"

Scott queried her with his gaze. "What's there to talk about?"

Joanna huffed. "I swear. Sometimes you're as thick as concrete."

"There's no need for name calling," he replied, unsmiling.

Her lips began to tremble. "Am I losing you? Tell me straight out. I'm woman enough to take it."

He didn't want to argue right out there on the

front porch. Arguing was all they'd been doing lately—even before Beth showed up. Fussing over little things. There was too much drama with Joanna. He had a business to run and a daughter to raise. He didn't have the time or patience for a relationship filled with distrust and arguments. Why did he continue to put up with it? So many thoughts raced through his mind just then.

I can't let this keep happening. I don't love her, so it's not fair to either of us. I should never have compromised my integrity and become involved with my best friend's ex-wife in the first place. I was a lonely man and she was attractive, familiar, and comfortable. I've let it go on far too long. I'll turn her loose—just as soon as the time's right.

He draped an arm around her shoulders in an effort to appease her. "I don't know what gets into you sometimes," he said, sidestepping his answer to her direct question. He pulled her into his shoulder and held her until he felt her body relax. "Let's not argue. Tell me what brings you to the ranch. What's in your hands?"

She shoved the garment bag into his arms. The hint of a tear glistened in her eyes. "I brought you a suit to wear tonight. I figured yours wasn't clean, or you can't find it, or something. I want my man to look good. This is an important night for me. I don't want you showing up to the dedication looking like a cowboy that's just come off the trail."

Scott accepted the garment bag and replied, "Thank you." No more, no less. The back of his throat burned, but he held his tongue. Though her comment was like a slap in the face, he decided to ignore it since he was about to give her a piece of news she wouldn't be happy about. With a bluntness he didn't intend, he said, "I've invited Beth and Willow to join us tonight."

"What?" Her mouth opened and closed like a

goldfish's. "I can't believe you invited *her*. And Willow? Children don't attend functions like this. She'll be bored to death."

"No, she won't. She's looking forward to dressing up pretty and going to a party."

"It's not a party, Scott. It's an *event*. For adults."

He stepped back and spoke sharply. "For God's sakes, you make it sound like we're going to a strip club. I've just about lost my patience, Joanna. The longer we date, the less I think I know you. I'm not sure we have that much in common besides growing up in the same town, and you sure don't want anything to do with my daughter."

She batted her eyelashes, surprised. "That's not true, darlin'. You know how I feel about Willow."

He dumped the garment bag into a rocker. "No. I don't. Willow and I come as a package deal, Jo. If she's not welcome at your damn hospital dedication, then I won't be able to attend either."

The doctor's eyes bulged as she grabbed his arm. She stammered, "Honey, don't be silly. Of course she's welcome. I'm just wondering why you invited that woman. She's not a member of our community. She doesn't know anyone, and the event will mean nothing to her." She blinked back tears.

"That woman has a name," Scott said, trying to stay calm. He thought a vein might burst in his forehead at any moment. "It's Beth. Her name's Beth. I invited her because she's going through a very stressful time and she could use a night out to take her mind off of her troubles. If you were more sensitive, you might have suggested it yourself."

"You know how uncomfortable she makes me feel," Joanna pouted.

"I'm sorry, but I can't help the way you feel."

"Why do you keep calling her Beth? That's not her real name. If she comes tonight, how will we introduce her to people? What will my colleagues think? What will I say about her? Am I supposed to tell everyone she's a woman you picked up off the road, and she has no idea what her name is or where she's from?"

Scott rolled his eyes. "*You* don't have to say anything. I'll make the damn introductions to your snobby colleagues. Besides, that's precisely what happened. Everyone in town knows the story. I never knew you could be so jealous. You're starting to become irrational. I'm not sure any of us should go tonight after all."

"You have to, Scott!" Joanna exclaimed. "You promised, and you never break a promise." She gripped his arm.

He sighed and resisted the temptation to break up with her at that very moment. "I'll go," he relented. "But only because I promised. Now, if you'll excuse me, I have a lot to get done around here."

Joanna expelled a long breath. "Of course, sweetheart." She wore a vexed expression, but tried to cover it with her most cheerful voice. "I have to get back to the office anyway. I just had a few minutes between patients." She pressed her lips to his cheek. When she got no reaction, she said, "Okay, then. See you tonight. I can't wait to see you in the suit! You'll be the best looking man in the place." She wiped her damp cheek with a hand.

Scott shook his head in frustration as she hurried to her car and drove away.

He took a deep breath and stepped into the foyer, leaving the garment bag right where it lay. When he went to Willow's bedroom, he found Beth fixing his daughter's hair into different styles.

"Hi Daddy! Beth's going to put my hair on top of my head for the party."

"You're going to look like a princess," he replied, flashing her a big smile. "Willow, could I steal Beth away for just a minute?"

"Okay. But just for a minute."

Beth stepped into the hall behind Scott and moved out of Willow's earshot. "Before you say anything," she began, "I really appreciate your inviting me to this hospital thing, but I've decided not to go. I think it would be better for you and Willow to spend the evening with Joanna."

His brow furrowed. "Don't say that, Beth. I want you to go with us." After a pause, he added, "Willow will be so disappointed if you don't come along."

"I'll explain to her and she'll understand. It'll give her an opportunity to spend time with Doctor Coleman. I think that's important since she may become her stepmother one day." She wouldn't back down from her position.

Eyebrows up, he asked, "Who told you that?"

"No one. She's your girlfriend, so I'm assuming…"

"Well, don't assume anything," he interjected, frowning. "I'm not even sure where Joanna and I stand right now. It's become complicated since you arrived."

She shook her head. "Don't involve me in whatever's going on between the two of you. I'm not going to get in the middle. I have my own problems to worry about."

"Beth, surely you can tell how I feel about you. Out there on the porch just now…"

"Don't say anything." She brought a finger to his lips to shush him. "I think it's best if you and I stop spending so much time together. Neither of us wants to get hurt—and I have a terrible feeling..." She met his gaze with deep sorrow.

"Please," Scott pleaded. "I swear. Hurting you is the last thing I'd ever do."

"I know you don't intend to, just as I don't want to hurt you. But, we both know it's bound to happen."

"Just say you'll come with us tonight. We can talk about all the rest later," he begged.

Beth knew she had to stay strong and do the right thing, for all their sakes. But the man made it very difficult. He stared at her with an intensity that turned her legs to rubber. And that low, sexy drawl...It was enough to convert a nun.

"Come on," he urged, grinning.

Cowgirl up, she told herself.

When the telephone rang, she heard Carmen answer it, and call out for Scott.

"I'm in here," he hollered.

The cook's footsteps were heavy as she treaded down the hallway.

"What is it?" Scott asked, still staring at Beth.

"That was Buddy Griggs on the phone. He wants you both to come to his office as soon as possible."

Scott's grin dissolved. "Did he say anything else?"

"*Si*. He says someone has shown up. Someone for Beth."

Chapter Seven

"There's no need to be afraid," Buddy told her. "I just want you to meet this man and see if anything strikes a chord with you. See if you remember his face, his voice, the way he walks, anything at all." The sheriff stood next to his secretary's desk with Beth and Scott. Speaking in a quiet voice, he assured her, "I wouldn't have called you in here if I didn't think his story was compelling."

"What's so compelling about it?" Scott asked.

"He brought something with him that could prove he knows her. It's an item he says belongs to her."

"What kind of item?"

"Linda, show them." Linda opened her hand and showed them a small blue suede jewelry box. Cushioned inside was a silver locket in the shape of a heart.

"What does this prove?" Scott questioned.

"Linda, open the locket."

Both Scott and Beth peered into the locket at the miniature photo tucked inside.

"It's so small, I can't even tell who it is," Scott complained.

"The man in my office claims it's his sister. He says the photo was taken two years ago. Look at it close. There's a resemblance."

Beth held the locket up to her eyes and squinted.

"Does the necklace look familiar to you?" Buddy asked.

She shook her head.

"Well, that doesn't mean it's not yours. I say, give this guy a shot. The locket is all we have to go on so far. Let's see what happens when you meet him."

"What if I don't remember this man? Will I have to leave with him?" She nibbled the bottom of her lip.

"No way. I'm not going to let any ole Tom, Dick or Harry waltz out of here with you. He has a photo I.D. on him, but I don't want to tell you his name yet. I'm hoping he's familiar to you. Maybe you'll remember the necklace after talking to him. The photo does resemble you."

"I'd never allow her to leave with someone without absolute confirmation," Scott stated firmly.

"I just said I wouldn't," Buddy repeated, frowning. "Are you questioning the way I'm handling this investigation, Scotty?"

"Nope. I'm just assuring her that she'll be protected. This could be the man who hurt her."

"My job is to protect and serve," Buddy reminded him. "I'm doing both for Beth. Are you ready?" he asked her.

"Yes." She took a deep breath and straightened her back.

Scott took a step forward, but the sheriff stopped him by pushing a hand onto his chest. "Where do you think you're going?"

"Inside, with the two of you."

"No. You'll stay right here. She has to do this on her own without any interference from you."

"I'm not going to interfere," Scott protested.

"You might be a distraction. You can keep my secretary company. She'll get you a cup of coffee, won't ya Linda?"

"Sure will." The legs of Linda's chair scraped as she scooted out from behind her desk. "Let's go back to the kitchen, Scotty. I've got some cinnamon-vanilla decaf in the pot."

He smiled at Beth and reluctantly followed Linda to the kitchen as Buddy opened the door to his office.

She walked into the small room. A thin man sat, with his legs crossed, in the hard wooden chair pulled up to the sheriff's desk. At the sound of the door squeaking open, he rotated his head. When Beth walked through, his face lit up. He bounded out of the chair and rushed toward her with his arms spread. "Dawn!" he cried.

Beth backed away and hid behind Buddy, like a child. The sheriff stuck out his arm to stop the tall man from coming closer. "Let's take this slow, sir. She's been through quite an ordeal. You don't want to scare her, do you?"

The fellow shook his head in a dramatic fashion.

"Okay, good. Let's all just have a seat and talk." Buddy motioned for the visitor to return to his chair and then offered Beth a seat. Then Buddy collapsed into the rolling chair behind the desk, folded his hands on top, and searched her face for any spark of recognition.

Beth stared at the man who had called her Dawn. Rail thin with a wide gap between his front teeth, he wore a plain white undershirt and pants that looked to be a size or two too large. His hair was dark, like hers, but it was wild and unruly, as if he'd been sitting in front of a fan.

The man leaned forward and spoke in a soft voice. "Do you remember me, Dawn? I'm your big brother David." He enunciated his words, as if she were hard of hearing.

"I have a brother?" she asked.

He grinned. "Of course you do, sweetheart. I'm three years older. I'm the one who gave you the pretty locket. The one the sheriff took from me." The man tossed an exasperated look at Buddy then smiled at Beth again. "I've missed you so much, ever since you went away."

"The locket is safe," Buddy assured him. "Will you tell us your last name, sir?"

"You already saw my I.D."

"Yes, I did, but I'd like you to repeat it for the lady."

The man laughed. "Dawn knows what my name is. She's my sister."

"Please just state your last name, sir," Buddy repeated. He was an easygoing man, obviously used to dealing with surly people.

The man folded his arms across his chest. "San Nicolas."

"My name is Dawn San Nicolas?" Beth asked. "That doesn't sound familiar at all." She began to fire questions at him. "Where do I live? Do I have a family? Am I married? How did you find me here?"

"You ask too many questions." David's hand flew to his head as his face contorted. "I'm getting a terrible headache."

Beth exchanged a questioning glance with Buddy, puzzled by the sudden odd behavior.

The sheriff asked the gentleman, "Would you like some aspirin? I can have my secretary get you some."

Adamant, San Nicolas replied, "No. I just want to take Dawn home—where she belongs. Can we go now?" He stood and shoved his hands into the pockets of his baggy pants.

Beth noticed his twitching mouth. "David...May I call you David?"

"Sure, but you always called me Davey, before you went away." He sat again.

"Oh, okay. Davey, can you tell me what happened on the day I disappeared? Where were you? Were we together that day? Did we have a disagreement?" She was racking her brains to remember whether he was the man she'd been seeing in the flashbacks. She searched his face and peered at his hands. He seemed frail. The man in the flashbacks was strong and muscular. Anxiety caused her pulse to throb in her neck.

"Disagreement? None of that matters," he shot back. "The important thing is I've found you now. When can I take her home, Sheriff?"

"Begging your pardon, Mr. San Nicolas, but we need answers to her questions and a whole lot more I have for you before you can take your sister home. I'm going to need to see some documents that belong to this lady that prove her identity—or perhaps another, larger photo. But first things first. Let's start at the beginning. Where do you live?"

"Siesta Springs." The man pouted like a child, refusing to look Buddy in the eye.

Buddy threw a curious look at Beth, as he asked the next question. "How did you find out your sister was here in Ghost Rock?"

"I saw her picture on TV."

"When was that? When did you see her picture?"

"Yesterday."

"Did you drive here from Siesta Springs?"

"No." The man drummed a finger on the arm of the chair. "I don't have a car."

"But you have a driver's license."

"Yeah. They let me keep it in my wallet, but they won't let me drive. I don't have a car, I just told you."

Buddy leaned forward. "Then, how did you get to Ghost Rock? Siesta Springs is a good, say...fifty miles from here."

"I hitchhiked." The man tapped his foot on the floor.

Beth shifted in her chair. Her stomach churned. She had a bad feeling. Something wasn't right. She glanced at Buddy and scooted to the edge of her chair. It was a subtle gesture, but she saw him lift his hand, and she realized he wanted her to stay put and remain calm.

"It's dangerous to hitchhike, Mr. San Nicolas. There are a lot of crazies out on the roads these days."

"You can say that again." A high-pitched laugh erupted from the fellow's throat as his wild eyes darted all around the room. "There might even be loonies hiding in here somewhere," he whispered.

Buddy rose and strolled to the front of his desk.

The man's face grew dark. He grimaced. "Are you going to let me take Dawn home now? I'm getting real tired of this interrogation."

"Could you please stand up, Mr. San Nicolas?" Buddy requested. When he received an ominous glare, Buddy placed a hand on his holster. "Beth, you go on out to the front. I want to ask this gentleman a few more questions."

Her head was spinning. She stood and stumbled toward the door. David yelled, "No! Stay right where you are, Dawn!" When he reached into his pocket, Buddy drew his gun.

"Put your hands up! Now!" Buddy took a defensive stance and aimed his gun. Beth screamed. As San Nicolas tried to scramble out of the chair, the sheriff barreled forward and shoved the chair with his foot, sending both San Nicolas and the chair hurtling to the floor. With Buddy towering over him and shouting for him to raise his hands, the frightened man broke into gut-wrenching sobs.

Paralyzed by the swift and weird turn of events, Beth stood rooted in the spot, staring, her face numb. Buddy pressed the intercom button and ordered, "Linda, call 911 and tell them to get an ambulance over here right away." He let up on the button. "Beth, go on out to the lobby." He kept his gun leveled at the man who lay sprawled on the floor.

When the door flew open and Scott burst in, Buddy told him to get her out of there.

Scott threw his arm around Beth's waist and ushered her out.

"No!" San Nicolas cried. "Don't take Dawn from me again." He brought his knees up to his chest and coiled himself into a ball.

The sheriff kept the gun on him. "Stay right where you are, Mr. San Nicolas. Help is on the way."

****

When the paramedics strapped San Nicolas into a straight jacket and administered a sedative, Beth asked if that was necessary. They assured her it was for his safety. He was a sick man. She, Scott and Linda watched as the ambulance drove off with him in the back.

Buddy stepped out of the office building into the sunshine. Removing his hat, he scratched a hand through his dark curls. "It sure is a balmy afternoon."

"So, what did you find out?" Scott asked him.

"I just got off the phone with the Director of the Siesta Springs Psychiatric Hospital. Here's the story. The fella's name *is* David San Nicolas and his sister's name was Dawn, but something unfortunate happened. She died in a house fire three months ago. The siblings were the only two in the house at the time and somehow he escaped, but the fire trapped her in an upstairs bedroom. Blaming himself for not being able to rescue her, Mr. San Nicolas became severely depressed. When he refused therapy and tried to commit suicide, his family had him committed to the hospital. From what the director can gather, San Nicolas was watching television in the recreational room yesterday and saw Beth's photo on the news, just like he said. The director assumes he had a psychotic break and really believed she was his sister. Another patient heard him say he was going to go look for Dawn, and several others even cheered him on as he escaped over the wall."

"That's a helluva security system they've got over there at the hospital," Scott replied, his voice dripping with sarcasm.

Beth queried Buddy. "Do I look like her? His sister? It was hard to tell from the tiny photo in the locket."

"Close enough, I guess. It doesn't matter one way or the other. In his mind, you were his sister, no matter what you looked like."

"It's so sad. I hope he gets the helps he needs," she said.

Buddy cleared his throat and apologized. "Beth, I'm *so* sorry for putting you in any kind of danger. The guy seemed perfectly normal when he stepped into my office. He had I.D. on him. I had no idea he'd escaped from a mental hospital." He pursed his lips and shook his head.

Beth patted his arm. "It's okay, Sheriff. You handled the situation with professionalism. I didn't feel in danger at all. I just feel so bad for the poor man."

"Let's hope he gets the help he needs," Buddy replied.

Scott glanced at his watch. "Well, now that the excitement is over, I guess we should be getting back to the ranch. Beth, I guess you'll be staying with us a little longer." He smiled.

"Looks that way," she agreed.

"Are you going to the dedication tonight?" Scott asked Buddy.

"Nope. Joanna and I try to steer clear of each other as much as possible. Are you two going?"

Scott looked to Beth. The sheriff's call had

interrupted them back at the house before she'd made her final decision. "Yes, we're going," she replied.

Scott beamed.

"Well, have fun," Buddy said. As he and Linda strolled back toward the office, he told Beth, "I'll keep you posted if any new developments occur."

Scott was opening the truck's passenger door when the sheriff spun on his heel and called out, "I know someone's out there looking for you, Beth. I feel it in my bones. Don't give up hope. I'll do everything in my power to get you back to your real life."

My real life, she thought. Which life is that?

She and Scott swapped glances, but neither of them offered Buddy a reply.

****

"My, my, my. Is this my daughter, or is it a fairy princess?" Scott beheld Willow in genuine bewilderment. Demure in a cornflower blue dress with capped sleeves and white lace around the collar and at the hem, she didn't look like the same girl. A big satin bow adorned her blonde ponytail, and she wore anklet socks and shiny white leather shoes with thin straps across the top.

"I wanted to wear my cowgirl boots, but Beth thinks these shoes make me look more grown up."

Her father grinned. "I totally agree—although I'm not sure I'm ready for you to grow up quite yet." He scooped the little girl into his arms and she buried her face in his neck. "You're so pretty, honey," he said with a voice choked with emotion. "You remind me so much of your mama."

Willow pulled back and gazed at him, baffled. "Are you crying, Daddy? Are you sad about something?"

"No, baby. I'm happy. You're as pretty as a picture."

"Do you like my hair?"

"Yes. The curl on the end of your ponytail looks like the tail of your little pony toy."

Willow laughed. "Beth used the curling iron on it. Wait till you see *her*. She's as pretty as a picture, too. I'll go get her!" Willow wiggled out of his arms and skipped down the hall. She returned a moment later grasping Beth's hand.

When Scott gazed upon Beth in a knee-length lilac wrap dress, which showed off her shapely legs and womanly curves, he swallowed hard. Her ebony hair tumbled down her back in soft waves. He couldn't take his eyes off her and found it difficult to contain the swell of joy rising inside.

"Do you remember this dress?" she asked twirling around.

His answer was an honest one. "No, I don't. Was it Maggie's?"

"It was hanging in the closet, so I assume so. Do you mind me wearing it?"

He shook his head. "It's yours. The dress is a perfect fit and you look gorgeous in that shade." He shoved his hands into his pockets, unable to utter another word.

"Thank you, Scott. You clean up real good yourself," she replied, smiling. He was dressed in a mahogany colored leather jacket, white shirt, black dress slacks and black ostrich quill boots.

Willow's head bobbed back and forth between them like she was observing a tennis match.

Carmen advanced around the corner with her old Polaroid camera in her hand and exclaimed, "*Ay yi yi*. Don't you all look like a million bucks! It's been a long time since I've seen you two dressed in anything but Wranglers and spurs," she accused, pointing a finger at Scott and Willow. "I have to take your picture for posterity. Stand together," she ordered, pressing the three of them together like a sandwich.

"What happened to that digital camera I bought you for Christmas?" Scott asked.

"This one works just fine," Carmen replied adamantly.

"Can't teach an old dog new tricks, I guess," he joked, shaking his head.

When the camera flashed, an image also popped into Beth's mind. She remembered posing for another photo, with the man—whose face she still could not recall—and the little brunette girl. The scene was reminiscent of the family photo she saw on Scott's dresser that first day. The image was gone in a second, but the face of the little girl lingered.

I know she's my child.

The hum of Carmen's camera brought her back to the present. "I want to take a couple more," Carmen said, as she pressed the button again and wiped a tear from her cheek.

"Why are you sad?" Willow asked.

"I'm not sad, *chiquita*. You and your daddy look so happy, and that makes *me* happy. These are tears of joy."

The photos slid out one after the other and she handed Beth one of them. "You keep this one. I want you to always remember your time at the High Lonesome."

Beth hugged Carmen, too moved to say more.

"Let's go, Daddy!" the little girl shouted.

"Good idea. We don't want them to run out of those tiny pinkie sandwiches," he said, causing them all to laugh.

****

Throngs of people were milling around when the trio arrived in the lobby of the new hospital wing. Glancing around, Scott saw he knew just about everyone there. He introduced his daughter and guest to a few ranchers and businessmen, not bothering to go into details when people stared. With all the flyers in town and Beth's picture having been on the news, he figured who she was or what had happened to her was no secret.

The three of them were checking out the buffet table when Joanna breezed up. "Hello, handsome," she drawled, snaking an arm around Scott's waist.

"Hi, Jo. Nice party you have here."

"Thanks. Hello, Willow. Hello, Beth." She shook both their hands in a formal manner and they replied with polite smiles. She stepped back and perused Scott from head to toe. Her forehead wrinkled. "Honey, where is the beautiful suit I brought out to the ranch? I thought you were going to wear it tonight."

"I never promised to wear it, Joanna. Formal suits aren't my style. You should know that by now."

"I like the way my daddy looks," Willow piped up.

Joanna fired the child a look that suggested she stay out of it. "This is big people talk, Willow," she replied in her iciest voice. Returning her gaze to Scott, she mumbled, "For once, I thought you could show up to one of my functions looking like a sophisticated gentleman instead of a trail cowboy."

"Daddy, what's a sophisticated gentleman?" Willow asked.

"A stuffy old toad."

Willow cackled.

"Scott!" Joanna jabbed him with her elbow. Even Beth visibly struggled to keep from laughing, her lips disappearing from biting them together.

"There's nothing wrong with the way I look," he replied. "I come from a long line of trail cowboys, and I'm proud of my heritage."

Jo sighed. "Everyone in this crummy little town is a cowboy. I married one, in case you don't remember. I thought you'd learn to..."

Scott cut her off. “That’ll be enough, Joanna.”

Her mouth twitched as her gaze darted between him and Beth. It was obvious she was considering her next move carefully.

“I’d advise you to think before you say more,” he said quietly. “Let’s not ruin the evening with harsh words.”

Willow stared at him with bug eyes. Beth stepped away and let her gaze drift across the crowd.

Joanna’s face flushed. In a heartbeat, she plastered on her best beauty pageant smile. Straightening her posture, she patted the top of Willow’s head.

Willow whined, “Don’t mess up my hair.”

Jo said, “Come with me, Scott. I want to introduce you to some important people.” She tugged on his arm. “You don’t mind if I steal him away for a few minutes, do you ladies?”

Beth spun around. Before she or Willow could answer, Joanna had dragged Scott off into the crowd of suits and ties.

“Let’s sample these finger foods,” Beth suggested to her young companion. “I love petite fours. How about you?”

Willow nodded and the two of them filled their plates with goodies. They had almost made their way down the buffet table when Joanna took her place behind the podium.

She tapped on the microphone and said, “Good evening ladies and gentlemen. I’m Doctor Joanna Coleman and I’d like to welcome you all here tonight. As a member of the Board of Directors of Ghost Rock Memorial Hospital, I would like to thank each and every one of you for attending this dedication of the brand new Marvin Cardiac Wing. The board wishes to express its sincere appreciation to Mrs. Clarice Marvin, who contributed the funds for the addition of this wing, in memory of her late husband, Doctor Elmer Marvin."

Beth joined the round of applause that erupted for the elderly Clarice, who stood to the right of the podium and nodded her head in thanks.

Joanna continued. "It's been two years since the design of this wing was approved and construction began, so we are very pleased to be here tonight celebrating the opening of this very important unit. It will benefit our community in so many ways."

Scott sidled up beside Beth during more applause and pressed his shoulder against hers. Willow yanked on his sleeve and he bent down to her cupped hand. She said in that loud whisper that all children think is quiet, "Can we go now? I'm bored."

"They're about to cut the ribbon. That's the most important part. They have a giant pair of scissors over there." He pointed across the room to where the scissors were propped.

"Oh. Cool."

Taking the arm of the benefactress, Joanna said, "Mrs. Marvin, if you'll come with me, we'll now conduct the ribbon cutting ceremony."

She led the woman over to a faux brick wall where a bronze plaque hung bearing the words, *The Elmer Marvin Cardiac Wing*. Clarice pointed to the plaque and smiled as a newspaper photographer snapped her photo. She then shuffled over to the wide red ribbon tied across the double-door entrance of the new wing. Joanna placed the gigantic pair of silver scissors in her hand and the room grew quiet.

Just then, Willow sneezed and all heads swiveled. The guest of honor shouted, "God bless you!" and everyone laughed. Then she positioned the scissors over the ribbon and cut. When the ribbon snapped and swirled to the ground, Beth, Scott and the other onlookers saluted her by erupting in cheers.

"Can we go now, Daddy?" Willow begged. "I

don't feel good. I think I ate too many pickles and cookies."

Scott dropped to his knees and pressed the back of his fingers to her forehead. "You do look a little green around the gills." He glanced at Beth, who shrugged her shoulders. "I guess the main event is over now anyway," he said. "Let me go explain to Joanna why we're leaving and tell her goodbye."

Beth watched him stroll over to his elegantly dressed and perfectly coiffured girlfriend. He stood behind Joanna, waiting until she excused herself from a circle of friends. As he spoke, Beth could tell from the expression on Joanna's face that she was not pleased with the news. She frowned, rolled her eyes and turned away from him in a huff.

When Scott returned, he told Willow, "Joanna is sorry we have to go so soon, but she wanted me to tell you she hopes you feel better."

Beth knew he was fibbing, but she understood his motive for doing so.

When the three of them stepped out into the tepid air, the child perked up as if a miracle had taken place. She slipped between Beth and her dad and grasped their hands. "Can we take a walk downtown?" she asked, swinging between them.

Beth received a sideways glance from Scott. He asked, "Are you sure you're up to it, kiddo? You were as green as a frog just a minute ago."

"Yep! I'm up to it. I'm feeling so much better already. I think I just needed some air."

He grinned. "Didn't we all? I wouldn't mind a walk. How about you, Beth?"

"It's a lovely evening," she noted, taking in a breath of air. "A walk would be nice."

As they strolled down the main avenue, hoards of people filled the streets in a deluge. Shop doors were open wide, music blared from a club on the corner, and enticing smells drifted out to Beth's nose from the many cafes and restaurants lining the quaint downtown row. As the golden sun floated below the horizon, colorful lights strung across shop doors warmed to a soft, inviting glow.

"This town is really hopping. Is it always so busy on a Friday night?" she asked.

"Yep. Main Street is the place to be. This is a small town, and what we offer may not be so cultured, but there's always something going on."

"I love the friendly, family atmosphere. It reminds me of when I was a girl, when life was simple. I grew up in a little town something like this."

He stopped, whirled, and put his hand on her arm. "What do you remember about your town? What was the name of it? Can you recall any landmarks?"

She stared down at his hand clamped upon her wrist.

He removed it and said, "I'm sorry. I just got so excited. I didn't hurt you, did I?"

"No, I'm fine." She smiled.

"So, what do you remember?" he asked.

"I remember a small town, but nothing specific. The words just slipped out of my mouth. It was more of a fond feeling rather than a true memory."

"Oh."

They began to walk again.

"What's going on over there?" Beth inquired, pointing to a building on the corner. There seemed to be a lot of activity and noise coming from inside.

"Bingo!" Willow shouted. "Can we go play, Daddy? Please, please, please." Willow wrenched his hand, pulling him down the walk toward the Bingo parlor. Beth followed along.

The doors were propped open and inside the hall were a dozen tables, lined one in front of the other with young and old hunched over their cards. The caller was an elderly lady with blue hair, done up in a beehive. She hollered "B, 14" as they entered.

"Please, Daddy. You know how I *love* Bingo." Willow cast him her best hangdog expression, which never failed to cause him to melt like snow on a spring day.

"Your tummy sure got better fast," he teased. He and Beth smiled at one another. "Have you ever played Bingo?" he asked her.

"When I was younger. Let's go in," she urged. "I feel lucky tonight."

"Me, too." Scott winked at his daughter.

The three of them found spots at the very back table, with Willow sitting in the middle. They poised their markers over their cards as the caller rapped her fist on the podium and hollered into the microphone. "Take your seats. A new game is starting." She was having a hard time getting people's attention because an older gentleman in a ten-gallon hat across the aisle had just won twenty dollars and was still being congratulated.

The new game commenced, and a teenage boy shouted "Bingo" almost as fast as the game had started. He won ten bucks then jumped into the aisle and celebrated by doing a few silly dance moves.

"Sit down, sonny," the lady yelled from up on the stage. "Next game is beginning!"

"This is fun!" Willow exclaimed. "Don't you think so, Beth?"

"Yes. I do. Is the parlor open every Friday night?"

"Yep. Do you want to come back next week?"

The adults glanced at one another. Beth wondered what the chances would be of her staying at the High Lonesome another week. Not likely, she figured.

The next game began. "N, 6," the lady yelled.

"Oh, I've got that one," Beth said, unbelieving.

"First one I've gotten so far."

"Lucky you," Scott said, shaking his head at his empty card.

"O, 23."

"What do you know? I've got that one, too." Beth wagged her head in amazement.

"Next number. G, 21."

"G, 21," Beth repeated. "Oh, my gosh. I've got it."

Scott and Willow grinned at her from across their blank cards.

"Next number coming up!" The lady shouted into the mike, "B, 63!"

"I've got B 63!" Willow cried.

Beth squeezed her shoulder. "You won't believe it, but so do I."

The child's mouth opened, forming an o. "One more and you've got Bingo."

Beth glanced at the next table and saw an old lady glaring at them. The lady was huddled over her card, protecting it like a mother bear would protect her cub.

The blue-haired lady caller declared the next number. "I, 85."

Beth's eyes swept over her card. "I, 85. I, 85. I've got it! Bingo!" she screamed. "Bingo! Right here, I've got a Bingo!" She shook Scott's shoulder and he and Willow both laughed.

The checker, an older gentleman wearing bib overalls, hobbled over and announced the marks on her card one at a time. His voice boomed.

"N, 6. G, 21. O, 23, B, 63, and I, 85. She's got 'em, Martha," he informed the caller. "She's got a Bingo!"

"Yippee!" Willow yelled. "Way to go, Beth!"

"What did I win? What did I win?" Beth asked. She was as excited as a child on Christmas morning.

The caller declared her the big winner of the night. "You've won fifty dollars! Congratulations, honey."

The old man who had checked her card pulled a fifty-dollar bill out of his pocket and placed it in Beth's open palm, as he flashed her a semi-toothless smile. "Don't spend it all in one place."

"Fifty dollars!" Beth jumped up and down like a little kid while hugging Willow. Scott stood and opened his arms. He was grinning that sexy, crooked grin. Without thinking, Beth melted into his embrace. She tossed her arms around his neck and kissed him on the cheek as the crowd of onlookers clapped and whistled.

His arms slipped around her waist and he pulled her tight against his chest. His body felt hard as steel. Beth held onto the taut muscles of his back and felt his fingers skim over her hips as he murmured something in her ear.

Her eyes slid shut. Having dreamed of his touch and strong loving embrace, she basked in the joy of the moment. Then, in a burst of light, Joanna's face flashed before her. Instantly, Beth disentangled herself from his hold.

"I can't believe I won," she said, brushing a strand of hair away from her face. She wouldn't look him in the eye. Guilt pierced her for desiring another woman's man. Her cheeks grew warm and she stammered, "It's hot in here. I could use some air. I'm going to step outside for a moment." She fanned her face with her hand and started for the door.

Scott replied, "Maybe we should all call it a night. What do you say, Willow? Had enough Bingo for one evening?"

Nodding, she stifled a yawn.

They left their cards and markers on the table, stepped out of the warm hall into the air that had grown cooler and began the trek back to the hospital parking lot. Willow begged her father to carry her. Scott hoisted her up, and she clung like a monkey with her arms around his neck and her legs around his waist.

The lemony moon dangled like a slice of pie, surrounded by millions of twinkling white stars. Beth looked up and sighed. She hugged herself and imagined being wrapped in Scott's arms again.

"Thank you, Scott," she said, trying to keep the conversation light and pretend their second close encounter of the day hadn't taken place. "I enjoyed that so much. I feel so comfortable here in this town."

Lost in his thoughts, Scott smiled but didn't reply.

When they reached his truck, Willow stirred and moaned. Keeping his hands securely clasped around her body, he asked Beth to grab the keys out of the front pocket of his jeans. She hesitated before slipping her fingers into the pocket to retrieve the truck keys. Although it was a legitimate request, given his hands weren't free, the act was an intimate one—one that caused her heart to race double-time as her fingers grazed his hard upper thigh through his pants. Her hand shook as she unlocked the passenger door. Scott deposited Willow in the middle of the seat and buckled her in. Beth slid in next to her.

She cranked the window halfway down and listened to the night sounds as the engine roared. They bounced along the back road toward the High Lonesome, the creamy moon as their guide.

Willow slumped over and laid her head in Beth's lap. Half asleep, she wiggled around until she found a comfortable position, where she stayed the rest of the way. Beth stroked the child's silky hair with her fingertips.

Silence filled the space between her and Scott, but Beth's pulse quickened as thoughts of his strong arms and firm body invaded her thoughts. Laying her head back against the seat, she also replayed the moment on the porch earlier that afternoon when they had come so close to kissing.

Stop! He's not yours. And you're not his. A tear slid down her cheek.

All was quiet at the ranch when they drove in. There were still lights on in a few of the small cabins below, but the main house was silent as a tomb when they entered. It was dark, except for the soft glowing night light in the hall. Scott carried Willow to her bedroom, with Beth following. Without asking, she undressed the child, slipped a nightgown over her head, and then Scott tucked the covers up under her chin. They lingered over her for a moment.

After clicking the room door shut, the two of them stood facing each other in the hallway. Moonlight shone through the windows of the great room and bathed them in silvery rays.

Scott whispered, "You're so good with her. Thank you for taking time to do her hair and help her get dressed. I know she felt like a little princess. Times like these are when I most regret she doesn't have a mother."

Beth was relieved that he was talking about Willow and not about what happened back in town. "She's going to be all right, Scott. You're a wonderful father."

"I know, but a little girl needs a mother." He surprised her when he added, "And a man needs a wife. Someone he can share life's ups and downs with. A woman who'll love him with her whole heart and soul, and accept all he has to offer in return. That's something I long for again. I didn't realize how badly, until you came along. I want a family. More children. And a woman—my soul mate."

Her heart fluttered and her stomach felt like a basket of butterflies had been set free inside. *Then, why don't you ask Joanna to marry you?* She wanted to shout it, but instead, she just clamped her mouth shut and began to march down the hall to her room. After the two near kisses that day, she didn't trust herself alone with him. Her reserves were growing weak. And now, here he was talking about soul mates. It was too much. She reached for the doorknob.

"Beth, wait." His voice was but a whisper. He came up behind her.

She turned, trembling, and wondered if she should tell him she sensed she was married with a child, and that he should go to his girlfriend and make up with her. But something in his soulful eyes caused her to wait. As he gazed with love and longing into her face, pins pricked at her spine and across her neck. At that very moment, time stopped, and she thought she'd go crazy if she didn't taste his kiss. She wanted his lips to devour hers. She needed his tongue to delve into her mouth and fill her with his heat. She ached for his hands to explore her body and set her on fire.

But none of it would come to pass. She *had* to push those thoughts out of her head. It wasn't meant for them to be. He had Joanna and she had…whom did she have? Was there anyone out there looking for her?

With all the tact and sincerity Beth could muster, she said, "Thank you for inviting me tonight, Scott. I had a wonderful evening. You've done so much for me. I don't know how I'll ever be able to repay you."

Anchoring his hands on his hips, he replied, "The best way to repay me would be to follow your heart."

The silence between them was deafening—broken only by the low hum of the central air conditioning whose condenser suddenly kicked on.

Beth questioned him with her gaze. "I'm not sure what that means," she managed to say.

She pressed her back against the wall, exhausted by the emotional turmoil of the day. When he put a hand on the wall and leaned in, she ducked under his arm and whispered, "Good night, Scott."

Without looking back, Beth flung open the guest room door and let it close with a firm snap behind her. Inside, she stood against it for several minutes—holding her breath—waiting for his steps to recede.

Scott stood in the shadows debating on whether to knock on the door and do what he'd wanted to do all day—kiss her and show her how bad he wanted her and needed her—but he knew if their lips touched even once, he'd never stop. His heart boomed inside his chest like thunder. He raised his fist, and then lowered it again.

Why am I doing this to myself? She's bound to remember more and more about her real life with every passing day. Someone's going to take her away. I know it.

The prospects of having to say goodbye to her caused him pain like he hadn't experienced in four years. With Maggie's death, he'd suffered unbearable, heartbreaking loss. It was the kind of loss intended to make him stronger, but it only made him realize how fleeting life was. He knew he was vulnerable, but he'd fallen in love. There was no denying it. And the thought of watching this woman walk away from his life scared him to death.

He climbed the stairs to his empty room, slipped off his clothes and crawled into bed—his limbs heavy and his mind spinning out of control. Sleep was slow to come, but when it did, hours later, he dreamed of a green-eyed angel that was flying away from him.

Chapter Eight

Jack West's muscular arms pumped from side to side. Every once in a while, he'd extend one and point it toward the television suspended from the ceiling in his home gym. He channel surfed between news stations. He liked to watch CNN or the local news as he ran. Jack punched a button and the belt speed picked up. His athletic shoes thumped on the hard rubber—left, right, left, right, left, right. He ran like a cougar on the treadmill, but barely broke a sweat. At six foot two and one hundred eighty-five pounds, the chiseled athlete considered himself more machine than man.

Exercising had always been a way of keeping his body in the shape he desired, but in recent years, it had also become a release—a stress reliever—from the daily grind of life. That kind of release was required now, more than ever, to channel the torture he'd experienced the past few days since his wife had disappeared.

Angela, his beautiful wife of eight years, had been missing for several days. Technically, she was his ex-wife, but Jack was not the kind of man to bother with technicalities.

He'd driven to his former home the morning she disappeared to visit with his daughter—time he'd been allotted by Court Order after the divorce. It was a magnificent brick home on a cul-de-sac in one of the ritziest neighborhoods in Tucson—a home he'd worked like a dog for years to provide for his family. Even when he thought about it now, it still pissed him off that the judge had just handed the house over to Angela as part of the divorce settlement.

As usual, he and Angela had disagreed—had a small argument over something—almost as soon as he'd stepped through the front door. He couldn't even remember what the fight was about now. He'd taken Heather to the park so both he and Angela could cool down. When he returned several hours later, he found Angie gone. At first, he'd thought she was off running errands, or visiting Faith, the neighbor next door. Then he remembered Faith was out of town and wouldn't be home for another week or so. He called the neighbor on the other side, but she hadn't seen his wife either.

After waiting a couple more hours, he'd started to worry. It was not like Angie to leave without a note, especially when she knew he'd be bringing Heather home. She had just a handful of friends, and when he called them, they told him they hadn't seen or heard from her.

This was the story he'd told the police later that evening. He explained how she had no immediate family living, and how he'd checked and realized her passport and birth certificate were missing. As the police investigated, they discovered no signs of forced entry into the home. Nothing was askew in the house, and there was no blood, no reason to believe she was kidnapped or taken by force.

When asked if she could have left on her own accord, Jack acknowledged that their relationship had been rocky for some time, and had disintegrated even further since the divorce. He said she had seemed restless and he'd noticed her being short and impatient with their young daughter. "It was tough to believe, but it was becoming more apparent that she no longer wanted to be a wife *or* a mother," he told the investigators.

Jack even wrung his hands and managed to

squeeze out a tear.

The trail grew cold fast, and the Arizona State Police soon considered it a case of a missing person by choice. Consensus was, Angela West had walked away from her family and vanished without a trace.

His plan had worked without a hitch.

Jack punched another button and the treadmill slowed. He stepped off and wiped his face with a towel. Sauntering over to the bar, he took out a bottle of cranberry juice from the mini fridge, filled a tumbler with ice and poured a glass, gulping it down without coming up for air.

Pausing in front of the television, he was about to flip it off when a familiar face stared out at him like a ghost. She was pale and innocent looking, with big green eyes. Her hair was glossy—as black as the night. A phone number, email address, and website address rolled across the bottom of the screen. Jack aimed the remote control at the set and pressed the volume to high.

His jaw clenched and the muscles twitched as he listened to a law officer offer up a plea to the greater Arizona community. The man was the sheriff of some hick town in New Mexico—the name of which he failed to grasp—and he was asking "anyone who knows this woman or has information about her, to please come forward or contact the number on the screen."

Jack's mind began to spin. He hit "Pause" on the DVR and grabbed a pad and pen from off the bar counter. Beads of sweat popped out on his face. He scribbled down the information and then pressed the start button and heard the word *amnesia*. Stunned, he wondered if he'd heard correctly. Angela, his former wife, was in New Mexico suffering from amnesia? Everything was jumbling together. He could hardly process the news.

He flicked off the television and ran down the

hall to the bedroom he'd once shared with her. The day she disappeared, after the police left, he'd driven to the apartment he'd been relegated to, packed his clothes and moved back to the house. He had Heather to look after, and there was no reason for him and his precious daughter to stay in that rented dump while his beautiful home stood empty. The same home the judge handed over to Angela without so much as a backward glance.

Jack reached for the picture frame that sat on Angela's vanity. It was a photo of her and Heather. Then he ran into the living room and searched the end table drawers for their wedding album. He hadn't looked at it in years and figured she'd stowed it away after the divorce, but he'd need a photo of the two of them as proof that she was his wife.

Finding it turned out to be easier than he thought. Locating it on the bottom shelf of the bookcase in the den, he flipped open the album, expecting to find their marriage certificate stuck in the front plastic cover. It wasn't there. He turned through the pages, but the certificate was not to be found anywhere in the album. No matter, he thought. A wedding photo of the two of them would suffice. He pulled out the top photo and gazed at it. A shiver ran through him. He could be sentimental. He'd given her the perfect wedding, and they'd been so in love at the time. But that was a long time ago.

Jack shoved the album back into the bookcase and searched the master bedroom for a duffle bag to carry a change of clothes, the wedding photo, and the framed picture.

He jumped into the shower and lathered up, his mind racing a hundred miles an hour. After drying his hair and slipping on some slacks, a white cotton shirt and loafers, he headed downstairs to place two phone calls. The first was to the older neighbor next door. Even though Angie was acquainted with her, he hadn't spoken to the woman often, but remembered she'd babysat for Heather a few times. He wondered if she even knew he and Angela were divorced. When he called, she told him she'd just seen the broadcast about Angie on TV and was in shock. When he asked if she could watch Heather overnight, the neighbor told him she'd do anything to help.

The second call was to the phone number of the sheriff's department in Ghost Rock, New Mexico. He got the answering machine. He didn't bother to leave a message, and he didn't have time to try again. He'd drive and spend the night in Ghost Rock—relax and polish his story—and call again in the morning.

When he was set, Jack locked up the house and jumped into the black BMW coupe that the divorce judge had also given to Angela. He sped down the interstate and crossed the state line, passing a sign, which read *You Are Now Leaving Arizona—Come Back Again*. Just ahead, he noticed a second sign, with the greeting, *Welcome to the Land of Enchantment*.

He mumbled, "God, I hate New Mexico."

Chapter Nine

Beth waltzed into the kitchen on Saturday morning to find Scott, Cody and Carmen having a pow-wow around the island.

"Good mornin'," Scott said, before taking a sip of coffee.

Her gaze connected with his, but only for a moment.

"Morning, everyone."

"Morning, Beth," echoed Carmen and Cody.

She meandered past Scott on her way to the coffee pot. She'd tossed and turned most of the night and wondered if he'd slept any better. He didn't look worse for the wear. In fact, he looked as sexy as ever. The early morning hours looked good on the man. His blue eyes were sparkling, his cheeks were rough and unshaven, and he smelled delicious—his scent a combination of soap, cologne, and pure masculinity.

She'd left her hair down and dressed in jeans and a snug plaid western shirt; clothes that felt second nature to her already. As she poured a cup of coffee and stirred in sugar, Beth felt Scott's gaze on her back. She turned and caught him staring—and not hiding the fact. His eyes traveled up and down her body, taking her all in. When he smiled, her heart began to hammer inside her chest.

She took a seat at the island, next to Cody, and reached for a blueberry muffin. From the look on Scott and his wrangler's faces, she guessed the conversation wasn't too serious. They both seemed relaxed as usual.

Then Carmen threw her arms into the air and began squawking a Spanish blue streak.

Beth took a bite of muffin and wondered what was going on.

"Calm down before you have a stroke," Scott joked after downing his coffee. "It's not the end of the world, Carmen."

"Is something wrong?" Beth asked.

"*Si*. We've got trouble with a capital T," Carmen told her, shaking her head.

"Rowdy and Amber have run off together." Cody soaked up some runny eggs with a piece of toast and offered the news as if he were giving the weather report.

"It was bound to happen sooner or later," Scott added.

"*Ai yi yi*." Carmen sighed. "Crazy kids. They didn't even have the decency to tell Mr. Scott face to face. They left a note taped to the back door." She made a stabbing motion with her finger toward the door for emphasis. She tapped the note lying in front of Scott. "Read it to her," she urged.

Scott unfolded the note. He read, "Dear Scott. Me and Amber are in love and have left for California. She has an uncle out there who works in the movie industry. He's going to give us both jobs and let us live in one of his apartments rent-free until we get on our feet. We're sorry for not telling you in person. We both feel real bad about leaving you stuck like this, cause you've been so good to us. We want to thank you for all you did, but we couldn't wait cause the uncle wanted us out there yesterday. Hope you understand. Sincerely, your wrangler, Rowdy. P.S. Tell my pardner Cody I said *adios*." Scott folded the note up again and laid it back on the counter.

Beth finally met his gaze. "Well, I'll be. It seemed to me they had it pretty good here," she said.

"You treated them both like gold and gave them fair wages."

"Ah, these kids are always looking for the next best thing. The grass is always greener, as they say." He leaned into the back of the bar stool and crossed one leg over the other knee.

Beth noticed he didn't seem too concerned for having just lost two out of three employees.

"Now, what are we going to do?" Carmen twisted her vein-ridden hands up in her apron. "We've got a business to run."

"Cody can handle the guests on his own for awhile, can't ya Cody?" Scott inquired.

"Yes sir. I won't be running out on you. I know which side my bread's buttered."

"I appreciate your loyalty, son." Scott leaned over and clamped a strong hand down on the young man's shoulder. "I suspect you've been the one to do the lion's share of the work around the ranch as it was."

"I just do my job." Cody shoveled a mouthful of sausage and eggs into his mouth.

"Humility is a good quality. You're a man of character," Scott praised. "I'd been thinking about upping your wages anyway. Now seems like a good time to put a raise into effect."

Cody's eyes lit up. He swallowed, then said, "Thank you, sir. I appreciate it."

"You're welcome. You deserve it. The guests all like you, and I like you. You're a good wrangler."

"Thank you, Scott." The young cowboy grinned and blushed.

"What are we going to do about a housekeeper, Mr. Scott?" Carmen asked. Her skin wrinkled in folds, and anxiety rimmed her dark, tired eyes. "I'm busy and too old to cook and do the cleaning, too. You need to put an ad in the paper today. It's going to be hard to find an honest girl around these parts.

Remember how we went through four housekeepers before we found Amber?"

Cody nodded and grabbed an apple out of the fruit bowl and crunched down on it. "I remember. One of them stole from the guests and another one was always sleeping on the job. The other two were just plain lousy at cleaning."

Scott agreed. "It's not easy finding and keeping good help. At least our current six guests are leaving this morning and we'll have a break for several days before the next group comes in."

"*Si*, but the bulk of the work in the cabins gets done after the guests leave," Carmen reminded him.

Beth cleared her throat and raised her arm, like a school kid asking permission to speak. "Excuse me. I don't know why you're all trying to figure out what you're going to do about a housekeeper when you have one right here. I won't steal from the guests, I won't sleep on the job, and I'm pretty sure I can clean a toilet and launder towels."

Three pair of eyes rotated toward her.

She faced Scott and begged. "Let me help, Scott. You and Carmen have done so much for me since I've been here. It's the least I can do until you can find someone to hire. Consider it partial payback for my room and board the past few days."

"Beth, you don't owe me anything," he responded.

"That's not the way I see it. Please. You'll insult me if you don't let me help."

"I don't know." He scratched a hand through his blond mop of hair.

"Well, I do. I'm *telling* you this is how it's going to be. I'm your new housekeeper, as of right now. No arguments." She crossed her arms and glared at him.

Carmen and Cody smiled and offered their approval with bobbing heads. "I guess Miss Beth just told *you*," Carmen said, chuckling.

"I guess she did." Scott and Beth locked eyes. "All right," he relented. "But, *only* until I hire a new girl."

Beth grinned. "You've got yourself a deal." The two of them grasped hands and shook on it.

****

Beth polished the cabin showers to a sparkle, scrubbed the toilets clean, and laundered, dried and stacked the towels for the arrival of the next guests the following week. She made up the beds with fresh sheets, vacuumed the floors, and swept the porches. She restocked the mini fridges and cleaned the coffee pots and mugs. After several hours of labor-intensive work, she plopped down on the front porch of the last cabin and wiped her brow with the sleeve of her shirt.

After resting a few moments, she took up the bucket of cleaning supplies and began to tread up the gravel drive toward the main house. Despite the physical labor, she'd never felt so energized and invigorated. She stopped at the pasture and stood at the fence to watch the horses. They were grazing, munching on grass with their tails swishing. She called to Sundance, and he ambled over and nuzzled her hand. The two of them had developed a bond of friendship and trust. Beth whispered in his ear and fed him a treat; one of several she had stashed in her pocket for quiet moments like this.

Admiring the red hills towering behind the cabins, she felt so at peace and thankful such kind people as Scott and Carmen took her in. Still, the truth about her life and how she ended up in the desert was never far from her mind. The dreams about the young dark-haired girl were intensifying—as were her feelings for the handsome rancher. She couldn't deny either—and both scared her to death.

"Hey, Beth. How's the cleaning business going?"

Cody was walking a dripping wet horse from the barn to the pasture. Both he and the horse were gnawing on spikes of grass.

"Great. Are all the horses getting baths today?"

"Yep. And it's not even Saturday night," he joked. "Scott and Willow are in the arena, if you wanna stop by. Willow's on Midnight practicing her pole bendin'."

"Thanks. I think I'll do that. I love watching her. Have a nice afternoon, Cody."

Beth wandered over to the arena. A slight breeze blew through her hair and cooled her neck and face. She set the cleaning bucket down, pulled her hair into a ponytail, and climbed up on top of the fence, hooking the toes of her boots under the wooden board.

She saw Scott at the end of the arena with a stopwatch in hand. When their eyes met, he waved. She waved back then set her attention on Willow and Midnight. Scott lifted his arm and shouted, "Go!"

Willow spurred her horse into a gallop. The big bay's muscles pulsated and his nostrils flared as they flew down the line of poles. Making a slight turn, the gelding zigzagged between the poles. Willow's pigtails flew like flags from under her pink hat. She smacked the horse's butt with a small whip, urging him to run full out down the final stretch. As they crossed the finish line, Beth clapped and whistled.

Scott's finger pressed down on the stopwatch. "Twenty-two point five!"

Willow beamed. "Did you hear that?" she yelled to Beth as she trotted the horse over to the fence.

"I sure did. You and Midnight are a winning team." Beth gave Willow a high five.

Scott strayed over and joined their conversation. "I think she has a pretty good chance of winning the

Little Wranglers competition. You did great, honey," he said, squeezing Willow's leg.

"My money would be on you. If I *had* any money," Beth added as an afterthought. Scott and Willow joined in when she chuckled.

"How's your morning been?" he asked, leaning against the fence close to her knee.

"Great." She ticked off the list of chores she had accomplished, her face warm with pride.

He shook his head. "You've done way too much work. You're supposed to be my guest, not my housekeeper."

She wagged a finger. "No arguments, remember? You promised."

"I remember, but that doesn't mean I have to like it. I feel terrible about this."

"You shouldn't. It makes me happy to contribute to the ranch this way. Besides, I really enjoyed the work, and I think I've done a pretty good job. Maybe I'm a housecleaner in my other life."

"I doubt that," Scott said, pulling a kerchief from his back pocket.

"Ranch life suits me. I sure am going to miss it here." Beth sighed and stared into the mountains.

Scott wiped his damp forehead and leveled a gaze at her.

"Why will you miss it?" Willow asked, puzzled. "Where are you going?"

Her father answered. "One of these days Beth will be going home. Back to where she came from."

"But we don't know where she came from," Willow replied, still confused.

He was slow to respond. "That's true, but Sheriff Buddy is working on it, and we both know what a good sheriff he is."

"Yep."

"He's sure to figure it out, sooner or later."

Willow frowned. "I hope it's later and not

sooner."

Beth felt tears welling up again. The thought of leaving the High Lonesome, not to mention Scott and Willow, was almost more than she could stand. She rubbed her eye with the back of her hand. "I think I got a piece of gravel in my eye," she fibbed.

"Let me help."

Before she could refuse, Scott had wiped his hands on the kerchief and was prodding her eyelid open with a gentle finger. His face was so close to hers she could feel his warm breath. The scent of cherry lip balm drifted off his slightly sunburned lips.

He didn't see a speck of gravel in her eye, as she knew he wouldn't, and he backed away. But not before letting his finger trail down her cheek. The gesture was so intimate and unexpected it caused Beth to quiver. Even after her brush-off last night, the man apparently would not be deterred.

"I think I got it out," he said, as a knowing smile tugged at his mouth.

"What are you going to do now?" Willow asked Beth. The girl was still sitting atop her well-behaved mount.

Beth found it difficult to answer. Scott's touch along her cheek had sent heat coursing through her body, distracting her. When Willow repeated the question, Beth stammered, "Uh. I'm headed up to the main house to ask Carmen what else I can do."

"Seems to me you've worked hard enough for one day," Scott said. "It's too pretty out to be stuck inside any longer. I have a great idea. Let's pack a picnic and ride the horses to the lake. I'd love to finally show it to you."

"That sounds tempting," Beth admitted. "But Carmen might need me. I'm on the clock now. Remember?"

Scott grinned. "Carmen practically runs this

entire ranch by herself. Let's throw caution to the wind. I think a little spontaneous fun would do us both good. I'm free the rest of the afternoon. And as your boss, I'm giving you the time off."

"What about you, Willow? Would you like to come along, honey?" Beth asked the girl.

Scott held his breath. As much as he loved his kid, he prayed she'd turn down the offer. He wanted to get Beth alone and tell her how he felt. That would be difficult to do with his little cowgirl tagging along.

Willow narrowed her eyes at her father. Fishing around in her jeans pocket, she retrieved a piece of bubble gum and tossed it in her mouth. "Nope. I don't believe I'll go along this time. Cody needs my help straightening up the tack room this afternoon. Right, Cody?" She winked at the cowboy who appeared like magic at her horse's side.

"Whatever you say, Willow. You're the boss."

"Where'd you come from?" Scott asked, baffled at the sudden manifestation of the wrangler.

"Been right here," Cody answered with a simple nod. "I need you to sign this, boss." He handed Scott a clipboard and pen.

After glancing over the paperwork, Scott scribbled his signature and chuckled. "I swear you weren't here a moment ago. You see, Beth. I *do* need an afternoon off."

"Willow, are ya coming up to the barn now?" Cody asked.

"Be right there."

Scott clapped his hands together. "Okay. It's settled then. Beth, I'll meet you at the barn in about a half hour. Does that give you enough time to clean up?"

She set her shoulders as though she might argue, but sighed and shrugged instead. "Yep."

Scott grinned. Yep. She was looking and

sounding like a cowgirl more each day. "Great. I'll ask Carmen to pack us a picnic lunch." He offered to assist her down from the fence, but she shook her head and climbed down on her own.

"See you soon." She picked up the cleaning bucket and began the short walk up the hill, humming as she went.

Scott's eyes followed the sway of her hips and another wide grin creased his lips.

Willow cleared her throat. "Will you please walk me and Midnight to his stall, Daddy?"

"Yes, ma'am. I sure will." He grabbed the gelding's halter and they made the short walk to the barn in silence. "Are you really going to help Cody with the tack room?" he asked her once they reached the stall. She dismounted.

"Yeah. Right after I eat lunch and play with my barn set and watch some cartoons."

"That's a lot of things to do. You may not have time to get around to the tack room," he teased with an arched brow.

"Maybe not," Willow agreed.

"Are you sure you don't want to ride to the lake with us?" he asked. He hadn't spent a lot of time with her lately and suddenly felt guilty.

"Nope. You and Beth can go by yourselves. I don't mind one bit." She slapped her pudgy hand across her mouth and started to giggle, as if she was hiding a secret.

Scott chuckled. "I swear. Sometimes you're too smart for your own britches."

****

Beth's first glimpse of the lake, a shimmering jewel set among juniper trees, mountains, and a sapphire sky, nearly took her breath away. She stood in her stirrups and took in the astounding setting, unable to speak for some time. A long breath escaped her throat.

Scott reined in beside her. "We call it Lake Tusi. In the Apache language, it's called *tusikanni doole.* Translated, that means Lake of the Butterflies. I'll show you why." They rode to the edge of the water and Beth could see where the lake got its name. Thousands of tiny butterflies flitted through the air, landing on wildflowers, purple thistles and the reeds that jutted up around the water.

She gasped again, and could feel Scott's smile before she caught sight of it out of the corner of her eye. "I've never seen any place like this. It's so...magical. I never want to leave," she whispered in a tone of reverence. "I'd like to build a little cabin right there on the edge of the water and stay here forever." She pointed to the spot across the way. "I would sit on my porch and look at this view for as long as I lived and never grow tired of it."

He chuckled, a low masculine sound.

When she stirred from her reverie, she said, "You speak the Apache language. I'm impressed."

"Ah, don't be. I've lived around the tribe all my life. I've worked with the people and employed a few of the men, as you know. I don't know a lot of the language, but I've picked up enough to communicate. The elders still speak it. Most of the young people don't."

"That's a shame."

His expression was serious when he turned back to her. "Maybe you could have your wish. Someday."

She looked at him, confused.

"The little cabin on the lake."

"Oh." His shining blue gaze penetrated her, causing her tongue to tie, so she gave Sundance a nudge with her spurs and trotted him over to a small clearing on the other side. Scott followed.

"This is the perfect place for our picnic," she called over her shoulder.

The spot was deep in luscious grass. They

climbed off and let their horses drink from the lake, then Scott tied them to a tree and both mounts dozed standing up.

Scott pulled the lunches from out of his saddlebags as Beth retrieved a soft blanket from hers. She spread it on the ground, sat and stretched out her legs. He sat cross-legged and handed her a sandwich wrapped in brown paper and a bottle of iced tea. They unwrapped their sandwiches and began to talk.

"This has always been one of my favorite places," he told her. "When I was a boy, Buddy and I would ride our horses up here and play cowboys and Indians. I think he and I could traverse these seven thousand acres with our eyes closed. We've been up every mountain and down every trail and in every cave there is. It sure was a great way to grow up."

"You were lucky. So is Willow. Children these days don't get enough fresh air and exercise. They're too busy playing video games or sitting at the computer, or engulfed in the television. I notice Willow doesn't watch much TV."

"Not much. She prefers the outdoors, just like her ole dad."

Beth took a bite of sandwich and brought up the subject neither liked discussing, but continued to weigh heavily on her mind. "Scott, I keep wondering what's going to happen to me. I can't keep imposing on you, but I'm not sure what my next step should be. Where I should go or what I should do. I'm beginning to wonder if anyone's out there looking for me. I can't figure out why Sheriff Griggs hasn't received any legitimate calls. Maybe it's because I'm all alone in the world."

"Don't say that. You're not alone at all. You'll always have me...and Willow, and Carmen," Scott added quickly. He didn't like talking about the possibility of another man in her life, but it was a reality, and he knew she needed him to listen to her concerns. He wanted to help relieve her worry. "Of course someone's looking for you. You know how hard Buddy has been working. I know it's just a matter of time now before someone shows up and you're on your way home."

His heart began to pound. He hoped he wasn't jinxing himself. The last thing he wanted was for a man to show up in Ghost Rock and take her away.

"Thank you for saying that," Beth offered with a warm smile. "Sometimes I'm so confused. I know I've only been here a few days, but I feel like such a part of your family—and the ranch. But, I keep wondering if I have a family of my own out there somewhere."

Scott took a swig of tea and didn't offer a response. That was something he didn't want to think about.

Beth continued to reflect. "There are so many people in this world who wouldn't have looked at me twice that morning, let alone stop and take me into their home the way you did. I feel so fortunate it was you who came along. Don't laugh, but I think it was destiny."

Scott took off his hat, ran his fingers through his hair, then pulled the Stetson back on. "I'm not laughing. I think we were meant to meet each other, too. But don't underestimate folks, Beth. I think there are a lot more good people than there are bad in the world. I was just doing what my folks taught me. I try to treat people the way I want to be treated."

"Don't they call that the golden rule?"

"Yeah. I try to live my life by it, but it's not an easy thing to do. I don't mean to hurt anyone, but I'm sure I have. I'm human. I've made plenty of mistakes, and I'm bound to make more."

She stared at him with the kind of intensity that

had become *his* trademark then said, "You're one of the best men I've ever known, Mr. Landry."

"Thank you, ma'am." He tipped his hat.

She stretched out her legs and leaned back on her elbows. She was glad he'd convinced her to come. "This is the kind of lazy afternoon that's good for doing nothing but enjoying the blue sky and warm sunshine. I bet you don't take many days to relax like this. You're such a hard worker."

"It takes hard work to keep a ranch solvent."

She removed her cowgirl hat and lay down on her back, cradling her neck in her clasped hands. "This was a great idea. I'm so glad you suggested it. Could a day be any more perfect?" She sighed and closed her eyes.

He watched her from underneath the shaded brim of his Stetson, recalling the morning he came upon her stumbling down the road, disoriented and frightened. She looked like such an angel then, and still did, he thought. Even more so, now that he'd gotten to know her. He lay on his side, leaned on one elbow and watched her. Her dark hair fell across her shoulders like a cascading waterfall, and her little heart-shaped mouth was pink and ripe for kissing.

Something powerful rose from the center of his gut. It was an odd mingling of joy and trepidation. Joy, because he was sure this was love he was feeling, and trepidation because of the uneasiness that came when he regarded the future as it related to her. Or, rather, without her. It scared the hell out of him to imagine her ever leaving.

When he'd held Maggie for the last time and felt the life drain from her body, he'd sworn there would never be another woman for him. He remained alone for a long time after her death—caring for his young child, the horses, the ranch, and then his dying father.

Despite friends and family urging him to move

on with life, he had no idea how to do that, when the one he was supposed to have spent his life with was gone. So, he became content with the simplicities of a day-to-day routine—allowing no woman to enter his wounded heart.

When Joanna divorced Buddy, she let Scott know she was interested. He'd been her high school crush, and they'd known each other all their lives. By that time, Scott had made peace with his loss and felt more comfortable about trying to move on. So he made a conscious decision to take a stab at dating.

Having gone to medical school out of state, Joanna had developed into an independent, intelligent, mature, sophisticated woman, knowledgeable about things other than horses and ranches. Scott was attracted to those qualities. He also thought she would be a good role model for Willow. And she was even prettier than she'd been in high school.

Maggie had been gone almost three years by that time, and three cowboys and an older Mexican cook had been raising Willow. The girl was a tomboy and tougher than most of the boys her own age, and Scott had fretted often over her and her needs. He thought Joanna could be someone his daughter could turn to when he was clueless about the wiles and whims of women.

Scott gazed out over the lake and thought about how funny and strange life could be. The relationship with Joanna had not worked out the way he'd thought. Sure, she was attractive and sexy. There'd never been a question about their compatibility in that way. He was a young, virile man—not cut out to be a monk for the rest of his life—but the trouble was she'd changed since they were kids in school together. Buddy had tried to warn him, but Scott hadn't listened. He'd been too focused on doing what he thought was right for his young daughter. He'd also had needs to satisfy. But he realized, in short time, that those needs went beyond the physical.

Now, though it had taken a while, he knew he'd been going about it the wrong way. He wasn't supposed to be looking for a mother for his little girl, or a familiar, trustworthy gal pal he could sleep with when it was convenient. He should have known when the time was right, he'd find the woman he was meant to fall in love with—the woman he'd recognize as his soul mate. If that happened, the rest of the pieces would fall into place.

I've found her.

He gazed down at the beauty by his side. *If I let myself love her, I'm going to get my heart broken, for sure and for certain. Watching her walk into another man's arms would tear me up as bad as feeling Maggie's lifeless body in mine. But if I don't take the chance, how will I ever know if this is meant to be?*

Scott sighed loudly—a rush of air escaping through his lips.

Opening her eyes, Beth didn't have to act innocent when she asked, "What is it?"

"I need to tell you something." His expression was somber.

She sat up and glanced around. "Have the horses escaped?"

"No. Nothing like that." He sat up, too. "Beth, I've been trying to fight this feeling, but I can't do it anymore. It's impossible. This couldn't have happened at a worse time, for both of us. I'm with Joanna, and I know we could find out, any day now, that…that you belong to someone else."

She drew a slow, deep breath in an effort to steady herself for what she suspected was coming.

Scott's gaze was full of heat and unbridled passion. "You've done something to me," he whispered in a husky voice. He leaned in close.

The very simplicity of the words made her shudder.

He placed his hand over hers. “We’ve only known each other a few short days, but it seems I’ve known you forever. I feel like my soul has found its mate.”

Beth couldn’t find her voice. Her throat went dry. Her pulse throbbed in her neck.

Scott pressed his hand to her cheek and held it there. The warmth of his imprint was like a brand on her. A brand she would be proud to carry. He drew her close and tilted her chin up.

She did not resist when his mouth came down over hers.

He opened her lips with his tongue, filling her with his breath, his heat. His fingers tangled themselves in her hair, and she reached around and clung to the hard muscles in his back. She pressed against his chest and could feel the rhythm of his heart pounding.

Their lips parted and he stared at her with a tenderness and fragility she’d never known before. Tears of joy stung her eyes.

“I’ve wanted to kiss you since the moment we met,” he told her, molding his lips to hers once more.

They parted again and smiled at one another, and then she kissed his eyelids, his nose, and the dimple in his chin.

There was no need for more spoken words.

Chapter Ten

Scott held her face in his hands. The breath caught in his throat, and a wild yearning swelled inside. The feeling was all-consuming, like needing air to breathe.

"I want all of you," he whispered, stroking her face. "More than you can imagine. But," he said, tentative, "I have to end it with Joanna first. And we have to find out who you are and whether you're free. If you are, then we can be together. That is, if you feel the same way I do."

Her eyes were wide, her hands clutching at him. "I do, Scott. I've been so afraid, trying to pretend there's no connection between us, but it gets stronger every day. I know this has happened fast, but it just feels so right. I'm finding it harder and harder to deny my feelings for you."

"I sure was hoping it wasn't one sided," he replied, sighing in relief.

They embraced, and he caressed her hair and the back of her neck.

"Beth, this is one of the happiest days of my life."

"Mine, too."

As the air began to cool and the sun threatened to set, Scott reluctantly led her from their magical oasis. They mounted their horses and he set a good pace all the way back to the High Lonesome with a soaring spirit. Their faithful horses carried them over creeks and across the mountains like the wind. It was near dinner by the time the barn came into his view.

He and Beth worked side by side in perfect harmony. As he unsaddled and brushed the horses, she tossed hay into the stalls and shook grain into the bowls. After she filled the tubs with water and he'd hung the tack, they strolled to house together—hand in hand—not taking their eyes off one another.

Carmen stood outside the kitchen door clanging the dinner bell. Beth startled at the loud ringing, and pulled away from Scott when she looked up at Carmen, but the housekeeper had to have seen them holding hands.

"It's about time you two show up," Carmen said, not bothering to keep the joy out of her voice. "I was starting to worry." She urged them to come inside and eat.

Scott displayed his dirty hands as they stepped into the kitchen. "I've got to wash up first. Sorry to keep you waiting, Carmen. We lost track of time."

"It's no problem. I just set the table." She winked at him and grinned. "Did you have a nice day?"

"It was perfect," he replied, sending an impassioned glance at Beth. She grew warm inside and felt her cheeks flame.

"Where's Willow?" he asked.

"Here I am!" The child skipped into the room, ran to Beth and squeezed her around the legs. "I missed you."

"I missed you, too, honey," Beth said, returning the squeeze. "I hope you had a nice afternoon."

Scott joked, "What about me, squirt? Did you miss me too?" Willow ran to her father and flung herself into his accommodating arms.

"Yes, Daddy. Did you have fun at the lake?"

"Yep, we sure did."

"Did you catch any bullfrogs?"

"No. We didn't look for any."

"Did you see the butterflies?" She was bursting with energy and fired out the questions like a Tommy gun.

"Yeah. Thousands of them."

"Did the horses go swimming?"

"No, but they just about drank all the water up."

"Did you go skinny dippin'?" Willow checked her dad's reaction and then busted out laughing as he picked her up and plopped her on the counter.

"No. Who told you about skinny dipping?"

"Nobody."

"Does this nobody have a name?"

"None of your bees wax." Willow chortled.

Carmen set a plate in front of the girl. "Willow, you're ornery. Don't be talking about skinny dipping. That's not a proper subject for the dinner table. *Ai yi yi,*" she sighed. "She's growing up too fast, Mr. Scott."

"You're telling me. I'm going upstairs to wash and change my shirt. Be right back, ladies." He winked at Beth.

"If you don't mind, Carmen, I need to clean up, too," she said. "I'll be just a minute, but you two go ahead and start."

Willow and the cook took their seats at the island and poured hot sauce over their enchiladas as Beth hurried out of the kitchen.

She breezed into the guest bedroom as if she were floating on air and stepped into the bathroom to wash her face and hands. Staring at herself in the mirror, she couldn't believe how her life had taken such a dramatic turn in a few short days.

What's going to happen now? Where do I go from here?

She'd been longing for Scott to kiss her, and now that it had happened, there were no doubts about her feelings for him. Taking a brush to her long hair, she realized she could not stop smiling.

What a relief it was when he told her he was ending it with Joanna. Up until the kiss, she hadn't been sure where the two of them stood. There was no way she was going to be the cause of any friction or disagreements between them—but he'd assured her this afternoon that his relationship with Jo was over—and it had been for some time. Beth's heart had almost jumped out of her chest when she heard those words.

Does he love me? He hadn't said the actual words, but he'd told her his soul had found its mate. If that wasn't an admission of love, she didn't know what was.

Everything was happening so fast. She grazed a finger over her lips and closed her eyes and conjured up the memory of his passionate kisses.

Have I ever been this happy before? She didn't think so.

A dull thud began to throb in her head as a picture flashed through her mind. In it, she saw the same tall, muscular man standing in the doorway yelling. He was arguing with a woman. He raised his hand and a shiny gold wedding band glistened on his finger.

Beth blinked hard and the image disappeared. She hung her head over the bathroom sink and retched, but her stomach was empty so nothing came up. Her hands trembled and she thought her legs might collapse beneath her. Mere moments ago she'd felt on top of the world. Now, reality shook her to the core of her being—the reality of what she'd feared and most recently suspected.

I'm married to the man in my flashbacks.

Once again, she splashed cold water in her face and fought to gain her composure before going into the kitchen to face Scott, Carmen and Willow.

As Beth tiptoed down the hallway in deep thought, voices interrupted her dream-like state—

voices that sounded familiar and were coming from the front porch. She peeked out the window and saw Scott and Joanna standing on the steps, huddled close together. She'd parked the Audi Roadster in the drive.

Why is she here? I wonder if Scott was expecting her tonight?

Knowing she shouldn't eavesdrop, but unable to stop herself, Beth cupped her ear to the window. Their words came in muddled whispers. *He must be telling her it's over.*

Beth took a deep breath in order to still her beating heart, which she feared they'd be able to hear straight through the glass pane. After several minutes, the conversation ended.

Joanna doesn't look upset or angry. I'd think she'd be showing some kind of emotion if Scott broke up with her. He said he was going to.

Beth watched Scott place his hand around Joanna's waist and lead her out to the Audi.

She could no longer hear their voices, but she could see their mouths moving. Scott opened the car door, Joanna spun and put her hands on his face and pulled him to her and—they kissed.

Beth's jaw dropped.

She turned away from the window and cradled her face in her hands. Fresh tears sprang to her eyes.

When the screen door squeaked open a minute later, she remained motionless behind the wall so Scott wouldn't hear her. Outside, Joanna's car sped down the driveway. Beth waited until Scott tramped down the hallway to the kitchen before letting out the breath she held.

She barely spoke during dinner and kept her eyes averted from Scott throughout the meal. After such a wonderful afternoon, her heart now felt heavy as a stone. First, she felt like a fool for believing he cared for her, when it was obvious he wasn't over Joanna. Second, she was certain the flashbacks were more than random dreams. They revealed the truth of her life in bits—like pieces of a puzzle.

It made her happy to imagine herself as the mother of the little brunette girl, but the thought of being married to the cruel man in the visions made her sick.

When she'd finished eating what little she could get down, Beth excused herself, claiming exhaustion. Scott excused himself as well and followed her down the hall to her room.

"Beth." He placed his hands on her shoulders.

She spun and shrugged free from his touch.

His expression was one of bewilderment. "What's going on? You didn't say a word all through dinner, and I get the impression you're either angry or sad—or both. Are you feeling all right? Do you want to talk?"

"No, I don't want to talk," she snapped. Upon seeing the stunned look on his face, she said "I'm just tired, Scott. I need to go to bed." She turned again.

"Wait a minute. I don't understand. You're acting so strange. This afternoon..."

"This afternoon never should have happened," she retorted.

Scott's mouth gaped, and a veil of silence fell between them.

Her lip trembled. "I'm sorry, Scott. I've just realized this will never work. It's crazy to think it would. You know nothing about me. *I* know nothing about me. You have a life and I don't belong in it."

Scott reached for her. "Don't say that. You *do* belong here, with me. My life is nothing without you."

She refused his touch. "Please, don't say another word. I don't want to hear anything else. I think it's better if I leave the ranch. In fact, I've made up my mind. Tomorrow I'll arrange for a room at the motel in town."

His brows drew together. "Beth, this is ridiculous. Talk to me," he pleaded. "Tell me what's changed in the past hour."

She pursed her lips and blurted, "What's changed is that I'm married and I have a child."

He stepped back, as if she'd shot him. "What? How do you know that for sure? Has your memory returned?"

"I remember enough. Now, I truly appreciate all you've done for me. I'll try to pay you back somehow, but I believe this is for the best. My leaving will be best for both of us."

He plowed a hand through his hair and looked down at the floor. When he raised his eyes to her again, he asked, "How's your leaving going to help? What about the things we said to each other this afternoon?"

She ignored the questions. "Don't try to change my mind, Scott. It's set. I'll ask Cody to drive me to town in the morning, if you don't mind giving him the time off to do so. I'll say goodbye to you now."

She closed the guest room door behind her, leaving him alone.

Standing on the other side, shaking, she waited until finally—thankfully—she heard his footsteps move down the hall. Throwing herself onto the bed face down, all the emotions of the past few days bubbled to the surface like an erupting volcano. The pillowcase grew damp as she allowed the tears to flow.

Chapter Eleven

Sunday morning, Beth heard the jangle of Cody's spurs before she saw him. He moseyed through the kitchen door and said, "Howdy."

She was huddled over cold eggs and ham wearing a green western plaid shirt, jeans and her cowboy boots. "Hi, Cody. Could I talk to you a minute?" She was ready to ask him to take her to town, but she hadn't yet told Carmen or Willow she was leaving, and had been trying to figure out the best way to bring it up. Willow was still in bed, but Carmen had been staring at her for the past ten minutes.

Carmen kept one eye poised on Beth as she filled a plate for the young wrangler. "You want blueberry pancakes with your ham, eggs and potatoes?" she asked Cody.

"Yes, ma'am. You can read my mind," he replied. He washed his hands at the sink and climbed onto a barstool.

Carmen set the maple syrup and a steaming plate in front of him.

"*Muchos gracias.*" He dug in with gusto. "What is it you want to talk about?" he asked Beth between mouthfuls.

"I want to ask you a favor."

"Sure. What is it?"

"Is Mr. Scott still in the barn?" Carmen interrupted.

Cody glanced over his shoulder at her. "Yep. Said he wasn't hungry."

"I wonder why." She looked at Beth again, who did not comment.

Cody shoveled potatoes and eggs into his mouth then said, "What were you saying, Beth?"

The phone pealed and the cook grabbed it on the second ring. In a robust voice, she said, "Good morning. High Lonesome Ranch. This is Carmen, may I help you?"

Beth whispered to Cody, "Could I ask you to do me a big favor?"

Carmen's voice rose an octave as she replied to the person on the phone. "*Si*, Sheriff. I understand. I'll tell them. *Adios*." She hung up and stared at Beth with wide eyes.

"What is it, Carmen?" Cody asked. "You look like someone just walked over your grave."

"That was Sheriff Griggs."

That grabbed Beth's attention. She swiveled to face Carmen. "What did he want?"

"He wanted me to tell you and Mr. Scott that there's a man in his office. He says to come quick. He says it's the real deal this time."

Beth's gaze darted back and forth between Carmen and Cody, whose fork hung suspended in the air. "Did he tell you who the man is?" Her voice quivered.

"*Si*. Sheriff Buddy says the man claims to be…your husband. And he's brought proof that it's so."

"I knew it," Beth uttered. "Cody, could you please drive me in to town?"

The wrangler looked confused. "Well, you know I'd be glad to take you, but Scott will want to himself. Won't he? I'll run out and get him." He jumped off the stool as he grabbed a sausage off his plate.

"No!" she barked. "I want you. Please."

Cody stopped dead in his tracks. "Sure, Beth.

Whatever you say." He exchanged a subtle glance with Carmen and then slid another egg down his gullet.

"Thank you. I'll be right back." Beth scurried out of the kitchen and returned wearing her cowboy hat. "Okay. I'm ready."

"Are you sure you don't want Scott to go with us?" Cody asked again, his young tanned face lined with concern. His jaw was grinding with another forkful of meat and potatoes.

"No. Carmen, you can tell Scott about the call later when he comes in. I have to do this by myself." She swooped in and gave the cook a big hug and kiss on the cheek.

"Why are you giving me a hug, Miss Beth? You're coming back, aren't you?"

"I don't know what's going to happen at the sheriff's office, but no matter what, I'll come back and say a proper goodbye to you and Willow. I just want to thank you for all you've done for me."

"You're welcome. Good luck." Carmen's bushy brows knitted together.

"Thank you. Let's go, Cody."

He plucked his hat off the coat hook near the door, and the two of them dashed outside, jumped into his pickup and Cody gunned it. They barreled down the drive, kicking up dust.

Hearing the truck pass by the barn, Scott stepped out and peered down the road. *Where the hell is he going in such a hurry?*

He'd been stabbing hay bales with a pitchfork—still reeling over Beth's odd behavior the evening before. Tossing and turning all night, he'd been unable to sleep or make sense of things. The questions flooded his mind. What had come over her so suddenly? Why had she shut him out? Had her memory returned? Why didn't she just tell him, if that was the case? What other explanation could there be for her telling him she's married? Did she really believe she was married, or was it just an excuse? Maybe the declaration of his feelings down at the lake scared her. Maybe her memory hadn't returned at all, and she was just confused and afraid.

Scott flung down the pitchfork and ambled into the house for some breakfast. The moment his boots crossed the threshold Carmen gave him the news.

"What? Why didn't someone come get me?" He kicked the bottom of the door.

"She wouldn't let us. She wanted Cody to take her. I'm sorry, Scott."

"It's not your fault," he relented. "She's a stubborn woman." He mumbled some curse words under his breath as he ran his hands under the sink. He dried them on a dishtowel, then lifted the Stetson off his head and ran his fingers through his hair before jamming the hat back down. "I'm going in to town. Can you watch Willow for me?"

"*Si*. But I don't think Miss Beth wants you there." Carmen narrowed her eyes at him. "What happened last night?"

"The hell if I know," he answered with a shrug. "I'll see ya later."

He slammed the door behind him and jogged out to the truck. He, too, left a trail of dust in his wake as he roared down the road toward Ghost Rock.

****

Beth's legs trembled as she swung them out of Cody's pickup. When her boots hit the pavement, she stood frozen, unable to take a step. The wrangler came around to her side. "You ready?"

"I don't know. I'm scared."

"I wish Scott was here. Why didn't you want him to bring you?"

"Never mind. Let's go in."

Cody held the door open for her. When he let go,

it banged behind them, sounding like a gunshot blast. “Gee whiz. Buddy needs some new hinges for that thing,” he complained.

Because it was Sunday, there was no one in front to greet them. The lobby was quiet except for the low buzz of the window air conditioner. At the sound of the front door banging shut, Buddy rushed out of his office, closing the door behind him. He was dressed casually in a pair of jeans and a button-down shirt. Touching the brim of his cowboy hat, he said, “Good mornin’ Beth. Mornin’ Cody. Where’s Scott?”

“Scott couldn’t make it,” Beth answered in a sharp tone. “Carmen said someone claiming to be my husband is here. Is he in your office?”

“He is. Why isn’t Scott with you?” Buddy repeated. He looked at Cody, who shrugged.

“Never mind about him. He’s busy. Can I please meet this man?” Beth was striding toward the door.

Buddy took a couple of steps and touched her arm. His voice was hushed. “Of course, but let me give you the story in a nutshell before you barge in. He saw your photo on one of the cable television stations. He drove in last night from Arizona and left a message on our machine. I listened to my messages this morning when I came in to do some paperwork and gave him a call at the motel.”

“Arizona?”

“Yeah. Tucson. I told him you’ve been staying out at the High Lonesome with the man who found you. I explained how Scott ran onto you disoriented and injured. He appears to be genuinely concerned about your well being and safety.”

“What’s his name?” she asked.

“Jack West. Does it ring a bell?”

She shook her head and took a deep breath. “You told Carmen he has some proof that I am who he says I am?”

"That's right." Buddy shifted from one foot to another.

"Okay then. Let's get on with this before I lose my courage."

Buddy put his hand on the knob and pushed the door open.

"Wait," she whispered, clamping her hand onto his wrist. "What if I don't remember him at all? What happens then?"

"Just take it one step at a time. Maybe you *will* remember something. I've got my fingers crossed for you."

She glanced at Cody, who was propped against the corner of Linda's desk. He gave her a thumbs-up sign.

When she entered the office, a man turned and rose from the chair.

Unlike the last time she'd walked into that room to face a strange man, this one didn't come rushing toward her, scaring her half to death. He was over six feet tall, good-looking, muscular, and was dressed like a preppie. A smile unfolded on his face, but he waited for her to make the first move.

"Mr. West, is this your wife?" Buddy asked.

"Yes. Yes it is," he said with excitement. "She's my wife, Angela."

"Angela?" Beth whispered the name, trying it on for size.

"Hi Angie," the man said. He stayed rooted to his spot. "Sheriff Griggs told me about the amnesia. It's unbelievable. It must have been a frightening few days for you, but I'm here now. I'll take you home and help you recover and everything will be okay."

"I don't remember you," she blurted. Her arms hung to her sides, her fists balled up.

His cool gray eyes swung to meet the sheriff's gaze.

Buddy cleared his throat. “The doctor here in town ran a CT scan on Beth…er, your wife, Angela, and although it showed no brain damage, her memory has still not returned. Have I got that correct, Mrs. West?”

“Not entirely.” She stared into Jack’s eyes. “My memory is starting to come back little by little. I’ve been having flashbacks on a regular basis.”

Jack looked surprised. “Well! That’s wonderful news. You can’t imagine how worried I’ve been since you went missing.”

“Since I went missing…,” she mumbled. Beth studied him, trying to remember something, anything familiar about the man—but all she felt was anxiety. “Your name is Jack West?” she asked.

He chuckled. “Yes, and you’re my wife, Angela.”

“The sheriff says you have proof that I am who you say I am. Could you please show it to me?”

“Why don’t we all have a seat,” Buddy suggested, as he offered her a chair and then leaned against the corner of his desk.

Jack said, “We have a daughter. Her name is Heather and she’s four years old.” He unzipped a small leather briefcase, which was sitting on the floor, and lifted out the framed photo of Beth and the little dark-haired girl and handed it to her.

As she stared at the picture, her eyes became moist. “I know her. I’ve been dreaming about her. She likes me to push her on the swing.”

A grin flashed across the man’s face, as well as Buddy’s.

“That’s right,” Jack acknowledged. “Swinging is one of her favorite things to do. She’s always begging you to take her to the park. That’s our little girl, Heather.”

Beth gazed around, as if the little girl might be hiding under the desk or behind a chair. “Where is she? Didn’t you bring her?”

He paused. "I left her with the neighbor. A lady you know well," he added. "I didn't want to overwhelm you all at once, and I didn't want Heather to be upset, in case you didn't remember her."

"Where does she think I've been these last few days?" Beth asked.

"I told her you were visiting a friend. I didn't know what else to say. She's so young, she didn't question it."

"Did you bring anything else with you? My birth certificate, a passport, or our marriage certificate?" The words came out choked. It was uncomfortable to be speaking about marriage to the total stranger.

"I looked, but couldn't find our marriage certificate." He chuckled again. "I don't know what you've done with it. It wasn't in the wedding album. I brought a photo taken of us on our wedding day instead. I figured it would suffice." Jack glanced at Buddy, received the go-ahead nod, then retrieved the picture from the briefcase and presented it to her.

There it was, in full color, the proof that she was indeed his wife. She set that photo aside and gazed longingly at the one of herself and the little brunette girl with the pixie haircut. She *was* that child's mother. She had known it; felt it so strongly.

I connected with Willow because of the bond I had with my own little girl.

"Jack? You don't mind if I call you Jack?" she asked.

"Of course not. Jack's my name, honey."

She cringed when he called her honey. "Sheriff Griggs says you drove in from Arizona. He said you came from Tucson."

"Yes. We live in a suburb of Tucson. You have a very nice home," he added, smiling at Buddy.

"Do you have any idea how I ended up here in New Mexico?" she asked with the directness of an investigator. “Ghost Rock is a long way from Tucson, isn’t it?”

He shook his head and hedged at the truth. “There were no witnesses, but we thought you were kidnapped. They must have driven all this way to throw the police off, and then left you in the desert when they had what they wanted. I suspect they were after money. I understand you had no purse or I.D. on you when you were found.”

“They? Who?”

“I don’t know,” he replied. “Whoever took you. The Arizona State Police considered the kidnapping theory, but the trail ran cold with no real leads. Still...what else could have happened? You didn’t just walk to New Mexico on your own.”

A puzzled look crossed her face. “Kidnapped? Who would have kidnapped me? Are we wealthy?”

Jack glanced Buddy’s way again and cocked his head. “Well, we’re quite comfortable,” he answered. “I’m the vice president of a bank. I was thinking your disappearance was drug-related.”

“Drug related? In what way?”

“I don’t know, Angie. It was just a theory that didn’t go anywhere. Thank God someone found you and you were safe. That’s all that matters now.”

“What was done to search for me? Were our friends and neighbors questioned? What were you doing to find me?” She fired questions at him with the relentlessness of a bulldog.

“Whoa.” Jack held up his hands. “I know you have a lot of questions, and I’ll try to answer them all for you. Let’s take them one at a time. This has been a trying time, for both of us.” He leaned forward and reached for her hand, but she kept hers folded in her lap.

“I’m sorry,” he said, his gray eyes clouding. “I forgot. I’m a stranger to you.”

“Give her some time,” Buddy suggested.

A shiver ran down Beth's spine. Her eyes searched the man's face as she tried to conjure up even one shred of a memory besides the terrible flashbacks. She couldn't be sure the visions were true memories. She wasn't even sure he was the man in them, but her intuition told her to be wary. As Doctor Coleman had explained, it was possible for dreams or idle imaginings to get mixed up with memories of one's real life. Her daughter, Heather, who she'd remembered in flashbacks, was real. But what about Jack? Should she be frightened of this man who called himself her husband?

She placed her head in her hands.

Whether I like it or not, I'm Angela, Jack West's wife. He has the evidence to prove it. There's nothing I can do but go back with him to my former life. Even if I don't remember him, I have a daughter. I do remember my baby, and I want to be with her again.

She scooted the chair back, causing the legs to scrape the floor with a squawk, and stood. "Seems there's nothing left here to do. If you're satisfied, Sheriff, I guess Jack and I should be getting on home."

Buddy lifted his rump off the desk and extended a hand to them both. "Okay then. Looks like we've got ourselves a happy ending."

Angela wasn't entirely sure about that, but she forced a smile and spoke with sincerity when she told him, "I want to thank you for all you've done."

"You're welcome, Mrs. West. Good luck to you both."

Jack opened the briefcase, stuck the wedding photo in, and then snapped it shut. Angela was still holding onto the picture of her and Heather.

As they stepped out of Buddy's office, Angela froze. Cody was gone but Scott was there in his place, leaning against the wall with his boot kicked up and his bright blue eyes shining from underneath his dusty Stetson. Their gazes fastened.

"Scott, it's about time you showed up." Buddy strolled over and clapped his friend on the back. "Scott Landry, I want you to meet Jack West. He's your friend's husband. Her real name is Angela West. They've just been reunited."

Jack stepped forward and offered a handshake as Buddy continued. "Mr. West, I'd like you to meet Scott Landry. He owns the High Lonesome Ranch just outside of town, and he's the man who happened upon your wife and kept her safe and sound for you."

"Mr. Landry, the pleasure is mine." Jack took his hand and pumped it vigorously.

Scott returned the shake, but never removed his eyes from Angela. His stare was strong and full of passion.

Her cheeks flamed and her gaze dropped to the ground.

Jack said, "It appears I owe you, Mr. Landry. I'd like to repay you for all you've done for Angie. Sheriff Griggs told me you've been taking excellent care of her." He reached into his jacket pocket and pulled out a checkbook. "Would a thousand dollars cover her expenses for the last few days?"

The rancher's eyes narrowed. "I don't want your money, Mr. West."

"I insist. It's the least I can do." Jack began to scribble on the check.

"Save your ink," Scott repeated. "I won't take money for doing what any decent person would have done."

Angela raised her eyes.

"Don't be ridiculous…" Jack began.

"I said that's the end of it." Scott sidled up next to Angela and looked her in the eye. "So, you're leaving with him? Just like that? No questions asked? No goodbyes?"

"I beg your pardon?" Jack exploded. His chest

puffed like a rooster as he took a step forward.

Angela stopped him from advancing by putting her hand on his arm. “Would you mind giving us a few minutes? I need to speak to Mr. Landry privately.”

“What?” Jack’s upper lip curled into a snarl.

“Please. I owe him a few minutes. I’ll be right out.”

Jack and Scott stared each other down. After a moment’s hesitation, Jack conceded. He jammed the checkbook back into his jacket pocket. “All right, but don’t be long.” He turned and fired a threatening look toward Scott as Buddy held the door open for him. The two of them stepped outside, leaving Scott and Angela alone in the reception area.

Scott threw his arms around her and pulled her close. “Why are you going with him? You don’t even know this man. What about us? What happened last night? Please talk to me.”

She shrugged out of his hold. “Scott, I’m begging you. Don’t make this harder than it already is. He’s my husband. He showed me a wedding photo. And I have a child—a daughter—just as I suspected.” She thrust the photo in front of him. “Look. She’s four years old. I have to go with him. I can’t abandon my little girl.”

“What about all the other flashbacks? The ones that scared you half to death?” he asked. “Is this the man that was yelling at you in those flashes? He’s probably the one who hurt you. I’d bet my life he dumped you in the desert and left you out there to die. I don’t know why, but I don’t trust him. You shouldn’t either.”

“Stop it, Scott!” Angela turned her back to him. “Maybe everything was just a bad dream. What am I supposed to do? I have to be with my baby. You, of all people should understand that.” When he spun her back around, her eyes were misting over.

He hugged her and she relaxed against his chest. His lips moved through her hair. "I meant what I said at the lake."

"I'm sure you did, at the time."

"What do you mean, at the time?" He pulled back.

Her eyes widened. "Never mind. I need to go." She took several steps toward the door. "Please tell Carmen and Willow goodbye for me. Tell them how special they are, and will always be to me."

"Don't walk away. Come back to the ranch with me and tell them yourself."

"I can't. I don't have the courage to face them," she admitted. "Jack's waiting for me. I have to go."

"You're afraid of him. I can see it in your eyes. Don't go. Stay with me."

"No." She turned so he couldn't see the tears pooling.

"What about your clothes? Your things?" he asked.

"They don't belong to me. *Nothing* at the ranch belongs to me." Angela glanced down at her outfit. "I'll mail these clothes back as soon as I get home."

"Keep 'em," Scott replied, his voice flat.

A pause hung in the air.

"Well, goodbye, Scott. This is for the best. For both of us. You'll come to understand that in time." She made a streak for the door, praying he couldn't see through her lies.

"Hold up a minute." He grabbed her hand—she whirled—and he forced a slip of paper into it.

Her skin singed at his touch.

"If you ever need anything, call me," he said. "And I mean *anything. Anytime.* I'll always be there for you."

She stuffed the paper into her back jeans pocket. "Thank you. I'll never forget you and Willow."

Angela flung open the door and rushed into the

glare of the sun while willing the tears not to fall. Jack was leaning against a black BMW with his arms crossed. The car looked familiar, but it didn't matter just then. Angela was grateful when Jack opened the door and helped her in. When she slid into the passenger seat, Jack bolted to the other side, hopped in and stuck the key in the ignition.

Scott marched outside and joined Buddy on the sidewalk as the beamer pulled out of the parking lot.

Angela graced him with one last, sweet smile.

Chapter Twelve

Despite the many questions Angela had for Jack, they didn't speak much on the drive to Arizona. As the miles clicked over on the odometer, she was becoming more anxious about returning to a house she didn't remember and a man who was a virtual stranger. There had been only one reason she made the hasty decision to go back to Arizona with him—because of her daughter—the little brunette child she *did* remember.

"What kind of getup are you wearing anyway?" he asked.

The sound of his voice made her jump. She'd been staring out the window, idly watching the saguaro and sagebrush fly by—consumed with memories of Scott and the moments they'd spent together. She'd also been mulling over the flashbacks, wondering about their true meaning. She began to tremble as she remembered the hand raised, the wildness of her assailant's eyes and the anger in his voice. A tremor ran the length of her body. She looked over to see Jack glaring at her.

"Pardon me?" she said.

His tone was accusatory. "I asked why you're wearing such an outlandish outfit."

She gave him a sideways glance. "It's a shirt and jeans. I don't see what's so outlandish about it."

"It's a plaid shirt with pearl snap buttons. And those boots." He cackled. "You look like you're dressed for Halloween. The old Angie wouldn't be caught dead in that silly cowgirl costume."

Dead. The very word would haunt her for the rest of her life. She'd come so close…

"You can burn those things when we get home," he continued with a smugness that she didn't find the least bit attractive. "You've got two closets full of designer clothes."

"I won't burn them," she replied adamantly. "I don't think you understand what I've been through. These clothes represent who I am now. I'm not sure what the *old* Angela was all about, or how the *old* Angela behaved or dressed, but I'm not that woman anymore." He'd hit a sore spot and she didn't care whether he liked the way she responded or not.

"I know this is a strange situation," she continued, "but things are not the same. You're going to have to get used to the new Angie." She turned her head back to the window and felt the tension melt off her shoulders.

Jack didn't utter another word until they reached Tucson.

They pulled up to a magnificent brick house in a posh gated neighborhood and news reporters inundated them. Angela was shocked to see a half dozen media trucks parked on the street and photographers camped out on the lawn.

"Damn paparazzi," Jack grumbled as people with microphones clamored around the car and banged on the windows. "Do you remember the house?" he asked through the noise.

She gawked at the mansion and shook her head.

"Get away!" Jack yelled through the glass. "Leave us alone!"

Angela shielded her face. "Why are they here? What do they want?"

"They want to interview you. You were on all the news stations. I guess you're a celebrity now."

She cast him a sour look. She had no desire to be a celebrity. She didn't want to be famous for going through the trauma she'd gone through.

Jack pressed a button on the console and the garage door rose. As he pulled the car in, the reporters swarmed around, shoving their microphones and cameras in Angela's face as she stepped out of the car. Jack rushed to her side and tossed his arm around her shoulder. The questions flew at her like bullets.

"Mrs. West, where have you been staying since you disappeared?"

"How did you end up in New Mexico?"

"Angela, they say you have amnesia. Do you remember your husband and child?"

"Were you kidnapped? Do you remember your kidnappers?"

"Were you harmed? Were you assaulted?"

"Who is the man who rescued you?"

"Is it true you don't remember anything about your life here in Arizona?"

She sunk her head into Jack's broad chest as he marshaled her through the garage. He fumbled with his keys to get the kitchen door open, then pushed her inside and faced the throng of media people and other curious onlookers. When he raised his hands, the noise of the crowd died down.

His speech was short and to the point. "Mrs. West will not be granting any interviews, now or ever. The matter of her disappearance is for the Arizona State Police to handle. As you can see, she's home and she's safe and that's all we care about. We request you respect our privacy and let us get on with rebuilding our lives."

Jack slammed the back door shut and locked it.

Angela stood in the kitchen, her feet fastened to the terracotta-tiled floor. "Thank you for handling those people. I wasn't expecting all that." Her voice trembled.

"What's a husband for, if not protecting his

wife?" Jack watched her behind heavy-lidded eyes. "Do you remember any of this?" He tossed the keys down on the granite countertop.

She glanced around the room. The appliances were top of the line stainless steel, and the cabinets were handcrafted cherry wood. There was recessed lighting in the ceiling, a built-in fireplace in the wall, and an expensive looking dinette set. The room was sparkling and neat as a pin, as if no one ever cooked in there. "I'm afraid not."

"Well, I'm sure it will all come back to you sooner or later."

"I hope. Some things have been coming in bits and pieces, just like the doctor in Ghost Rock said. She told me it's also possible that all my memories could return at once."

Jack had no comment.

"Where's Heather?" Angela asked. She bordered on brusque, she knew, but she was anxious to hold the little girl in her arms. "I'd like to see her now."

"I thought you'd want to relax and settle in first." Jack took a glass out of the cabinet and filled it with tap water. He gulped it down then asked, "You want some?"

She shook her head. "I just want to see Heather. She's the only person I remember. Where is she?"

Jack's tongue dripped with acid. "I told you she's with a neighbor." A muscle ticked along his jaw line, and then he stalked out of the room.

Her mouth gaped. *What was that about? I just want to see my child. Why won't he let me see her right now?*

She trailed him to a room that looked like a den and stood in the middle studying the leather furniture, corner bar, hardwood floor, and stone fireplace. She watched as Jack ripped a bottle out from under the bar sink against the wall. Ice cubes clinked together as he poured a drink with a shaking hand.

Stung by his harsh tone and taken aback over his behavior since leaving Ghost Rock, her head began to ache as a recollection flashed before her.

They were arguing again. She and the man. She held some papers in her hand, and was waving them in front of his nose. Liquor splashed into a cut glass tumbler, and then he threw the glass against the wall, shattering it. He yelled, "You'll always be my wife. It doesn't matter what some damn judge says."

"What's the matter?" Jack barked.

Angela's eyes blinked. "Excuse me?" She felt the color drain from her cheeks as she snapped back to reality.

"You're holding your head. What's wrong?" He stepped toward her with the drink in his hand and softened. "You must be exhausted. Why don't you go to our bedroom and lie down and rest? We can pick up Heather later."

Angela backed away from him. The flashback frightened her. It seemed so real, and the mere mention of their bedroom made her ill.

Surely, he won't expect anything of me tonight.

He was a different man from the one she met in Ghost Rock. There, he was a concerned husband, accommodating and comforting. Now, Jack was intimidating and critical. No matter what he said or did, there was no way he'd bully her into sharing a bed with him.

"I don't want to rest," she told him. "I want to see Heather, and I'd like to discuss the sleeping arrangements. Is there a guest room in this house?"

"Of course there is." Jack snorted and rolled his eyes. "I assumed you'd want to sleep there tonight," he answered with sarcasm.

"Thank you. I hope you can understand..." She breathed a sigh of relief. "Since that's out of the way, can we please get Heather now?"

He slammed his drink down on a side table, causing her to jump again. Alcohol sloshed out of the tumbler. "Damn it. You're nagging already. Let me make a phone call." He strode to the other side of the room, grabbed up the phone receiver and then punched in some numbers. His voice was low as he spoke to the person on the other end. When he hung up, he said, "We can go over and get her now if you want. She's right next door, but you know we'll have to wade through the paparazzi again. That's why I thought we should wait."

Angela's boots clicked across the wood floors as she hurried to the front door. He caught her arm and swung her around. She flinched at his tight grip. Another picture exploded in front of her eyes. A man was twisting her arm then shoving her to the floor. She saw herself falling...striking her head against the wall.

In the vision, she lay on the floor, moaning from the head injury, and looked up into her attacker's eyes. His face materialized for the first time. It *was* Jack!

Her heart seized. She peered at the arm that still showed the faint signs of a past struggle. Her eyes widened as she jerked and cried, "Please let go! You're hurting me."

His gray eyes searched her face as he let loose. Softening his tone once again, he said, "I'm sorry, honey. Sometimes I don't know my own strength."

She rubbed her arm. "Don't grab me like that."

"I said I was sorry. I was just trying to stop you. Some of the reporters are still out on the front lawn. Let's go out the back door."

She glared at him, wrought with confusion over his Jekyll and Hyde personality, but followed him to the back door.

He stuck his head out to make sure the coast was clear before they scrambled across the lawn to the neighbor's home.

An older woman answered the door and shepherded them in. A tiny brunette girl sat at a table, coloring. She jumped off the chair when she saw Angela.

"Mommy!" She ran and leaped into Angela's waiting arms. "Mommy, I missed you."

Angela's fist flew to her mouth. Her heart burst with love. "I missed you, too, sweetheart." She smothered the child with kisses, then cradled her in her arms and smelled her hair. "I'm so happy to be with you again!" Tears sprang to her eyes as she hugged her daughter to her breast.

I do remember her! I remember my child. This is Heather, my baby.

"Why are you crying, Mommy?" Heather touched her mother's hair, then her cheek.

When Angela replied, her voice was tight and choked. "These are tears of happiness, pumpkin. I'm just so glad to be home."

"I'm glad too, Mommy." Mother and daughter cuddled again, and then Heather squirmed out of her arms and ran to Jack. "Daddy, can we go home now? I want to play with my toys."

"Of course."

He thanked the neighbor for watching Heather and the three of them snuck back to the house, cunningly avoiding the reporters still camped on the front lawn.

****

Miles away, Scott tucked Willow into bed.

"Why did Beth leave without telling me goodbye, Daddy?" The girl had refused to remove her pink cowgirl hat, so she sat propped up in bed against her pillows with the hat tilted across one eye. She tugged on an unraveling thread from her pajama top.

"I explained it to you twice already, Willow. Her

husband drove all the way from Arizona to pick her up. They had to get on the road right away because it was going to take them a long time to get back home. They didn't have time to come out to the ranch. She asked me to tell you goodbye."

"It's not the same," she said, pouting.

"I know." He plucked the cowgirl hat off her head, hung it over the bedpost and then kissed her forehead. As he patted down tiny flyaway hairs caused by static electricity, he said, "I know Beth didn't mean to hurt your feelings. She would never do that on purpose."

"Her name's not Beth." Willow's lip protruded and quivered a bit.

"You're right. I'm glad you remembered. It's Angela. Angela West is her real name." He felt exhausted. "We'll talk more about this in the morning, baby. You go to sleep now and have sweet dreams about racing Midnight."

Willow gave him a weak smile then lay down and curled her legs up to her chest. "Okay. Daddy?"

"Yes?"

"Are you going to miss Angela?"

Scott pulled her comforter up and tucked it around her small shoulders. "Yes, honey. I'm going to miss her. She was a very special person."

"I thought she was going to become my new mother." Willow's big round eyes grew wet.

"Oh, Willow," Scott drawled. "Whatever gave you that idea?"

"I thought she loved us. I thought she was going to stay with us forever."

He sighed and hugged her tight. "I think she did love us, all of us, but she has her own family. They missed her. They wanted her back home. That's where she belongs. We did a good thing by taking care of her while she was here. She will never forget us. And we'll never forget her."

"Are you going to marry Joanna now? Is she going to be my mother?" Willow gazed into her father's blue eyes with expectant anticipation.

Scott's face flushed. A nervous chuckle bubbled up from his throat. "You say the darndest things sometimes."

"What's so funny about asking if she's going to be my mother?" Willow asked. She gave the impression of being much older than her seven years.

"Nothing, I guess. You just surprised me with the question."

"Well, what's the answer?"

"To be honest with you, I hadn't given it much thought. You need to get to sleep now. It's been a long day for all of us." When he kissed her cheek, she didn't even comment about the scratchy bristles.

"I don't want you to marry Joanna. I don't like her, and I don't want her to be my mommy. I want Beth. I mean, Angela." Willow scooted up in bed again and crossed her arms in a defiant fashion.

"Willow, it's not nice to speak about Joanna like that. She's been very kind to you, and I already told you, Angela has her own family. I can't marry her."

The child started to cry. "Why did she have to leave, Daddy? We love her. It's not fair. When do *we* get to have a mommy again?"

Scott folded his daughter into his arms and rocked her back and forth until her sobs subsided. He had no answers for her, but he could understand how her heart was breaking, because his was, too.

Chapter Thirteen

Angela spent the night in Heather's canopy bed, snuggled against her daughter's soft, warm little body. She was so thankful and glad to reunite with her child. She couldn't bear the thought of being separated from her again.

Sleep evaded her because her mind replayed all the beautiful memories of the moments they'd spent together—none of which she ever wanted to forget. There weren't any gaps in Angela's life when it came to Heather. Amongst all the wonderful memories, however, was one frightening image she couldn't erase—the one of Jack twisting her arm and pushing her against the wall.

Doctor Coleman had told her that with head trauma, it was possible for true memories to be mixed up with crazy dreams or even images she'd seen on television or in the news. She'd said the brain was a complicated and fascinating organ, and amnesia worked in strange and unusual ways.

Angela desperately wanted to believe the terrifying flashbacks had been just that—mixed-up signals in her brain. The possibility of her husband, the father of her child, intentionally hurting her was hard to bear. But could she forget the terrifying visions? The knot on her head had been real, as well as the marks and bruising on her arm. Who did that to her? And why?

There had to be someone who knew the truth. Who could she turn to? Why didn't Jack seem happier to have her home? She'd been missing for four days. He acted annoyed with her—not like a loving husband, relieved to have his wife back safe and sound. His strange split personality gave her serious pause and made her reluctant to trust him.

She tried to put herself in his shoes. It had to be difficult for a man to see his wife on television, bring her home, then realize she remembers nothing about him and won't let him touch her. A caring man would understand and be sensitive to what she'd experienced. He'd do anything to find out the truth of what happened. Was Jack that kind of man? He wasn't coming across that way.

A nagging suspicion settled in her gut. Angela couldn't erase the flashbacks. She just wanted to push them out of her mind and start over, now that she was home and with Heather again. But would she be able to put her fears to rest and stop suspecting Jack of causing her harm? She was determined to try, for Heather's sake, though he hadn't made it easy on her first night back home.

Angela eased herself away from Heather's sleeping little body, pulled a pair of jeans and tee shirt on, and padded down to the kitchen to start some coffee. She surprised herself when she walked straight to the cabinet where the coffee can was stored. As she spooned coffee grounds into the filter and added water, she wondered what kind of mood Jack would be in that morning.

She was not surprised when he entered the kitchen in jeans and told her he was staying home from work that day. But she was mystified when he proceeded to spend the morning in the office behind closed doors, away from her and Heather. She'd thought he'd taken off work to spend time with her.

Early that afternoon, she bucked up her courage and stepped into the home gym where Jack was working out. She'd decided to make the best of the situation and try to make amends with him.

Standing at the back of the room watching him pump iron, an icy chill crept down her spine. She didn't want to interrupt his workout since he'd already shown himself to be someone with a short fuse.

I shouldn't feel afraid to talk to my own husband, but I am.

When he finished his reps, she handed him a towel to wipe his face. "I wondered if you'd like to have lunch with Heather and me," she said with a timid smile. "I fixed grilled cheese sandwiches and canned tomato soup I found in the pantry."

He hesitated before responding. "I'll pass. Not hungry, but thanks for asking." He hopped onto the treadmill. The machine started up with a whine. Angela stood in front of him.

"Is there something else?" he asked. His athletic shoes bounced on the rubber tread.

"Is this the way our relationship was before I disappeared?" she asked.

"What do you mean?" Jack's arms pumped in rhythm at his sides and he blew short puffs of breath out of his mouth.

"You do your own thing and Heather and I do ours?"

"I don't know what you're insinuating, Angie."

She made her tone less accusatory. "Never mind. Forget I brought it up. Would you like to play a game with us after you're finished with your workout? Heather's setting up the Candy Land game."

"I have some business to take care of," he replied, not looking at her.

"I thought you'd want to spend time together—as a family. After all, I just got home, and I thought that's why you took the day off. So we could be together—get to know each other again."

"Yes, you're home," he snapped. "Now things can

go back to the way they were, which means I have things to do. In case you've forgotten, my whole routine was messed up while you were gone. I don't have any time to waste. I'm not interested in playing games."

She couldn't speak. He'd been moody and irritable ever since leaving New Mexico, but this was a new low—one she didn't understand and didn't appreciate.

He couldn't care less about me or what I went through, and he obviously isn't interested in his daughter either.

She blurted, "I'd hardly call your wife and daughter a waste of time, Jack."

He ignored the jab and retorted, "Besides, it was obvious you didn't want to spend time with me last night. By the way, how was the bed in the guest room?"

Angela took a deep breath, to calm down, and answered. "I slept with Heather in her room. You told me you understood. It's not my fault I don't remember you, Jack. It's natural for me to need time to..."

He cut her off by aiming the remote control at the television and clicking it on. CNN hummed in the background.

She leveled a fierce gaze at him. "Jack, why haven't you asked about my injuries, or wanted to know where Mr. Landry found me? Aren't you interested in how I ended up at the High Lonesome, or what happened while I was there? You haven't even looked at my head—or my arm. You don't seem the slightest bit interested in what I've gone through. To be honest, I can't figure out why you bothered to come to New Mexico to get me."

He pushed the "mute" button on the remote and looked her in the eye, but continued to jog on the treadmill. "I haven't wanted to upset you by bringing it all up. I know it was traumatic—getting kidnapped and all. I figured you would talk about it when you were ready."

She questioned him again. "Jack, you keep talking about my being kidnapped, but I don't have any recollections at all about being abducted. If that were the case, why aren't the police over here talking to me right now? What makes you think that's what happened to me? Don't you think I'd have *some* kind of flashback, if that had happened? I've had many other flashbacks and I'm remembering more and more things each day."

His eyes widened. He bellowed, "I don't know. I'm not a doctor, for Christ's sake." He turned the TV volume control up until the news program was blaring.

After a few moments, Angela left the room, disheartened and angry.

What a jerk! How could I ever have loved such a selfish man?

That evening, after a dinner of Chinese take-out with silent tension between herself and Jack, she bathed Heather, dressed her in pajamas, tucked her in, and read a story before kissing her good night. Her maternal instincts were as strong as ever, and she felt blessed and grateful to have been given another chance at taking up right where she left off with Heather.

After leaving her daughter's room, Angela went in search of Jack and found him in the office, his head bowed over a pile of paperwork. He didn't bother to raise his head, but she suspected he knew she was in the doorway, so she told him good night and headed upstairs to the guest room, where she locked herself in.

She changed her clothes and crawled in between the covers. It had been another long and trying day, and she was exhausted. Despite being tired, sleep wouldn't come. She couldn't stop thinking about Scott. Her attempts to forget about him had failed. No matter how she tried, his easy smile, brilliant blue eyes, wonderful sense of humor, caring personality and sexy body kept invading her thoughts.

An immediate longing pierced her heart and a flush of heat crept into her loins at the recollection of the long, passionate kisses they shared at the lake. She knew to continue thinking about the ranch—and the man she'd never have—was cruel torment, but she couldn't help herself. She hadn't been able to erase him from her mind.

At the lake, he'd told her his soul had found its mate, and when they kissed, she'd soared into another realm. He'd gazed into her eyes as if he'd been waiting for her all his life. Her body had burned with a fiery desire to satisfy him. She'd wanted him with a quiet desperation she'd never known before. He'd wanted her, too, but he was a man of integrity—too much of a gentleman to do something they'd both regret later. He'd told her they couldn't make love until they settled the matter of both their relationships. For her, that meant learning who she was and whether she was single and free. For him, it meant breaking up with Joanna.

That day, Scott said he was going to tell Joanna they were through, but Angela saw them kiss in the moonlight that very same night. Even now, the memory caused her to break out in a cold sweat. Her hands started to shake. Her heart beat fast. She closed her eyes, wanting to forget all of it had happened—meeting Scott, falling in love with him, seeing him kiss Joanna...

She'd realized right then, when she watched them kiss, that he wasn't over Joanna, and that it would be better for her to leave the ranch. When she'd made that decision, she never would have guessed she'd actually be leaving the next morning—for good.

Angela crawled out of bed and dug through the clothes she'd worn home from New Mexico, which lay on the floor. She stuck her hand into the back pocket of the jeans and retrieved the slip of paper with Scott's phone number and the Polaroid picture Carmen took the night of the hospital dedication. She held both in her hand like precious artifacts. Flipping on a bedside lamp, she stared at the images of Scott, Willow and herself for a long time, feeling her heart shatter into a million pieces.

I have to forget him. He's not mine and I'm not his.

She sunk onto the bed, tucked the photo and paper under her pillow and shut off the light. There were some memories better left in the past after all.

Chapter Fourteen

When Angela woke the following morning, she turned on her side and expected to see Scott's rugged face looking at her. She'd dreamt about him again. She could even feel his fingers caressing her skin. She jerked up. This had to stop.

Jack was her husband and Heather was their daughter. The little girl deserved a home with both parents. Even if it wasn't a perfect marriage, Angela knew she had to do all she could to make it work, for Heather's sake. But she couldn't concentrate on the relationship if Scott Landry kept popping up in all her sleeping and waking moments. Besides, she knew it would serve no purpose, nor do any of them good, if she continued to pine over a man she could never have.

She decided to offer Jack a truce.

Again, she found herself puzzled, but this time thankful, when Jack came down to the kitchen dressed in a suit and tie, ready for work. She'd been standing at the sink, washing a few dishes and thinking about how she was going to approach him.

The day before he'd told her he planned to take several days off to help her adjust to her old life, but it looked like he'd changed his mind. It was just as well, she thought. She didn't need looking after. She just wanted to get back to living a normal life again. There would be less tension and stress for both of them if he was gone during the day.

She had coffee brewing and bread in the toaster. Heather was still sleeping, so Angela determined this to be a good time to speak to him about a fresh start. She poured him a cup of coffee and flashed him a warm smile. "Good morning, Jack."

"Good morning." He wasn't bright-eyed and bushy-tailed, but he wasn't surly either.

"Would you like some toast?" she asked, buttering a hot slice.

"No thanks. The coffee's fine." He adjusted his tie. "You and Heather seemed to settle in fine together yesterday," he said, eyeing her.

"We did. It's wonderful to be with her again. It was like I was never gone."

"Thanks for the coffee." He stirred in sugar and took a sip. "Did you sleep well?"

"Yes. Tired as I was, I think I could have fallen asleep on a bed of bricks." She joined him at the table and sipped at her own cup of coffee. So far, so good, she thought.

His mouth turned up at the edges. "As you can see, I've decided to go back to work today. I got to thinking I don't need to be under your feet all day. You can readjust just as easy without me looming over you."

Grateful that he seemed to be in a good mood, she replied, "You wouldn't be looming, but I understand if you want to get back to the office."

He threw her a surprised look.

"You do work in an office, right? I think you told me you're a bank manager." She wondered why he had a funny expression on his face. Had she misunderstood him before?

His posture relaxed as he shifted on his feet. "A vice president. Yes."

"Oh. Sorry. Vice President is a more prestigious position than a bank manager, isn't it? Obviously you've worked hard to be able to afford all this." She let her eyes drift around the well-appointed room. "I'll remember everything, sooner or later."

He didn't answer, and she wondered if she'd said something wrong again.

"What do you plan to do today?" he asked, opening the pantry door and fishing a granola bar out of a box.

"I expect Heather and I will just putter around the house. Read together. Play some games. Maybe we'll go to the park. I know she likes to swing, and I think the paparazzi have all given up and gone home."

"Yeah, they're gone. I suppose they've moved on to the next big story." Jack stuck the granola bar in his inside jacket pocket, then picked up his cup and drained it. "You two have a good time." He leaned over and hesitated before giving her a quick peck on the cheek.

Angela reached for his arm. "Jack. I was hoping we could forget whatever happened between us in the past. I'd like it if we could make a fresh start. Heather deserves two committed parents, and we must have been in love once. Maybe we can get those feelings back again. All I need from you is a little patience. Do you think we can try? I'm willing, if you are."

He considered the offer. "Yes, we can try, Angie. I appreciate the fact that you're willing to give me another chance. You won't regret it this time. I'll see you this evening."

"Okay. Have a good day." She patted his arm in a friendly way then closed the door behind him.

That went easier than I expected, she thought.

As she watched the BMW back out of the driveway, there was a lift in her spirits at having made the decision to do what she felt was the right thing. But her curiosity was piqued. He'd thanked her for giving him another chance. Another chance at what? She wouldn't regret what this time? It seemed an unusual choice of words.

Angela opened the refrigerator door to conduct an inventory of groceries and realized she and Heather would need to run to the store today.

Jack hadn't been gone ten minutes when a rap sounded at the back door. Angela tossed the grocery list onto the counter and peeked out the peephole in the back door. The pleasant, ruddy-complexioned face of a woman with short brown hair greeted her. When she opened the door, the slender woman smiled and threw her arms around Angela.

"Oh, Angie. It's so good to see you! Did you miss me? I just saw Jack leave the house in the Beamer. What in the hell was *he* doing here at this hour?" She barged into the kitchen, plucked a mug out of the cabinet and poured herself a cup of coffee. Turning and noting the odd expression on Angela's face, she said, "What's wrong? Why are you looking at me that way? What happened over here?"

Angela rolled her tongue over her bottom lip. "I'm sorry, but do I know you?"

The woman laughed. "Do you *know* me? Is that a joke?"

"Excuse me," Angela said. "It's no joke. Could you please tell me who you are?"

The woman gave her a perplexed look and set the coffee mug on the table. "Angie, it's me. Faith. Your neighbor and best friend. What's going on here? Why are you acting weird?"

"You're my best friend?" Angie searched her face, trying to remember.

Faith's jaw twitched. She chuckled. "Yes. We've been friends ever since you and Jack moved into this house six years ago." She moved in close and stared into Angela's green eyes. "What's happened to you? Why don't you remember me?"

"I'm sorry. I guess you don't know."

"Know what?"

Angela gave her another quizzical look. "When

you walked in, you asked if I missed you. If we're friends, shouldn't you be telling me how much you missed *me*?"

Faith backed up and shook her head. She raised her hands as if she was surrendering. "Whoa. Let's start at the beginning. I haven't the slightest idea what you're talking about. You said, *I guess you don't know*. What don't I know?"

Angela told her straight. "Something happened to me about a week ago. For reasons still unknown, I disappeared from this house and was discovered wandering the desert outside a town called Ghost Rock, New Mexico with a big knot on my head. I was recuperating there with a rancher and his daughter until Jack saw me on television and came to get me a couple of days ago."

Faith gasped. "Oh, my God! I don't believe it. And now you...you don't..."

"I have amnesia. Some memories are starting to return. I remember Heather, thank goodness, but I don't remember much about Jack, and I'm sorry to say I don't remember you. But it's strange. I have a feeling about you...I'm not afraid of you."

Faith collapsed into a dining chair and held her head in her hands. She mumbled, "Of course you wouldn't be afraid of me. We're friends! Oh, I was worried something like this *might* happen, but I never in a million years dreamed it really would."

"What are you talking about?" Angela pulled out a chair and sat down across from the woman. "You were worried *what* would happen?"

Faith looked her square in the eye. "I've been out of state for the past two weeks. I just got home late last night. That's why I had no idea."

"Tell me what you were worried about."

Faith covered Angela's hand. Her brow furrowed when she asked, "Angie, you say you don't know what happened to you? What did the police say?"

"I haven't spoken to the police, but Jack thinks I was kidnapped."

"Kidnapped?" Faith did not hide her surprise. "By whom?"

"I don't know. I don't believe that's what happened." She looked deep into her neighbor's eyes and felt more than a flicker of remembrance. "For some reason, I feel I can trust you."

"You can. We're best friends. We've always told each other everything. What do you believe happened to you?"

Angela hesitated. "Well, I've had some flashbacks. The doctor who saw me in Ghost Rock told me it's perfectly normal—that they could be actual memories coming to the surface."

"What kind of flashbacks?" Faith leaned close.

Angela paused again. "I hate to say. They've scared me. I don't know what's real and what's not."

"Have they been about Jack?" Faith asked with bluntness.

Angela blinked. "How did you know?"

Faith sighed. "Angie, tell me why he was here this morning."

Angela's face expressed confusion. "I don't know why you're asking me that. He was here because he lives here. That's obvious. He's my husband. He was leaving for work."

Faith slammed her hand on the table. "That son of a bitch!"

Angela jumped and her eyes grew wide. "What? Tell me. Faith, if you're truly my friend, tell me what you know."

"Of course I'm going to tell you. Brace yourself." Faith's eyes flashed. "Angie, Jack is not your husband."

"What?"

"He's your *ex*-husband. You divorced him. The divorce became final right before I went out of town."

Angela's mouth gaped. She leaned forward in the chair and the hairs on her arms pricked. A cold shiver raced down her spine. She whispered, "He led me to believe we were still married. He lied to me."

"Of course he lied to you!" Faith exclaimed. "He's a lying drug-addicted creep who lost his job and threatened to get even with you for getting the house and taking Heather away from him."

Angela's hand splayed across her heart. "Heather! She's been here with him the whole time I was away. He's never hurt her, has he?" Panic coursed through her.

"No, no. Jack used to be a good father. He's always claimed to love her more than anything or anyone else. That's why he was so angry when the judge refused to grant visitation rights until he'd completed the drug rehab program."

"Drug rehab?" Angela widened her eyes in disbelief.

"Yeah. He was also upset that you got the house and the Beamer."

"I did?"

"Yes. This house and the car he's driving, it's all yours—not that you wanted it. You didn't care about any of the material things. You just wanted out of the marriage. You'd put up with Jack's lies for far too long. He was always selfish, in my opinion. I saw how he put himself before you and Heather even before he started using, but the drugs just made it worse."

"Jack's an addict?" Angela shook her head. "I guess that would explain his erratic behavior, but I'm in shock. I can't believe I'd be married to a drug addict. What's he addicted to?"

"Cocaine. It's been going on for a long time. And I hate to toss more wood on the fire, but Jack did not go to work today. About a month ago he was fired for embezzling funds from the bank where he was employed."

"Oh, my God. He lied about that, too. Why isn't he in jail?"

"He and the president of the bank are golfing buddies, so Jack cut a deal. The deal was, Jack would quietly leave his position and agree to pay back all the money, and in return, the bank president would not prosecute."

Angela's forehead puckered. "If he hasn't got a job, how will he pay back the money he stole? Where'd he go this morning if not to the bank? Did he get another position somewhere?"

"I'm afraid I haven't got the answers to any of those questions. I'm only aware of what you told me before I left town."

"As far as you know, he didn't go to rehab?" Angela asked.

"No. He outright refused. He doesn't think he has a problem. Idiot. He blames all his troubles on everyone but himself."

Angela took a deep breath and lowered her voice. "Faith, have I ever confided in you about being physically abused by Jack?"

"No, but you were afraid he might start. You said he was getting more volatile and he'd threatened to take Heather away from you. I never saw bruises or marks on you. Angie, I hated to leave when I did, because you have no family to turn to, and I was so worried about you and Heather. My aunt was having surgery and she had no one else. I had to care for her. But maybe if I'd been here, I could have helped somehow. You wouldn't have been *kidnapped*." Faith spit the word out with sarcasm.

Angela patted Faith's hand. "Don't blame yourself for the things Jack did. You're helping now by telling me the truth. I wonder how much Jack owes the bank."

Faith sighed again. "I *do* know the answer to

that one. Get ready for this. He owes close to half a million."

Angela's fist flew to her mouth. "He must be a desperate man. I don't see how he could come up with that kind of money, especially if I received the house and car in the divorce. He'd have to figure out another way..."

Another vision popped into her head. She remembered finding a document—a life insurance policy—stuck inside his suit jacket pocket one evening when he was at the house to collect some personal items. She remembered confronting him, an argument ensuing, and him shoving her against the wall. The whole scene flashed before her in horrible living color.

Dear God. Could it be?

"What is it, Angie?" Faith shook her arm. "You look like you've seen a ghost."

"Not a ghost, Faith. A monster. I've seen a monster. And he lives in this house."

Chapter Fifteen

"You remember finding a life insurance policy in his coat? A policy that was taken out on you?" Faith's mouth formed an "o" and she slammed her hand on the table again.

"Yes!" Angela said. "It's all coming to me now. When I confronted him, we argued. I waved the policy in his face, angry that he'd forged my signature. He didn't deny forging it. He grew quiet. When I demanded he tell me why he'd taken a life insurance policy out on me for one million dollars, his eyes grew so hard and cold."

"What are you saying?" Faith asked.

"I was kidnapped all right—by Jack. He wanted me to die out in that desert. I think Jack intended on murdering me for the money. It was the only way he could possibly pay back the bank. We'd just gotten divorced, he'd been denied visitation rights with Heather, and he lost the house and his precious car. He must have lost his mind. As they say, desperate causes call for desperate measures."

"Oh, honey. I'm so sorry. What are you going to do now?"

"If he's pretending to be at work all day, he'll be home around six o'clock this evening. I can't let him know I remember anything, but I have to find that insurance policy and our Divorce Decree. I have a strong feeling they're here in the house. It's obvious that he moved back in once he thought he'd gotten rid of me last week. Once I find those documents, I'll go to the police and tell them all I know and remember. But I have to have the evidence to back me up."

"You can't let him know you suspect anything," Faith reminded her. "He might try to hurt you again. You're going to have to be a damn good actress tonight when he gets home."

"I will be."

"I hate to leave you alone with him. What else can I do to help?"

"You've done it already, by telling me the truth and being my friend. Now, if you'll excuse me, I've got to start looking for that policy." Angela pushed back from the table and stood.

Faith scratched her phone number on a slip of paper and stuffed it in Angela's hand. "This is my number. Call me if you need me—anytime, day or night. I'm just across the lawn."

"I will. Thank you."

"Be careful." They hugged and Faith left, though reluctant.

Angela's head began to spin. She *had* to find that insurance policy and the divorce documents. Her very life depended on it.

She peeked in on Heather, who was still snoring away in the pink canopy bed. She glanced at her watch. She might have an hour to search the house for the insurance policy before Heather woke up. She started in the master bedroom, where Jack had strewn his clothes all over the floor. After going through all the dresser drawers, she rummaged around the closet and found nothing.

Moving on to the office, Angela dug through the desk drawers and looked in the credenza. Next, she ran a critical eye over the shelves of the built-in bookcases, which flanked both sides of a brick fireplace. He could have hidden the document in any one of the dozens of books on the shelves, she realized. She began pulling the books off the shelves one by one—flipping through the pages swiftly.

"Mommy. I'm hungry."

Angela spun around, the blood pumping through her veins. "Oh, Heather. You scared Mommy."

Heather crossed the room in her pajamas, dragging her blanket behind her. "I'm sorry, Mommy." She stuck a fat thumb in her mouth and plopped down on the floor on her belly.

"It's okay, sweetie." Angela took a deep breath and stuck the book she was holding back onto the shelf, then walked over and scooped the child into her arms and smothered her with tiny kisses. "How would you like some French toast with strawberries?"

"I would!"

"Your wish is my command, fairy princess."

Heather giggled. Angela closed the office door and carried her daughter down to the kitchen. As she whipped up the French toast, her mind scattered like the four winds. She needed to locate the life insurance policy to prove Jack had tried to kill her for the money.

Where could he have hidden it?

When Heather finished her breakfast, Angela said, "Let's gather up some of your toys, honey. You can play on the floor in Daddy's office while I do some cleaning in there."

After picking out a few playthings, Heather sat on the rug in the middle of the room and began to play. Angela once again began searching through the books. She had gone through two dozen volumes when the phone rang. Her pulse raced as she grabbed the receiver. "Hello?"

"You sound out of breath."

Her heart stopped beating when she recognized Jack's voice. The lie she fed him came easy. "I was just running a bath for Heather when I heard the phone. I ran to grab it."

"No you weren't, Mommy," Heather said. The little girl had sidled up beside her and gave her a puzzled look.

Angela placed a finger on her lips and mouthed, "Shhh."

"Is Heather there with you?" Jack asked.

"No. The television's on. How's your morning going?" She wanted to change the subject without arousing his suspicions.

"Same ole, same ole. I'm just calling to make sure everything's okay there."

Angela tried to sound as normal as possible. "That's nice of you. We're just fine." Her hands were trembling. "Heather and I just finished breakfast. We're going to go shopping later. We're running low on groceries."

"I'm afraid I didn't keep up with that while you were away."

It could have been a conversation between any couple. He sounded very calm for a man hooked on drugs and pretending to be at work. Almost too calm, she thought.

"Are you still going to the park?" he asked.

"Maybe. I'll see how the day goes."

A pause hung between them.

"Well, I was just checking in," he repeated.

Heather reached for the phone. "Can I talk to Daddy?"

"Not now, baby. Daddy's very busy," Angela whispered, cupping her hand over the receiver mouthpiece.

In her ear, Angela heard Jack say, "Let me talk to her."

She took another deep breath and placed the phone up to the little girl's ear. "Say hello to Daddy." She lowered her ear to the receiver so she could listen in while Heather talked.

"Hi Daddy!"

"Hi baby. What have you been doing?"

"I'm playing with my toys."

"And what's Mommy doing?"

"She's cleaning."

"Cleaning? Where is she cleaning? What room are you in?"

"We're in your—"

Angela cut her off by pulling the phone away. "Jack, there's a knock on the door," she fibbed. "I've got to go. See you when you get home tonight." She hung up the phone and closed her eyes. She was afraid Heather might have tipped him off.

"Why'd you hang up the phone, Mommy?" Heather stuck her thumb in her mouth.

"I'm sorry, honey. I thought I heard someone at the door. Why don't you go back to playing with your Legos while I finish cleaning?"

After rifling through every book in the bookcase, Angela came up empty.

Bored with playing by herself, Heather begged Angela to help her build towers with blocks. After that, Angela and a stuffed teddy bear and rabbit became guests at a tea party. She read Heather some stories, they colored in coloring books, and then she fixed lunch and put Heather down for a nap.

Heather balked at first, claiming she wasn't tired and too big to take naps. Angela felt terrible, trying to force her down, but she needed time alone to hunt for those papers. She rubbed Heather's back and sang her some lullabies, and soon her daughter was fast asleep and snoring.

Angela tiptoed out of the bedroom and made quick time, poking around every room in the house, looking in every space, dark corner, and nook and cranny for the policy.

Maybe he's moved it. Or it's in the car. I never thought of that! Oh, I hope that's not the case.

She was standing in the den with her hands on her hips, pondering her next move. While thinking, she stared at the oil painting above the sofa and suddenly remembered she'd never liked that particular piece of art. It always seemed to be off balance for some weird reason—hanging askew, as it was now.

That ugly painting is out of here.

She kicked off her shoes then stepped onto the sofa and lowered the painting off the wall. When she saw the wall safe, she gasped.

This has to be the place! This must be where Jack has hidden the life insurance policy. I bet he never thought I'd remember the safe was here in the wall!

Angela's hand landed on the combination lock. She squeezed her eyes shut and searched her mind to remember the combination. They had never had a use for the safe, she recalled, since Jack worked at the bank and stored their valuables in a safe deposit box there. The safe deposit box! She hoped the bank made him clear out the safe deposit box when he was let go. Where else would he keep important documents, but here at home?

She didn't know whether she'd remember the combination, even if she weren't suffering from amnesia. Her mind was blank.

Think. Think. Think. The combination could be any group of numbers—Jack's birthday, my birthday, our wedding date...I don't know any of them.

She ran out of the den and up the stairs to the master bedroom and spied their wedding album sitting on the vanity, just where she'd seen it on the day she returned home and showed herself around. Panting from running up the stairs, she flung the album open and memorized the date imprinted in cursive gold letters on the front page. Hurrying back to the den, she put her fingers on the lock. Right six, left seven, right ninety-nine. It didn't open. *Damn!*

Angela ran back up the stairs and frantically dug through the closet once again. Maybe she'd missed something the first time around. When she opened a cardboard box she thought contained boots, she discovered packets of letters she'd written to Jack before they married, some loose photos of the two of them, her passport, and her birth certificate.

With a safe in the house, why would her important documents and sentimental memorabilia be packed into a box and hidden in the closet? Jack must have planned to destroy them at some point to rid himself of everything associated with her. She didn't have time to consider all the possible scenarios.

Angela rushed back to the den with her passport and birth certificate in her hands. She read her birth date out loud while turning the combination lock. Right ten, left four, right seventy-nine. Bingo! Glancing at her birth record again, she took a double take at the name printed on the certificate: Angela Elizabeth Turner. *Beth!*

She stuck her hand inside the opening in the wall and pulled out a gray metal strongbox. Her heart sank when she saw the box was bound by another lock. Convinced the strongbox held the life insurance policy, and perhaps even the Divorce Decree, she leapt off the sofa and ran to the basement, carrying the strongbox under her arm. She searched for a tool, any tool she could use to break the lock. Spying a claw hammer on the work table, she began to whack at the lock. When it broke open, she lifted the lid and fanned through the documents. There they were—the life insurance policy and Divorce Decree—at the bottom, just as she suspected.

Angela skimmed through the contents of the

insurance policy, frowning when the realization hit her. She leaned heavily against the basement wall and slid down to the hard concrete floor. Her eyes drifted shut. Her head began to swim with clear memories of that fateful day.

He'd shown up at her door the day after their divorce was final, begging to see Heather. She'd let him in, but told him he could spend only fifteen minutes with the child, in the living room where she could monitor them. She didn't trust him at all, and he wasn't even supposed to be there.

As father and daughter sat on the sofa together reading a book, Angela had checked the pockets of his jacket, which he'd slung over the back of a chair in the foyer. She'd wanted to see if he was carrying any drugs. That's when she discovered the life insurance policy.

When the story was over, Angela fixed Heather a snack and sat her in front of cartoons in the kitchen. She asked Jack to follow her to their bedroom, out of hearing range of Heather, and she confronted him about the policy. They argued and he swung his fist in front of her face. He grabbed her arm and twisted it, then shoved her against the wall, after which, her world went black.

The next time she woke, she was in a cramped, hot, dark space—realizing in one horrifying moment that she was locked in the trunk of a car. When the trunk popped open, she caught a glimpse of Jack's cool, calculating face in the glint of the sun, right before he brought something hard down on her head.

He *had* tried to kill her, and no doubt, he'd try again.

Angela scrambled up from the concrete floor. She had no time to lose. She had to replace the lock that she'd broken, just in case Jack opened the safe and looked in. She yanked open the drawers of his work table and rummaged around, finding a bicycle lock. She knew it would do. It was about the same size and required a combination to open it, just like the other one. She carried the strongbox upstairs and hid it back in the wall safe. After replacing the oil painting, she ran upstairs and checked on Heather, who was still—amazingly—sound asleep. Then she rushed into the guest room. One more thing she had to do.

She flew to the bed then tossed her pillow aside and kissed the little slip of paper. As she picked up the phone and punched in the cell number, she prayed to God Scott would answer.

Chapter Sixteen

Scott had been unable to sleep. Angela's long soft hair, sparkling emerald eyes, and heart-shaped lips pervaded his dreams—both while sleeping and awake.

It had taken a while, but after racking his brains, he'd realized she must have seen him and Joanna kiss that night before she left. What he still didn't understand, however, was why she didn't say something when he asked her what was wrong. At that moment, he'd had no idea she even knew Joanna had come by.

All he could think about now was how hurt Angela must have been. Over and over, he castigated himself for letting her leave without knowing the truth.

He was outside swinging a hammer and pounding nails into a fence. Sweat dripped down his brow, rolled off his shoulders, and down his muscular bare back.

The chiseled face of Jack West played before his eyes. He didn't like the guy one bit. There was something fishy about him. What had the man done to try to find his missing wife? Scott wondered. Why didn't he ask about her injuries? According to Buddy, he was nonchalant during their whole interview. And what kind of ridiculous story was that he told about her being kidnapped? If she'd been kidnapped, why hadn't the Arizona police plastered her face all over creation the same way Buddy had? Something just didn't add up and Scott was worried about Angela.

He stuck one nail in his mouth and slammed another one into the fence. Hell. Angela had gone with the guy willingly, after all. They were husband and wife. What else was she supposed to do? It had turned out just as she thought it would.

It's a good thing I didn't tell her I loved her after all.

Scott whacked at the nail and hit his thumb. "Shit!"

He needed to get away from the ranch and clear his head before he maimed himself. He flung the hammer in the dirt and kicked over the box of nails. Wiping sweat from his face with his forearm, he tugged on his shirt, then plodded to the barn and grabbed Pepper's bridle. After saddling her, he scribbled a note to Cody.

Gone for a ride. Have my cell phone if you need me.

The sun rode high in the cloudless sky as Scott galloped across the mountain on Pepper. She was lathered from the hard ride, but of all the horses he'd ever owned, he knew the mare could handle it. He had to ride out his frustrations, and he'd go to the edge of the earth if that's what it took.

The horse's nostrils flared and she blew air out in loud puffs. Scott finally slowed and walked her down the hill to the lake. He hadn't ridden here on purpose. He'd just struck out—needing to feel the wind at his back—and this is where Pepper took him.

His heart swelled as he neared the sapphire pool, aching with the remembrance of holding Angela and searing her with hot, burning kisses. When she was ensconced in his arms, he felt everything was right with the world. But since she'd left, he couldn't sleep, couldn't eat, and he couldn't stop thinking about her fast smile, soft voice and pleasant laugh. Hadn't he warned himself from the very beginning not to get close to her? Not to let himself fall for her? He had only himself to blame for the emptiness he was feeling now. But it didn't make him feel any better to admit it.

He reined Pepper over to the field of wildflowers and swung off her back. After leading her into the marshy reeds at the edge of the water, she drank her fill, and then he ground-tied her. Sitting cross-legged in the tall grass, he listened to the wind carry its ancient tune across the rippling water.

His thoughts soared back to Angela. She'd been happy on the ranch. She loved the horses and had taken to riding as if she'd been born in the saddle. She treasured the red mountains and felt a sacred connection to the caves and the ancient spirits who still wandered the woods. But she was most at peace there at the lake—smelling the sweet grass, watching the butterflies, gazing upon the water and hearing the wind whistle through the canyon.

Scott lay down on the carpet of grass and clasped his hands behind his neck. The sun beat down on him. His skin was already brown as a nut, but he didn't care if he turned as dark as an Apache. He'd lay there in the sun until the burning in his heart and loins ceased.

He tossed his hat on the ground, and before long, he'd drifted off.

The blare of his cell phone ringing woke him. Half asleep, he wondered how he could be receiving any service when there were no cell towers for miles. He rose up on his elbows, plucked out the phone and flipped it open. "Hello."

"Scott?"

"Yeah, this is Scott." The phone crackled with bad reception. "If you can hear me, hold on a minute." He sat up, got to his feet, and walked a few yards. He was amazed when the connection became crystal clear. "Hello? This is Scott."

"Scott, it's Angela."

His heart sunk to the pit of his stomach and blood pumped through his veins. "I'm here," he shouted. "I can hear you. Tell me I'm not dreaming. Is it really you?"

"Yes, it's me."

"I haven't been able to stop thinking about you. I know it's wrong, since you're married and all, but—"

"I'm not married," she blurted.

Scott stared into the phone. "Come again? Our reception must be bad. I thought I just heard you say you're not married."

"That's exactly what you heard, Scott. My memory has returned and I know what happened to me. It's a long story, which I'll explain when you get here."

"When I get there?" He scratched his head.

"Yes. I'm calling because I need your help. Jack's not my husband. He's my ex-husband."

"Your…ex-husband?" Scott repeated, making sure he'd heard correctly.

"That's right. I was already divorced from him when you and I met."

Scott's tongue was tied.

"Are you still there?" she asked. "Did you hear what I said? I'm not married."

A wide smile spread across Scott's face. "I heard you, darlin', and that's the best damned news I've ever heard."

"It is?"

"Of course!" He knew she'd taken a chance by calling him. He recalled Jack's attitude when they left together and realized his instincts had been right.

"I don't have much time," she told him, "but it's so good to hear your voice. You're one of the few people I feel I can trust right now."

"I've been thinking of you every minute since you left," Scott confessed. "I'm so glad you called."

"You're not just saying that, are you?"

"No, I'm not, Angela. I've missed you more than you know."

"I've missed you, too. Although I know I shouldn't. Because of Joanna," she added.

Scott ran a hand through his tousled hair. His heart melted. If he could have reached through the phone and taken her in his arms right then, he would have. "You saw her kiss me the night before you left with West. Am I right?"

There was a pause before she answered. "Yes. I knew then, you weren't over her. But I don't want to get into that right now, Scott. I need your help. If you're willing to give it."

He waited.

"I know now that Jack tried to kill me, and I think he's going to try again. Very soon. That's why I'm calling."

Rage boiling, his empty hand in a fist, Scott said, "I knew something wasn't right the moment I met that creep. Pack your bags, honey. I'm on my way. I'll be there first thing in the morning."

****

Angela stood at the kitchen sink washing the dinner dishes. Jack and Heather were at the table playing Go Fish. He hadn't said more than a dozen words throughout the meal; but when Heather asked him to get out the cards, he did so without hesitation.

Angela thought back to the number of times he'd played with their daughter on his own like this—and she couldn't fill up the fingers of one hand. It was strange, she thought, how she hadn't been able to remember anything about her life for more than a week, and now she could recall every last detail, down to the hours Jack had spent interacting alone with Heather.

Although he was all smiles while playing with Heather, Angela could sense his dark mood. He seemed distracted—but why wouldn't he be? He was hiding so many secrets—ones that any normal human being wouldn't be able to live with. It hurt her to think of how Jack had changed. She had loved him once. But the drugs had turned him into a liar, a thief and an attempted murderer.

She was distracted as well. It took every bit of her strength and composure to keep from shaking. She had to pretend she still suffered from amnesia so as not to tip Jack off. Her very life depended on it.

Running through her mind was the list of things to do before Scott arrived the next morning. Since Jack was pretending to go to work, she and Scott had arranged for him to be at the house at eight-thirty. They would take the forged life insurance policy, the divorce documents, the information about Jack's bank embezzlement, and her memories of being attacked—and waking up in the trunk of the car—to the police. Faith was ready to be a witness if need be. If all went as they hoped, Jack would be arrested, and she and Heather would be safe and free to start a new life.

Until then, it was imperative that she behave as if nothing had changed. If Jack suspected she remembered anything about what he'd done to her already, there was no telling what he'd be capable of this time. Under all conditions, she had to keep her daughter safe.

He strolled into another room as Angela carried Heather to bed. She tucked the covers up to Heather's chin and kissed her forehead, then stroked the little girl's hair as she sang her a lullaby. Once Heather closed her eyes, she began snoring. Tomorrow, Angela thought, everything would change, for both of them.

For one brief moment, she felt guilty about taking Heather away from her father, but the guilt soon vanished. Jack had brought all this on himself. His selfish, and ultimately evil, choices had caught up with him. Not only had he lost his family, but he'd also lost his ability to distinguish right from wrong, not to mention his freedom, once the police got a hold of him.

Angela wanted to sleep in the bed with her little girl. She didn't trust Jack not to steal her away in the middle of the night. She walked to the guest room to collect her toiletries and nightclothes. She was ticking off the list of things to do in the morning when she entered the bedroom. Her heart stopped when she saw Jack lying half-naked on the bed. He was propped against the pillows on top of the bedspread, bare-chested with briefs on.

"Is Heather asleep?" he asked.

She nodded, averted her eyes, and walked straight to the bathroom. She had no idea he'd snuck into the guest room, and the sight of him so flustered her she couldn't even speak to tell him to get out. She thought he'd gone into his office or into the den to pour himself a drink.

She pushed the bathroom door partway closed and turned on the water faucet to splash her face, to stall as she considered how to handle the situation.

"I tucked her in and she was out like a light," she answered from behind the door. Her voice trembled.

"Good. I thought we might try sleeping together tonight. I think it's time. I've missed you. Don't you miss me that way?"

Angela's stomach began to roll. She was sickened by the truth of what he'd done to her and what he'd become. It made her flesh crawl to think of him touching her.

Scott's face flashed before her and hot tears

sprang to her eyes. He was coming for her in the morning, and he'd told her to pack her and Heather's bags. He wanted them to return to the High Lonesome with him. But that was tomorrow, more than twelve hours away. Right now, she had to figure out what to do about Jack. She wasn't sure how to get him out of the room without upsetting him or causing him suspicion. No matter what, she vowed, he would not lay a hand on her.

"Angie, I'm waiting for you," he called. "You told me you wanted a truce. You said you wanted us to start over again. Well, we always connected in bed. At least, in the early years...Maybe that will bring back some memories. What's taking you so long in there?"

"I don't feel well," she lied from behind the door. Moaning for emphasis, she said, "I guess my dinner didn't settle." She glanced at her image in the bathroom mirror and saw she'd grown pale. She opened the door a sliver and leaned against the frame, letting her tongue loll out of her mouth. "I have a feeling I'm going to be up tonight." She placed a hand on her stomach.

"Angie!" The sharp tone of Jack's voice caused her to jump.

"What is it? I just told you I'm feeling nauseous."

Glaring, he asked, "Do you remember when we were first married?"

"I'm sorry, but you know I don't."

His eyes took on a distant, dreamy look. "We were happy then, and so in love. We used to make love every day. Please tell me you remember."

Another woman who didn't know Jack might have been moved by the genuine look on his face. But not Angela.

She didn't answer.

"What happened to us?" he asked rhetorically. "What went wrong? Our marriage is not what it should be. You must know that. Whose fault is that?"

"I'm sorry, Jack." Angela acted as if she was going to throw up and closed the bathroom door shut. Pressing her back against it, she took several deep breaths in order to regain her composure. You already know the answers to those questions, she thought with bitterness.

"Are you coming out?" he called again, his voice curt.

"I'm sick," she replied.

After a few moments, she heard him roll off the bed and pad out of the room. When she thought he'd gone, she peeked out of the bathroom, then dashed to the door and snapped the lock. She waited until she heard the master bedroom door slam shut. Forgoing her sleep shorts and tee shirt, she unlocked the door, crept down to Heather's room, climbed into the bed with all her clothes on, and held her hand over her heart. It hammered inside her chest.

Scott's on his way.

Chapter Seventeen

The morning sun streamed in through the kitchen bay window. Much to Heather's delight, a kaleidoscope of rainbow colors danced upon the shiny glass. She spooned a bite of oatmeal into her mouth as she watched, mesmerized. "I see fairies, Mommy."

"I see them, too, honey." Angela absent-mindedly wiped the counter with a rag as she glanced at the clock. *Why isn't Jack up yet?* It was six forty-five and he hadn't come down for coffee. Her stomach was reeling with anxiety—made worse by the fact that Heather woke earlier than usual and couldn't get back to sleep.

Why hasn't he come downstairs? The thought occurred to her he might not be "going to work." What if he'd decided to stay home and try to make peace? Worse yet, what if he'd caught on to her?

Angela's heart sank. She feared her plan was about to unravel like a sweater with a loose thread. Wringing her hands, she told Heather, "I'm going to go check on Daddy. Stay here and finish your cereal."

"Okay, Mommy." The little girl was in her pajamas and her dark hair stuck up on end with static electricity. She giggled as she watched the jeweled colors flit across the window.

Angela walked down the hallway and stood at the bottom of the stairs. She heard no movements upstairs. Her heart pounded in her chest as she took one anxious step at a time, climbing the stairs until she reached the top. The master bedroom door was closed. Gathering her courage, she took a deep breath and pushed open the door and peered in. The bed was made up, as if he hadn't slept in it.

"Jack?" She entered the room and rapped on the bathroom door. "Jack? Are you in there?"

There was no answer.

Glancing around the room, she noticed her vanity drawer was open and some of her belongings were scattered on the floor. He'd been looking for something. She slid the drawer shut.

Where is he?

Her throat tightened. Was this a ploy? What if this was a distraction, so he could grab their daughter and run? There was no telling what the drug-addicted man was capable of. *Heather!*

Angela dashed out of the bedroom shouting out his name. "Jack! Jack!" They nearly collided in the hall as he materialized before her like a phantom. Her hand clutched at her chest as she gasped, "You scared me!"

"I'm sorry." His demeanor was cool.

She tried to catch her breath. "Where have you been? I've been calling you. Aren't you going to be late for work?"

He glared at her. His eyes were bloodshot and the pupils wide open. She remembered seeing that look before—all the times he was high on cocaine, which she remembered now, clearly.

She ran her eyes up and down and was relieved to see he was dressed in business attire, wearing slacks and a dress shirt and tie. "Are you feeling all right?" she asked.

"Of course I'm feeling all right," he barked. "Never better." He peered around her into the bedroom, and suspicion covered his face like a blanket. "Why were you in my room?"

Thinking fast, she stammered, "I came up to

look for you. I got worried when you didn't answer me when I called. I thought you were ill."

"Oh. Well, as you can see, there's no need to worry. I'm just running a little late. What are you and Heather planning to do today?" His veined, bloodshot gaze bored into her.

"It looks like it's going to be a beautiful day. We'll probably go to the park. We got so busy we didn't make it yesterday." Her heart thumped.

"I guess you had more important things to do." He fired a disgusted look her way before stomping down the stairs.

His despicable behavior irked her—and confirmed that she'd made the right decision when she divorced him. She followed him down the stairs and watched him strut through the front door. Sighing heavily, she rushed into the kitchen and watched the BMW back out of the driveway and careen down the street. She picked up the phone and dialed Faith.

When the neighbor answered, Angela filled her in. "I found the life insurance policy and the divorce documents yesterday. Jack was acting very strange last night and this morning. I'm afraid."

"What are you going to do?"

"I'm going to the police. I've called the man I stayed with in Ghost Rock for help. He's going to be here at eight-thirty."

"The rancher?" The octave in Faith's voice rose.

"Yes. His name's Scott Landry. He wants Heather and me to return to the High Lonesome with him."

"Oh, honey. I'm thrilled for you," Faith declared. "After all you've been through, you deserve love and happiness."

Angela didn't have time to explain to Faith the complicated relationship she shared with Scott. "He's willing to help us out," was all she said. "I don't have much time," Angela went on. "Jack's gone, but Heather's already up. Could you keep her at your house for about an hour while I pack? She won't understand what's happening."

"Of course. I'll be right over."

Heather had switched on the portable TV and was laughing at cartoons. When Faith entered through the back door, Angela picked up Heather and told her, "Mommy has something important to do right now, so Faith is going to take you over to her house for a little while, okay? It won't be long."

"Okay, Mommy."

Faith scooped the little girl into her arms. "Is that SpongeBob SquarePants on TV?"

"Yes." Heather giggled. "He's funny."

"He's on my TV, too. We can watch him together. Then we can put some puzzles together. Would you like that?"

Heather nodded.

"You two have fun," Angela said. "I'll come get you in a little bit, honey." She kissed the child on the cheek and told Faith, "I don't know how I'll ever be able to thank you."

"I just want you and Heather to be safe and happy. This rancher must be someone special."

"He is. He's a good man."

"As your friend, I just want the best for you, but I'm sure going to miss you and this little kid so much." Faith nuzzled Heather's static-cling hair with her nose.

"We'll see each other again," Angela promised. "I don't even know how long we'll be staying at the ranch. It's all up in the air, until a few things get sorted out." She squeezed her friend's shoulder. "Faith, I want you to know that all my memories have returned, and I remember the bond we share. You are a dear friend."

Tears sprang to the Faith's eyes. "So are you.

Now, hurry and get your bags packed. Your cowboy will be here soon to carry you off into the sunset."

As Faith scurried across the lawn with Heather, Angela flung open the basement door and tramped down to get a couple of suitcases. She hauled them upstairs and started in Heather's room. She pulled her clothes out of dresser drawers and off hangers, grabbed all of Heather's favorite toys and games and tossed them into one suitcase, closed and zipped it, and then ran into the master bedroom with the other case.

She didn't care if she ever returned to this house. All she could think about at that moment was leaving with Scott and starting new. She didn't even want to think about Joanna. She'd take it one day at a time.

Leaving the luggage, Angela ran down the stairs to the den and removed the oil painting from the wall. As she worked the combination lock, she prayed Jack had not opened the safe and removed the strongbox. She reached in, pulled out the metal strongbox and noted the new bicycle lock had not been tampered with. *Thank God.* Closing the wall safe, she relocked it and returned the painting to the wall—making sure to straighten it so it appeared untouched.

Angela returned to the bedroom and unzipped the suitcase. She tossed in some clothes, her makeup, toiletries, and the important personal papers from the cardboard box she'd found in the closet. Satisfied she had all she needed, she set the strongbox on the floor next to her as she knelt and zipped up the suitcase.

"Leaving again so soon?"

She froze. She hadn't heard the car pull up nor had she heard his feet on the stairs.

"I asked you a question," Jack said. "At least have the courtesy to look at me when I speak to you."

Realizing he could see the strongbox on the floor beside her, she scooped it up into her arms and stood, clutching it against her chest. "Jack."

"Are you going somewhere, Angie? Back to that cowboy?" His glare was menacing, but she refrained from answering. "Do you take me for an idiot?" he continued. "Do you think I didn't see how the two of you looked at each other in that hick sheriff's office? I'm not stupid."

She ignored the sarcasm that dripped from his tongue.

"I'll take that box," he said darkly, as he stretched out his arm. "I can't collect on your death policy without it."

Her eyes grew large as he stepped forward.

"Stay right where you are, Jack. I know everything. I remember what happened, and you're not going to get away with it."

"I figured that out already. You never were a good liar."

"No, but you were—and still are. We're not even married anymore. This document is no good. You forged my signature."

"No one but you knows that. It's a perfect match. I practiced for weeks. The insurance agent couldn't even tell."

"What are you going to do? Try to murder me again? You'll never get away with it a second time."

"If you remember everything, then you know I have to pay back the bank or go to prison. I no longer have a job—which, I assume, you've figured out already—and you got the house and the car in the divorce. I have no other options. I have no money—no way to live. You've taken everything from me. Don't you see? I *have* to collect on that policy. I've been forced into a terrible situation here."

He took another step closer.

"I'm warning you, Jack. Don't come any closer." Reading the danger and desperation in his wild eyes, she held the strongbox tight to her chest.

"Give me that box!" he yelled.

When he lunged, she swung the box and hit him on the side of the face. He screeched. She bolted for the door but he whirled and blocked her with his body then grabbed her arm and twisted. The box fell from her hands.

"Let go!" she screamed, while pummeling him with her other fist. In a scene reminiscent to the one she'd experienced before, he gritted his teeth and shoved her hard. He slammed her petite body against the wall. She slid to the floor and willed herself not to pass out.

As he reached down for the box, she ignored the pain she felt in her back and stumbled to her feet. Glancing around, she saw he had backed her into the corner. Trapped between the bed and the bathroom, she looked around, wondering how she was going to escape.

Realizing she was no match for his brute strength, she opted for reverse psychology. She needed a moment to come up with a plan. She'd try to appease him. "Jack, we can work this out," she wheezed. Her eyesight was blurry. She steadied herself against the wall to keep from falling down. "The judge wasn't fair when he gave everything to me in the divorce. You can have the car and the house."

Taken aback, he asked, "What about Heather?"

"Once you get the help you need—go to rehab and get clean," she said tentatively, "then you can spend more time with Heather. I'll go back to court and have new documents drawn up. I promise."

He considered that a moment, then said, "No. It's too late." He lumbered forward and Angela crossed her hands to protect her face from the blow that was sure to come.

"It's never too late," she cried.

He stopped mid-stride.

"You don't want to hurt me, Jack. Please think about Heather. She needs me. I'm her mother. Remember how you felt when your mother died? You were twelve—she's only four. You told me your world was never the same after that. You don't want Heather to go through that same kind of pain."

"Heather will be just fine," Jack grumbled. "I'm all she needs. I'll take care of her."

"I know you love her, Jack, but you can't take care of her until you take care of yourself. You have to get help for your addiction."

"Shut up!" he yelled. "I'm sick of your nagging. Why didn't you die out in the desert where I dumped you?"

A trickle of blood dripped from his nostril. Angela wasn't sure if it was from where she smacked him with the strongbox or if it was from the coke. He wiped it away with the back of his hand and said, "I'm sorry, Angie, but there's no other way." He tossed the strongbox on the floor. Rushing forward, he raised his hands in a chokehold position.

"Jack! Don't!"

He strode right up to her and wrapped his hands around her neck. Angela looked to her right. With a burst of adrenaline, she yanked the lamp off the bedside table next to her and smashed it into his head.

With a low moan, he crumpled to the floor and fell unconscious. A gash on his scalp began seeping blood the color of dark berries. Angela dropped to her knees and felt a weak pulse in his neck, then picked up the phone and dialed 911.

Leaning over his body, she said, "I'm sorry, too, Jack."

****

Scott pulled up to a scene straight out of the movies. He parked along the curb because an ambulance was coming out of the driveway. Two police cars were parked in front and onlookers were both gathered on the street and congregated on the lawn, gawking. He jumped out of the pickup and jogged up to the front door, banging on it with his fist. Realizing it was ajar, he stepped inside and a slender woman with short dark hair appeared from around the corner. "Where's Angela?" he asked, forgetting his manners.

"You must be Mr. Landry. I'm her friend, Faith. Come in."

"Where is she? What happened here? Is she all right?"

"Shhh. Come with me." Faith linked her arm through his and led him into the kitchen via the back hallway. "Angie's fine. It's Jack who's been carted off to the hospital. She had to defend herself against him, but she wasn't hurt—just a sore back. She'll explain everything to you when she finishes up with the police."

Scott glanced around, noting the high-end interior surroundings. "She wanted me with her when she spoke to the police. We planned to go to them with the insurance policy. Does she have it?"

"Yes. She wanted me to ask you to wait here in the kitchen. I think the interview with the police is going well. Go ahead and sit down." She motioned toward the dining table. "Would you like a cup of coffee?"

"No. I'm good." He removed his Stetson and laid it in the chair next to him. "You're sure she's okay? That bastard didn't hurt her?"

"No. I think he meant to kill her though. She walloped him with a metal box and cold cocked him with a lamp. She's a courageous woman, our Angie."

Scott shook his head.

Angela stepped into the room a half hour later. When her gaze locked with Scott's, there was no hesitation. She walked straight into his arms then rested her head on his chest, and he held her as if he'd never let go again. They didn't speak for several moments—just clung together—holding each other in a lover's embrace.

Faith cleared her throat and excused herself. "I'll go check on Heather while you two get reacquainted."

They sat at the table and he placed his hand over hers. He said nothing as she told him what it'd been like since she returned to Tucson with Jack. How she remembered everything that had happened, and how she'd narrowly escaped Jack's evil clutches.

"I'm not a lawyer," she said at the end, "but I'm pretty sure Jack's going to be incarcerated for a long time. He's got some serious charges facing him. I just hope he'll be able to receive the help he needs to kick the drugs."

"I'm so proud of you," Scott said, his voice warm. "You didn't need me at all."

She begged to differ. "Yes, I did." Angela gazed into his blue eyes. "You were the first person I thought to call. You were the *only* one. I know I shouldn't have contacted you, but you told me you'd always be there for me."

"That's right," Scott said. "I meant it."

Angela closed her eyes for a moment then opened them again. She had to speak her heart. "Scott, I was heartbroken when I realized our afternoon at the lake was nothing more than physical attraction."

"You're wrong about that, Angela. The passion I felt when we kissed—it was real and my words were true. What you saw Jo and I share that evening before you left was a farewell kiss between old friends. After I washed up, I saw her sitting in her car in the driveway. I couldn't believe it. The timing couldn't have been more perfect. I went out to tell her it was over between us, but you'll never guess what happened."

"What?"

"She beat me to the punch." Scott chuckled.

"What do you mean?" Angela asked.

"She broke up with me before I got the chance. She said she realized it hadn't been working for some time, and she thought it would be better if we dated other people."

A grin broke through her heartbreak. "So, are you telling me it's over between you two?"

"Absolutely. One hundred percent."

He looked into her eyes. "Angela, I wanted to tell you something before you left the ranch, but I didn't get the chance." He leaned forward and sifted his fingers through her silky hair.

"Tell me now," she whispered.

He stroked her cheek. "From the first moment I laid eyes on you, I knew you were meant for me. I felt like I'd known you all my life, but I was afraid to get close to you, for the obvious reasons. I didn't want either of us to get hurt. But the more I got to know you and the more time we spent together, I knew I could never say goodbye. When we kissed at the lake, my whole world turned upside down. I've thought about you twenty-four seven. Since you left the High Lonesome, I haven't slept, I can't eat, and I can't keep my mind on business. I'm like a lovesick teenager."

She smiled and her heart fluttered with anticipation.

"I haven't felt this way about a woman since Maggie." He slid off the chair then got down on one knee and folded her hands into his. "I'm no longer afraid of telling you how I feel. This feels so right.

You feel so right. I love you, Angela, with all my heart and soul. I wanna be married to you. Will you marry me, darlin'?"

Tears welled in her eyes as she nodded and exclaimed, "Yes!"

He took her face in his hands, pulled her close, and seared her lips with burning kisses. When they parted, he grinned and said, "I'm in love for the last time in my life, baby."

She returned the smile. "I'm in love for the *first* time."

Chapter Eighteen

Three Days Later.

As they pulled up to the log house, a welcoming committee stood on the front porch and greeted the old pickup with smiles wider than the Rio Grande. Scott hopped out of the driver's seat and ran around to the other side. He opened the squeaky door, unbuckled Heather and lifted her onto the ground. The little girl gazed around, holding her silk blanket snug between her fingers. Angela stepped out and took her daughter's tiny hand.

Willow bounded down the porch steps and skidded to a stop right in front of the trio. She was wearing her signature pink cowgirl hat and boots. "Daddy! I missed you!" She coiled her arms around his legs and squeezed.

"I missed you, too, sweetie. Give your dad a kiss. Right here." He bent down and tapped his unshaven cheek. After kissing him, she wrinkled her nose.

"Scratchy. But that's just the way I like it." She raised her eyes to meet Angela's. "Beth! I mean, Angela. My daddy called when he was in Arizona. He told me you're going to marry him. I'm *so* happy!"

"So am I, Willow. So am I. We're going to hold the wedding right here on the ranch." She squeezed Willow's hands then knelt on one knee. "I want to apologize for not saying goodbye when I left before. I'm very sorry for hurting your feelings."

"It's okay. My dad explained it to me. The important thing is you're back and you're staying forever."

"That's right." The two hugged. "Willow, I want you to meet my little girl. This is Heather. I've told her all about you and Midnight and the other horses. She's never been on a ranch before, but she likes horses, too."

Willow stretched out her hand to welcome her. "Howdy, Heather. I'm pleased to meet ya."

The pixie brunette stared silently.

"It might take a little time for Heather to adjust to all the new changes, and to living on a ranch, but I'm hoping you can help her with that," Angela told Willow.

"I sure can! I have something for you, Heather. Stay right here!" Willow dashed up the porch steps and slung the screen door open. It banged against the doorframe.

"Take it easy," Carmen cried, rolling her eyes in mock annoyance.

She and Angela waved and shouted hellos to each other.

Willow ran out the door and back down the stairs holding something behind her back. She stood in front of Heather and looked up at her father. When he winked and nodded, Willow offered the little girl the gift. It was a pink cowgirl hat, an exact replica of hers.

"Do you like it? It's just like mine. When my daddy and your mommy get married, we're going to be sisters. Did you know that? I've never had a sister before. I think we're gonna have loads of fun together. I'll teach you how to ride. And we can catch bullfrogs at the lake. And we can play in the caves. You're gonna love it here at High Lonesome. This is your new home."

A slight smile creased Heather's lips as Willow plopped the hat on her head.

"Do you like it?" Willow asked again.

The child nodded and softly said, "My Mommy says you're a cowgirl. Can I be a cowgirl like you?"

"Yep. I'll teach you all the ropes. Okay?"

Heather nodded again then looked to her mother, who bent and hugged her. Scott patted his daughter on the shoulder and hollered up to Carmen. "Would you mind watching these two girls for a while? I have something I want to show Angela."

"No problem, Mr. Scott. Come, little ones. Follow me to the kitchen. I was just about to ice some cupcakes. You can both help."

Willow reached for Heather's hand and whispered in her ear, "We'll help all right. We'll help ourselves to eating a bunch of cupcakes!" Giggling, the seven-year-old led the four-year-old onto the porch.

Carmen patted Heather on the head and said, "*Buenos dias*, little lady. Welcome to the High Lonesome."

Angela waved and blew Heather a kiss, then gave Scott a sly look. "What is it you want to show me?"

"You'll see. It's a surprise."

They saddled Pepper and Sundance and climbed at a leisurely pace into the mountains. When they reached the top of the hill, they brought their horses to a halt. Angela peered down at the magnificent Lake Tusi and surrounding fields of wildflowers and butterflies. The first time Scott had brought her here, she'd become overwhelmed by the beauty. This time, the breath caught in her throat for another reason. Something was different about the view. She spurred Sundance into a trot down the long hill, with Scott and Pepper close on their heels.

The two of them got off their horses and left their mounts ground-reined. Angela jogged through the carpet of grass to the other side of the lake.

Sticking out of the ground were iron stakes with orange flags tied to them. String wrapped around the posts—forming a large square—marked the area where a foundation was to be built.

"What's all this?" Angela asked. Her pulse quickened in anticipation.

"Do you remember telling me you wished you could have a little cabin right here? You said you'd look out over the lake and never leave."

She nodded, tears pooling in the corners of her eyes.

"In less than a week, we'll be breaking ground. It's my early wedding present to you. It'll be our little hideaway."

"When did you do this?"

"Right after you left. I always knew you'd come back to me. I wanted to be ready when that day came."

Angela flew into his arms and branded him with kisses. "Oh, Scott. I love you with all my heart."

"I love you, too." He locked his arm around her waist and they stood gazing out over the shimmering blue lake.

"Welcome home, darlin'."

About the author...

Stacey lives in rural Maryland with her husband, daughters, horses and dogs. She enjoys horseback riding, photography, scrapbooking, and traveling, especially out west, where many of her stories take place. Her debut contemporary romance novel, *Lucky in Love*, was published by Asylett Press in May 2008, as was her TWRP Faery Rosette, *Chasing Her Dreams*. She is also the author of two books for children.

Visit Stacey at www.staceycoverstone.com

Contact Stacey at info@staceycoverstone.com

Other Yellow Rose titles you might enjoy:

THAT MONTANA SUMMER by Sloan Seymour
Samantha Matthews has everything but love. Head wrangler Dalton MacLaine has only one thing on his mind: land. The last thing Samantha needs is a dusty cattleman. The last thing Dalton wants to be is a summer fling.

A CHANGE OF HEART by Marianne Arkins
Jake Langley returns to Wyoming to find more than changes in the family ranch. His discovery of a well-kept secret sets duty against his heart's desire and changes hearts and lives forever.

ALWAYS A COWBOY by Cindy Spencer Pape
When old friends reunite, danger threatens and sparks fly! Trip Hall had a nice life in Hollywood until a stunt crash went wrong. Beth Corcoran learned her lesson about Trip's playboy ways back in high school. But when a stalker threatens, everything changes. Will Trip be able to save her? Can they trust each other with their hearts, as well as their lives?

TO TAME A COWGIRL: SARA [THE DOUBLE B]
by Roni Adams
They've always been buddies, no hint of romance. But then Sara's father dies and stipulates in his will that she must marry Buck's older brother or lose her life's goal—controlling interest of the Double B. Should Buck risk his heart by telling Sara how he feels, or watch the love of his life marry his brother in order to secure what she has worked so hard to earn? Will Sara choose to marry for love of the land, or will she realize that the one man who has always had her back also has her heart?

Printed in the United States
146786LV00001B/4/P

9 781601 544735